Lord of Misrule

The Morganville Vampires

BOOK FIVE

RACHEL CAINE

This edition first published in 2009 by
Allison & Busby Limited
13 Charlotte Mews
London, W1T 4EJ
www.allisonandbusby.com

A CIP catalogue record for this book is available from
the British Library.

First published in the USA in 2009 by NAL Jam,
an imprint of New American Library,
a division of Penguin Group (USA) Inc.

10 9 8 7 6

ISBN 978-0-7490-0757-7

Typeset in 11/17pt Century Schoolbook by
Allison & Busby Ltd.

The paper used for this Allison & Busby publication
has been produced from trees that have been legally sourced
from well-managed and credibly certified forests.

Printed and bound in Great Britain by
CPI Bookmarque Ltd, Croydon, Surrey

...ville Vampires series

'Rachel Caine brings her brilliant ability to blend witty
dialogue, engaging characters, and an intriguing plot'
Romance Reviews Today

'A rousing horror thriller that adds a new dimension to the
vampire mythos...a heroine the audience will admire and root
for... The key to this fine tale is...plausible reactions to living
in a town run by vampires that make going to college in the
Caine universe quite an experience'
Midwest Book Review

'An electrifying, enthralling coming-of-age supernatural tale'
The Best Reviews

'A fast-paced, page-turning read packed with wonderful
characters and surprising plot twists. Rachel Caine is an
engaging writer; readers will be completely absorbed in this
chilling story, unable to put it down until the last page... For
fans of vampire books, this is one that shouldn't be missed!'
Flamingnet

'Weaves a web of dangerous temptation, dark deceit, and loving
friendships. The non-stop vampire action and delightfully sweet
relationships will captivate readers and leave them craving more'
Darque Reviews

'Throw in a mix of vamps and ghosts, and it can't get any
better than *Dead Girls' Dance*'
Dark Angel Reviews

'It was hard to put this down for even the slightest break... Forget
what happens to the kid with the scar and glasses; I want to
know what happens next in Morganville. If you love to read about
characters with whom you can get deeply involved, Rachel Caine
is so far a one hundred percent sure bet to satisfy that need. I love
her Weather Warden stories, and her vampires are even better'
The Eternal Night

Rachel Caine is the international bestselling author of thirty novels, including the *New York Times* bestselling Morganville Vampires series. She was born at White Sands Missile Range, which people who know her say explains a lot. She has been an accountant, a professional musician, and an insurance investigator, and still carries on a secret identity in the corporate world. She and her husband, fantasy artist R. Cat Conrad, live in Texas with their iguanas, Pop-eye and Darwin, a *mali uromastyx* named (appropriately) O'Malley, and a leopard tortoise named Shelley (for the poet, of course).

www.rachelcaine.com
www.myspace.com/rachelcaine

To Ter Matthies, Anna Korra'ti, and Shaz Flynn –
courageous fighters, each one.
And to Pat Flynn, who never stopped.

Acknowledgments

This book wouldn't be here without the support of my husband, Cat, my friends Pat, Jackie, and Sharon, and a host of great online supporters and cheerers-on.

Special thank-you recognition to Sharon Sams, Shaz Flynn, and especially to fearless beta readers Karin and Laura for their excellent input.

Thanks always to Lucienne Diver.

THE STORY SO FAR

Claire Danvers was going to Caltech. Or maybe MIT. She had her pick of great schools, but because she's only sixteen, her parents sent her to a supposedly safe place for a year to mature – Texas Prairie University, a small school in Morganville, Texas.

One problem: Morganville isn't what it seems. It's the last safe place for vampires, and that makes it not very safe at all for the humans who venture in for work or school. The vampires rule the town...and everyone who lives in it.

Claire's second problem is that she's gathered both human and vampire enemies. Now she lives with housemates Michael Glass (newly made a vampire), Eve Rosser (always been Goth), and Shane Collins (whose absentee dad is a wannabe vampire killer). Claire's the normal one...or she would be, except that she's become an employee of the town Founder,

Amelie, and befriended one of the most dangerous, yet most vulnerable, vampires of them all – Myrnin, the alchemist.

Now Amelie's vampire father, Bishop, has come to Morganville and destroyed the fragile peace, turning vampires against one another and creating dangerous new alliances and factions in a town that already had too many.

Morganville's turning in on itself, and Claire and her friends have chosen to stand with the Founder, but it could mean working with their enemies...and fighting their friends.

CHAPTER ONE

It was all going wrong, and Morganville was burning – parts of it, anyway.

Claire stood at the windows of the Glass House and watched the flames paint the glass a dull, flickering orange. She could always see the stars out here in the Middle of Nowhere, Texas – but not tonight. Tonight, there was—

'You're thinking it's the end of the world,' a cool, quiet voice said behind her.

Claire blinked out of her trance and turned to look. Amelie – the Founder, and the baddest vampire in town, to hear most of the others tell it – looked fragile and pale, even for a vampire. She'd changed out of the costume she'd worn to Bishop's masked ball – not a bad idea, since it had a stake-sized hole in the chest, and she'd bled all over it. If Claire had needed proof that Amelie was tough, she'd certainly got it tonight. Surviving an assassination attempt definitely gave you points.

The vampire was wearing grey – a soft grey sweater, and *pants*. Claire had to stare, because Amelie just didn't do pants. Ever. It was beneath her, or something.

Come to think of it, Claire had never seen her in the colour grey, either.

Talk about the end of the world.

'I remember when Chicago burnt,' Amelie said. 'And London. And Rome. The world doesn't end, Claire. In the morning, the survivors start to build again. It's the way of things. The human way.'

Claire didn't particularly want a pep talk. She wanted to curl up in her warm bed upstairs, pull pillows over her head, and feel Shane's arms around her.

None of that was going to happen. Her bed was currently occupied by Miranda, a freaked-out teenage psychic with dependency issues, and as for Shane...

Shane was about to *leave*.

'Why?' she blurted. 'Why are you sending him out there? You know what could happen—'

'I know a great deal about Shane Collins that you don't,' Amelie interrupted. 'He's not a child, and he has survived much in his young life. He'll survive this. And he wishes to make a difference.'

She was sending Shane into the predawn darkness with a few chosen fighters, both vampire and human, to take possession of the Bloodmobile: the last reliably accessible blood storage in Morganville.

And it was the last thing Shane wanted to do. It was the last thing Claire wanted for him.

'Bishop isn't going to want the Bloodmobile for himself,' Claire said. 'He wants it destroyed. Morganville's full of walking blood banks, as far as he's concerned. But it'll hurt *you* if you lose it, so he'll come after it. Right?'

The severe, thin line of Amelie's mouth made it clear that she didn't like being second-guessed. It definitely couldn't be called a smile. 'As long as Shane has the book, Bishop will not dare destroy the vehicle for fear of destroying his great treasure along with it.'

Translation: Shane was bait. Because of the *book*. Claire hated that damn book. It had brought her nothing but trouble from the time she'd first heard about it. Amelie and Oliver, the two biggest vamps in town, had both been scrambling to find it, and it had dropped into Claire's hands instead. She wished she had the courage to grab it from Shane right now, run outside, and toss it in the nearest burning house to get rid of it once and for all, because as far as she could tell, it hadn't done anybody any good, ever – including Amelie.

Claire said, 'He'll kill Shane to get it.'

Amelie shrugged. 'I gamble that killing Shane is far more difficult than it would appear.'

'Yeah, you are gambling. You're betting his life.'

Amelie's ice grey eyes were steady on hers. 'Be clear on this: I am, in fact, betting all our lives. So be grateful, child, and also be warned. I could concede this fight at any time. My father would allow me to walk away – only me, alone. Defeated. I stay out of duty to you and the others in this town who are loyal to me.' Her eyes narrowed. 'Don't make me reconsider that.'

Claire hoped she didn't look as mutinous as she felt. She pasted on what was supposed to be an agreeable expression, and nodded. Amelie's eyes narrowed even more.

'Get prepared. We leave in ten minutes.'

Shane wasn't the only one with a dirty job to do; they were all assigned things they didn't particularly like. Claire was going with Amelie to try to rescue another vampire – Myrnin. And while Claire liked Myrnin, and admired him in a lot of ways, she also wasn't too excited about facing down – again – the vampire holding him prisoner, the dreadful Mr Bishop.

Eve was off to the coffee shop, Common Grounds, with the just-about-as-awful Oliver, her former boss. Michael was about to head out to the university with Richard Morrell, the mayor's son. How he was supposed to protect a few thousand clueless college students, Claire had no idea; she took a moment to marvel at the fact that the vampires really could lock down the town when they wanted. She'd have thought keeping students on campus in this situation would be impossible – kids phoning home, jumping in cars, getting the hell out of Dodge.

Except the vampires controlled the phone lines, cell phones, the Internet, the TV, and the radio, and cars either died or wrecked on the outskirts of town if the vampires didn't want you to leave. Only a few people had ever got out of Morganville successfully without permission. Shane had been one. And then he'd come *back*.

Claire still had no idea what kind of guts that had taken, knowing what was waiting for him.

'Hey,' Claire's housemate Eve said. She paused, arms full of clothes – black and red, so they'd almost certainly come out of Eve's own Goth-heavy closet – and gave Claire a quick once-over. She'd changed to what in Eve's world were practical fighting clothes – a pair of tight black jeans, a tight black shirt with red skull patterns all over it, and stompy, thick-soled boots. And a spiked black leather collar around her throat that almost dared the vampires, *Bite that!*

'Hey,' Claire said. 'Is this really a good time to start laundry?'

Eve rolled her eyes. 'Cute. So, some people didn't want to be caught dead in their stupid ball costumes, if you know what I mean. How about you? Ready to take that thing off?'

Claire looked down at herself. She was honestly surprised to realise that she was still wearing the tight, garish bodysuit of her Harlequin costume. 'Oh, yes.' She sighed. 'Got anything without, you know, skulls?'

'What's wrong with skulls? And that would be a no, by the way.' Eve dumped the armload of clothing on the floor and rooted through it, pulling out a plain black shirt and a pair of blue jeans. 'The jeans are yours. Sorry, but I sort of raided everybody's stash. Hope you like the underwear you have on; I didn't go through your drawers.'

'Afraid it might get you all turned on?' Shane asked from over her shoulder. 'Please say yes.' He grabbed a pair of his own jeans from the pile. 'And please stay out of my closet.'

Eve gave him the finger. 'If you're worried about me finding your porn stash, old news, man. Also, you have really boring taste.' She grabbed a blanket from the couch and nodded towards the corner. 'No privacy anywhere in this house tonight. Go on, we'll fix up a changing room.'

The three of them edged past the people and vampires who packed the Glass House. It had become the unofficial campaign centre for their side of the war, which meant there were plenty of people tramping around, getting in their stuff, who none of them would have let cross the threshold under normal circumstances.

Take Monica Morrell. The mayor's daughter had shed her elaborate Marie Antoinette costume and was back to the blond, slinky, pretty, slimy girl Claire knew and hated.

'Oh my God.' Claire gritted her teeth. 'Is she wearing my *blouse*?' It was her only good one. Silk. She'd just bought it last week. Now she'd never be able to put it on again. 'Remind me to burn that later.' Monica saw her staring, fingered the collar of the shirt, and gave her an evil smile. She mouthed, *Thanks*. 'Remind me to burn it *twice*. And stomp on the ashes.'

Eve grabbed Claire by the arm and hustled her into the empty corner of the room, where she shook out the blanket and held it at arm's length to provide a temporary shelter.

Claire peeled off her sweat-soaked Harlequin costume with a whimper of relief, and shivered as the cool air hit her flushed skin. She felt awkward and anxious, stripped to her underwear with just a blanket held up between her and a dozen strangers, some of whom probably wanted to eat her.

Shane leant over the top. 'You done?'

She squealed and threw the wadded-up costume at him. He caught it and waggled his eyebrows at her as she stepped into the jeans and quickly buttoned up the shirt.

'Done!' she called.

Eve dropped the blanket and smiled poison-sweet at Shane.

'Your turn, leather boy,' she said. 'Don't worry. I won't accidentally embarrass you.'

No, she'd embarrass him completely on purpose, and Shane knew it, from the glare he threw her. He ducked behind the blanket. Claire wasn't tall enough to check him out over the top – not that she wasn't tempted – but when Eve lowered the blanket, bit by bit, Claire grabbed one corner and pulled it back up.

'You're no fun,' Eve said.

'Don't mess with him. Not now. He's going out there alone.'

Eve's face went still and tight, and for the first time, Claire realised that the shine in her eyes wasn't really humour. It was a tightly controlled kind of panic. 'Yeah,' she said. 'I know. It's just – we're all splitting up, Claire. I wish we didn't have to do that.'

On impulse, Claire hugged her. Eve smelt of powder and some kind of darkly floral perfume, with a light undertone of sweat.

'Hey!' Shane's wounded yell was enough to make them both giggle. The blanket had drooped enough to show him zipping up his pants. Fast. 'Seriously, girls, *not cool*. A guy could do serious damage.'

He looked more like Shane now. The leather pants had made him unsettlingly hot-model gorgeous. In jeans and his old, faded Marilyn Manson T-shirt, he was somebody down-to-earth, somebody Claire could imagine kissing.

And she did imagine, just like that. It was, as usual, heart-racingly delicious.

'Michael's going out, too,' Eve said, and now the tension she'd been hiding made her voice tremble. 'I have to tell him—'

'Go on,' Claire said. 'We're right behind you.'

Eve dropped the blanket and pushed through the crowd, heading for her boyfriend, and the unofficial head of their strange and screwed-up fraternity.

It was easy to spot Michael in any group – he was tall and blond, with a face like an angel. As he caught sight of Eve heading towards him, he smiled, and Claire thought that was maybe the most complicated smile she'd ever seen, full of relief, welcome, love, and worry.

Eve crashed straight into him, hard enough to rock him back on his heels, and their arms went around each other.

Shane held Claire back with a touch on her shoulder. 'Give them a minute,' he said. 'They've got things to say.' She turned to look at him. 'And so do we.'

She swallowed hard and nodded. Shane's hands were on her shoulders, and his eyes had gone still and intense.

'Don't go out there,' Shane said.

It was what she'd been intending to say to *him*. She blinked, surprised.

'You stole my paranoia,' she said. '*I* was going to say, *Don't go*. But you're going to, no matter what I say, aren't you?'

That threw him off just a little. 'Well, yeah, of course I am, but—'

'But nothing. I'll be with Amelie; I'll be OK. You? You're going off with the cast of *WWE Raw* to fight a cage match or something. It's not the same thing.'

'Since when do you ever watch wrestling?'

'Shut up. That's not the point, and you know it. Shane, *don't go*.' Claire put everything she had into it.

It wasn't enough.

Shane smoothed her hair and bent down to kiss

her. It was the sweetest, gentlest kiss he'd ever given her, and it melted all the tense muscles of her neck, her shoulders, and her back. It was a promise without words, and when he finally pulled back, he passed his thumb across her lips gently, to seal it all in.

'There's something I really ought to tell you,' he said. 'I was kind of waiting for the right time.'

They were in a room full of people, Morganville was in chaos outside, and they probably didn't have a chance of surviving until sunrise, but Claire felt her heart stutter and then race faster. The whole world seemed to go silent around her. *He's going to say it.*

Shane leant in, so close that she felt his lips brush her ear, and whispered, 'My dad's coming back to town.'

That *so* wasn't what she was hoping he'd say. Claire jerked back, startled, and Shane put a hand over her mouth. 'Don't,' he whispered. 'Don't say *anything.* We can't talk about this, Claire. I just wanted you to know.'

They couldn't talk about it because Shane's father was Morganville's most wanted, public enemy number one, and any conversation they had – at least here – was in danger of being overheard by unfriendly, undead ears.

Not that Claire was a fan of Shane's father; he was a cold, brutal man who'd used and abused Shane, and she couldn't work up a lot of dread for seeing him behind bars...only she knew that Amelie and Oliver wouldn't stop at putting him in jail. Shane's father was marked for death if he came back. Death by burning. And while Claire wouldn't necessarily cry any big tears over him, she didn't want to put Shane through that, either.

'We'll talk about it,' she said.

Shane snorted. 'You mean, you'll yell at me? Trust me, I know what you're going to say. I just wanted you to know, in case—'

In case something happened to him. Claire tried to frame her question in a way that wouldn't tip their hand to any listening ears. 'When should I expect him?'

'Next few days, probably. But you know how it is. I'm out of the loop.' Shane's smile had a dark, painful edge to it now. He'd defied his dad once, because of Claire, and that meant cutting the ties to his last living family in the world. Claire doubted his dad had forgotten that, or ever would.

'Why now?' she whispered. 'The last thing we need is—'

'Help?'

'He's not *help*. He's chaos!'

Shane gestured at the burning town. 'Take a good look, Claire. How much worse can it get?'

Lots, she thought. Shane, in some ways, still had a rose-colored view of his father. It had been a while since his dad had blown out of town, and she thought that Shane had probably convinced himself that the guy wasn't all that bad. He was probably thinking now that his dad would come sweeping in to save them.

It wasn't going to happen. Frank Collins was a fanatic, car-bomb variety, and he didn't care who got hurt.

Not even his own son.

'Let's just—' She chewed her lip for a second, staring at him. 'Let's just get through the day, OK? Please? Be careful. Call me.'

He had his cell phone, and he showed it to her in mute promise. Then he stepped closer, and when his arms closed around her, she felt a sweet, trembling relief.

'Better get ready,' he said. 'It's going to be a long day.'

CHAPTER TWO

Claire wasn't sure if *get ready* meant put on her game face, brush her teeth, or pack up a lot of weapons, but she followed Shane to say goodbye to Michael first.

Michael was standing in the middle of a bunch of hard-looking types – some were vampires, and many she'd never seen before. They didn't look happy about playing defence, and they had that smelling-something-rotten expression that meant they didn't like hanging out with the human help, either.

The non-vamps with Michael were older, post-college – tough guys with lots of muscles. Even so, the humans mostly looked nervous.

Shane seemed almost small in comparison – not that he let it slow him down as he rushed the defensive line. He pushed a vampire out of his way as he headed for Michael; the vampire flashed fang at him, but Shane didn't even notice.

Michael did. He stepped in the way of the offended vamp as it made a move for Shane's back, and the two of them froze that way, predators facing off. Michael wasn't the one to look down first.

Michael had a strange intensity about him now – something that had always been there, but being a vampire had ramped it up to about eleven, Claire thought. He still looked angelic, but there were moments when his angel was more fallen than flying. But the smile was real, and completely the Michael she knew and loved when he turned it on them.

He held out his hand for a manly kind of shake. Shane batted it aside and hugged him. There were manly backslaps, and if there was a brief flash of red in Michael's eyes, Shane didn't see it.

'You be careful, man,' Shane said. 'Those college chicks, they're wild. Don't let them drag you into any Jell-O shot parties. Stay strong.'

'You too,' Michael said. 'Be careful.'

'Driving around in a big, black, obvious lunch wagon in a town full of starving vampires? Yeah. I'll try to keep it low profile.' Shane swallowed. 'Seriously—'

'I know. Same here.'

They nodded at each other.

Claire and Eve watched them for a moment. The two of them shrugged. 'What?' Michael asked.

'That's it? That's your big goodbye?' Eve asked.

'What was wrong with it?'

Claire looked at Eve, mystified. 'I think I need guy CliffsNotes.'

'Guys aren't deep enough to need CliffsNotes.'

'What were you waiting for, flowery poetry?' Shane snorted. 'I hugged. I'm done.'

Michael's grin didn't last. He looked at Shane, then Claire, and last – and longest – at Eve. 'Don't let anything happen to you,' he said. 'I love you guys.'

'Ditto,' Shane said, which was, for Shane, positively gushing.

They might have had time to say more, but one of the vampires standing around, looking pissed off and impatient, tapped Michael on the shoulder. His pale lips moved near Michael's ear.

'Time to go,' Michael said. He hugged Eve hard, and had to peel her off at the end. 'Don't trust Oliver.'

'Yeah, like you had to tell me that,' Eve said. Her voice was shaking again. 'Michael—'

'I love you,' he said, and kissed her, fast and hard. 'I'll see you soon.'

He left in a blur, taking most of the vampires with him. The mayor's son, Richard Morrell – still in his police uniform, although he was looking wrinkled and smoke stained now – led the humans at a more normal pace to follow.

Eve stood there with her kiss-smudged lips parted, looking stunned and astonished. When she regained the power of speech, she said, 'Did he just say—?'

'Yes,' Claire said, smiling. 'Yes, he did.'

'Whoa. Guess I'd better stay alive, then.'

The crowd of people – fewer now than there had been just a few minutes before – parted around them, and Oliver strode through the gap. The second-most badass vampire in town had shed his costume and was dressed in plain black, with a long, black leather coat. His long greying hair was tied back in a tight knot at the back of his head, and he looked like he was ready to snap the head off anyone, vampire or human, who got in the way.

'You,' he snapped at Eve. 'Come.'

He turned on his heel and walked away. This was not the Oliver they'd known before – certainly not the friendly proprietor of the local coffee shop. Even once he'd been revealed as a vampire, he hadn't been *this* intense.

Clearly, he was done pretending to like people.

Eve watched him go, and the look in her eyes was boiling with resentment. She finally shrugged and took a deep breath. 'Yeah,' she said. 'This'll be *so* much fun. See ya, Claire Bear.'

'See you,' Claire said. They hugged one last time, just for comfort, and then Eve was leaving, back straight, head high.

She was probably crying, Claire thought. Eve cried at times like these. Claire didn't seem to be able to cry when it counted, like now. It felt like pieces of her were being pulled off, and she felt cold and empty inside. No tears.

And now it was her heart being ripped out, because Shane was being summoned impatiently by yet another hard-looking bunch of vampires and humans near the door. He nodded to them, took her hands, and looked into her eyes.

Say it, she thought.

But he didn't. He just kissed her hands, turned, and walked away, dragging her red, bleeding heart with him – metaphorically, anyway.

'I love you,' she whispered. She'd said it before, but he'd hung up the phone before she'd got it out. Then she'd said it in the hospital, but he'd been doped up on painkillers. And he didn't hear her now, as he walked away from her.

But at least *she* had the guts to try.

He waved to her from the door, and then he was gone, and she suddenly felt very alone in the world – and very...young. Those who were left in the Glass

House had jobs of their own, and she was in the way. She found a chair – Michael's armchair, as it turned out – and pulled her feet up under her as humans and vampires moved around, fortifying windows and doors, distributing weapons, talking in low tones.

She might have become a ghost, for all the attention they paid her.

She didn't have to wait long. In just a few minutes, Amelie came sweeping down the stairs. She had a whole scary bunch of vampires behind her, and a few humans, including two in police uniforms.

They were all armed – knives, clubs, swords. Some had stakes, including the policemen; they had them, instead of riot batons, hanging from their utility belts. *Standard-issue equipment for Morganville*, Claire thought, and had to suppress a manic giggle. *Maybe instead of pepper spray, they have garlic spray.*

Amelie handed Claire two things: a thin, silver knife, and a wooden stake. 'A wooden stake in the heart will put one of us down,' she said. 'You must use the silver knife to kill us. No steel, unless you plan to take our heads off with it. The stake alone will not do it, unless you're very lucky or sunlight catches us helpless, and even then, we are slower to die the older we are. Do you understand?'

Claire nodded numbly. *I'm sixteen,* she wanted to

say. *I'm not ready for this.*

But she kind of had to be, now.

Amelie's fierce, cold expression seemed to soften, just a touch. 'I can't entrust Myrnin to anyone else. When we find him, it will be your responsibility to manage him. He may be—' Amelie paused, as if searching for the right word. 'Difficult.' That probably wasn't it. 'I don't want you to fight, but I need you with us.'

Claire lifted the stake and the knife. 'Then why did you give me these?'

'Because you might need to defend yourself, or him. If you do, I don't want you to hesitate, child. Defend yourself and Myrnin at all costs. Some of those who come against us may be those you know. Don't let that stop you. We are in this to survive now.'

Claire nodded numbly. She'd been pretending that all this was some kind of action/adventure video game, like the zombie-fighting one Shane enjoyed so much, but with every one of her friends leaving, she'd lost some of that distance. Now it was right here in front of her: reality. People were dying.

She might be one of them.

'I'll stay close,' she said. Amelie's cold fingers touched her chin, very lightly.

'Do that.' Amelie turned her attention to the

others around them. 'Watch for my father, but don't be drawn off to face him. It's what he wants. He will have his own reinforcements, and will be gathering more. Stay together, and watch each other closely. Protect me, and protect the child.'

'Um – could you stop calling me that?' Claire asked. Amelie's icy eyes fixed on her in almost-human puzzlement. 'Child, I mean? I'm not a child.'

It felt like time stopped for about a hundred years while Amelie stared at her. It probably had been at *least* a hundred years since the last time anybody had dared correct Amelie like that in public.

Amelie's lips curved, very slightly. 'No,' she agreed. 'You are not a child, and in any case, by your age, I was a bride and ruled a kingdom. I should know better.'

Claire felt heat build in her face. Great, she was blushing, as everybody's attention focused on her. Amelie's smile widened.

'I stand corrected,' she said to the rest of them. 'Protect this *young woman*.'

She really didn't feel like that, either, but Claire wasn't going to push her luck on that one. The other vampires looked mostly annoyed with the distinction, and the humans looked nervous.

'Come,' Amelie said, and turned to face the blank far wall of the living room. It shimmered like an asphalt road in the summer, and Claire felt the connection snap open.

Amelie stepped through what looked like blank wall. After a second or two of surprise, the vampires started to follow her.

'Man, I can't believe we're doing this,' one of the policemen behind Claire whispered to the other.

'I can,' the other whispered back. 'My kids are out there. What else is there to do?'

She gripped the wooden stake tight and stepped through the portal, following Amelie.

Myrnin's lab wasn't any more of a wreck than usual. Claire was kind of surprised by that; somehow she'd expected Mr Bishop to tear through here with torches and clubs, but so far, he'd found better targets.

Or maybe – just maybe – he hadn't been able to get in. Yet.

Claire anxiously surveyed the room, which was lit by just a few flickering lamps, both oil and electric. She'd tried cleaning it up a few times, but Myrnin had snapped at her that he liked things the way they were, so she'd left the stacks of leaning books, the piles of glassware on counters, the disordered piles of curling paper. There was a broken iron cage in the corner – broken because Myrnin had decided to escape from it once, and they'd never got around to having it repaired once he'd regained his senses.

The vampires were whispering to one another, in sibilant little hisses that didn't carry even a hint of meaning to Claire's ears. They were nervous, too.

Amelie, by contrast, seemed as casual and self-assured as ever. She snapped her fingers, and two of the vampires – big, strong, strapping men – stepped up, towering over her. She glanced up.

'You will guard the stairs,' she said. 'You two.' She pointed to the uniformed policemen. 'I want you here as well. Guard the interior doors. I doubt anything will come through them, but Mr Bishop has already surprised us. I won't have him surprising us again.'

That cut their forces in half. Claire swallowed hard and looked at the two vampires and one human who remained with her and Amelie – she knew the two vampires slightly. They were Amelie's personal bodyguards, and one of them, at least, had treated her kind of decently before.

The remaining human was a tough-looking African American woman with a scar across her face, from her left temple across her nose, and down her right cheek. She saw Claire watching her, and gave her a smile. 'Hey,' she said, and stuck out a big hand. 'Hannah Moses. Moses Garage.'

'Hey,' Claire said, and shook hands awkwardly.

The woman had muscles – not quite Shane-quality biceps, but definitely bigger than most women would have found useful. 'You're a mechanic?'

'I'm an everything,' Hannah said. 'Mechanic included. But I used to be a marine.'

'Oh.' Claire blinked.

'The garage was my dad's before he passed. I just got back from a couple of tours in Afghanistan – thought I'd take up the quiet life for a while.' She shrugged. 'Guess trouble's in my blood. Look, if this comes to a fight, stay with me, OK? I'll watch your back.'

That was so much of a relief that Claire felt weak enough to melt. 'Thanks.'

'No problem. You're what, about fifteen?'

'Almost seventeen.' Claire thought she needed a T-shirt that said it for her; it would be a great time-saver – that, or some kind of button.

'Huh. So you're about my kid brother's age. His name's Leo. I'll have to introduce you sometime.'

Hannah, Claire realised, was talking without really thinking about what she was saying; her eyes were focused on Amelie, who had made her way around piles of books to the doorway on the far wall.

Hannah didn't seem to miss anything.

'Claire,' Amelie said. Claire dodged piles of books

and came to her side. 'Did you lock this door when you left before?'

'No. I thought I'd be coming back this way.'

'Interesting. Because someone *has* locked it.'

'Myrnin?'

Amelie shook her head. 'Bishop has him. He has not returned this way.'

Claire decided not to ask how she knew that. 'Who else—' And then she knew. 'Jason.' Eve's brother had known about the doorways that led to different destinations in town – maybe not about how they worked (and Claire wasn't sure she did, either), but he definitely had figured out how to use them. Apart from Claire, Myrnin, and Amelie, only Oliver had the knowledge, and she knew where he'd been since her encounter with Mr Bishop.

'Yes,' Amelie agreed. 'The boy is becoming a problem.'

'Kind of an understatement, considering he, you know...' Claire mimed stabbing with the stake, but not in Amelie's direction – that would be like pointing a loaded gun at Superman. Somebody would get hurt, and it wouldn't be Superman. 'Um – I meant to ask, are you—?'

Amelie looked away from her, towards the door. 'Am I what?'

'OK?' Because she'd had a stake in her chest not

all that long ago, and besides that, all the vampires in Morganville had a disadvantage, whether they knew it or not: they were sick – really sick – with something Claire could only think of as vampire Alzheimer's.

And it was ultimately fatal.

Most of the town didn't have a clue about that, because Amelie was rightly afraid of what might happen if they did – vampires and humans alike. Amelie had symptoms, but so far they were mild. It took years to progress, so they were safe for a while.

At least, Claire hoped it took years.

'No, I doubt I am all right. Still, this is hardly the time to be coddling myself.' Amelie focused on the door. 'We will need the key to open it.'

That was a problem, because the key wasn't where it was supposed to be. The key ring was gone from where Claire kept it, in a battered, sagging drawer, and the more Claire pawed through debris looking for it, the more alarmed she became. Myrnin kept the weirdest stuff... Books, sure, she loved books; small, deformed dead things in alcohol, not so much. He also kept jars of dirt – at least, she hoped it was dirt. Some of it looked red and flaky, and she was really afraid it might be blood.

The keys were missing. So were a few other things – significant things.

With a sinking feeling, Claire pulled open the half-broken drawer where she'd kept the bag with all the tranquilliser stuff, and Myrnin's drug supplies.

Gone. Only a scrape in the dust to indicate where it had been.

That meant that if – *when* – Myrnin turned violent, she wouldn't have her trusty dart gun to help her. Nor would she have even her trusty injectable pen, so cool, that she'd loaded up for emergencies, because it had been in the bag with the drugs. She'd lost the other supplies she'd had with her.

But even worse, she didn't have any medicine for him, other than the couple of small vials she had with her in her pockets.

In summary: so very screwed.

'Enough,' Amelie said, and turned to her bodyguard. 'I know this isn't easy, but if you would?'

He gave her a polite sort of nod, stepped forward, and took the lock in his hand.

His hand *burst into flame*.

'Oh my God!' Claire blurted, and clapped her hands over her mouth, because the vampire guy wasn't letting go. His face was contorted with pain, but he held on, somehow, and jerked and twisted the silver-plated lock until, with a scream of metal, it ripped loose. The hasp came with it, right off the door.

He dropped it to the floor. His hand kept burning.

Claire grabbed the first thing that came to hand –
some kind of ratty old shirt Myrnin had left thrown
on the floor – and patted out the fire. The smell of
burnt flesh made her dry heave, and so did the sight
of what was left of his hand. He didn't scream. She
almost did it for him.

'A trap,' Amelie said. 'From my father. Gérard, are
you able to continue?'

He nodded as he wrapped the shirt around the
ruin of his hand. He was sweating fine pink beads
– blood, Claire realised, as a trickle of it ran down
his pale face. She realised that as she was standing
there right in front of him, frozen in place, and his
eyes flashed red.

'Move,' he growled at her. 'Stay behind us.' And
then, after a brief pause, he said, 'Thank you.'

Hannah took her by the arm and pulled her to the
spot in the back, out of vampire-grabbing range. 'He
needs feeding,' she said in an undertone. 'Gérard's
not a bad guy, but you don't want to make yourself
too available for snack attacks. Remember, we're
vending machines with legs.'

Claire nodded. Amelie put her fingers in the hole
left by the broken lock and pulled the door open...on
darkness.

Hannah said nothing. She didn't let go of Claire's
arm.

For a long moment, nothing happened, and then the darkness flickered. Shifted. Things came and went in the shadows, and Claire knew that Amelie was shuffling destinations, trying to find the one she wanted. It seemed to take a very long time, and then Amelie took a sudden step back. 'Now,' she said, and her two bodyguards charged forward into what looked like complete darkness and were gone. Amelie glanced back at Hannah and Claire, and her black pupils were expanding fast, covering all the grey iris of her eyes, preparing for the dark.

'Don't leave my side,' she said. 'This will be dangerous.'

CHAPTER THREE

Amelie grabbed Claire's other arm, and before Claire could so much as grab a breath, she was being pulled through the portal. There was a brief wave of chill, and a feeling that was a little like being pushed from all sides, and then she was stumbling into utter, complete blackness. Her other senses went into overdrive. The air smelted stale and heavy, and felt cold and damp, like a cave. Amelie's icy grip on one arm was going to leave bruises, and Hannah Moses's warmer touch on the other seemed light by contrast, although Claire knew it wasn't.

Claire could hear herself and Hannah breathing, but there was no sound at all from the vampires. When Claire tried to speak, Amelie's ice-cold hand covered her mouth. She nodded convulsively, and concentrated on putting one foot in front of the other as Amelie – she hoped it was still Amelie, anyway –

pulled her forward into the dark.

The smells changed from time to time – a whiff of nasty, rotten something, then something else that smelt weirdly like grapes? Her imagination conjured up a dead man surrounded by broken bottles of wine, and Claire couldn't stop it there; the dead man was moving, squirming towards her, and any second now he'd touch her and she'd scream...

It's just your imagination; stop it.

She swallowed and tried to tamp down the panic. It wasn't helping. *Shane wouldn't panic. Shane would* – whatever, Shane wouldn't be caught dead roaming around in the dark with a bunch of vampires like this, and Claire knew it.

It seemed like they went on for ever, and then Amelie pulled her to a stop and let go. Losing that support felt as if she were standing on the edge of a cliff, and Claire was really, really grateful for Hannah's grip to tell her there was something else real in the world. *Don't let me fall.*

And then Hannah's hand went away. A fast tightening of her fingers, and she was gone.

Claire was floating in total darkness, disconnected, alone. Her breath sounded loud as a train in her ears, but it was buried under the thunder of her fast heartbeats. *Move,* she told herself. *Do something!*

She whispered, 'Hannah?'

Cold hands slapped around her from behind, one pinning her arms to her sides, the other covering her mouth. She was lifted off the ground, and she screamed, a faint buzzing sound like a storm of bees that didn't make it through the muffling gag.

And then she went flying through the air into the darkness...and rolled to a stop facedown, on a cold stone floor. There was light here. Faint, but definite, painting the edges of things a pale grey, including the arched mouth of the tunnel at the end of the hall.

She had no idea where she was.

Claire got quickly to her feet and turned to look behind her. Amelie, pale as a pearl, stepped through the portal, and with her came the other two vampires. Gérard had Hannah Moses's arm gripped in his good hand.

Hannah had a bloody gash on her head, and when Gérard let go, she dropped to her knees, breathing hard. Her eyes looked blank and unfocused.

Amelie whirled, something silver in one hand, and stabbed as something came at her from the dark. It screamed, a thin sound that echoed through the tunnel, and a white hand reached out to grab Amelie's shirt.

The invisible portal slammed shut like an iris,

and severed the arm just above the elbow.

Amelie plucked the still-grabbing hand from her shirt, dropped the hand to the ground, and kicked it to the side. When she turned back to the others, there was no expression on her face.

Claire felt like throwing up. She couldn't take her eyes away from that wiggling, fish-pale hand.

'It was necessary to come this way,' Amelie said. 'Dangerous, but necessary.'

'Where are we?' Claire asked. Amelie gave her a look and ignored her as she took the lead, heading down the hall. Going through this didn't give her any right to ask questions. Of course. 'Hannah? Are you OK?'

Hannah waved her hand vaguely, which really wasn't all that confidence-building. The vampire Gérard answered for her. 'She's fine.' Sure, he could talk, having one hand burnt to the bone. He'd probably classify himself as fine, too. 'Take her,' Gérard ordered, and pushed Hannah towards Claire as he moved to follow Amelie. The other bodyguard – what was his name? – moved with him, as if they were an old, practiced team.

Hannah was heavy, but she pulled herself back on her own centre of gravity after a breath or two. 'I'm fine,' she said, and gave Claire a reassuring grin. 'Damn. That was not a walk in the park.'

'You should meet my boyfriend,' Claire said. 'You two are both masters of understatement.'

She thought Hannah wanted to laugh, but instead, she just nodded and patted Claire on the shoulder. 'Watch the sides,' she said. 'We're just starting on this thing.'

That was an easy job, because there was nothing to watch on the sides. They were, after all, in a tunnel. Hannah, it appeared, was the rear guard, and she seemed to take it very seriously, although it looked like Amelie had slammed the doorway behind them pretty hard, with prejudice. *I hope we don't have to go back that way,* Claire thought, and shivered at the sight of that pale severed hand behind them. It had finally stopped moving. *I really, really hope we don't have to go back there.*

At the mouth of the tunnel, Amelie seemed to pause for a moment, and then disappeared to the right, around the corner, with her two vampire bodyguards in flying formation behind her. Hannah and Claire hurried to keep up, and emerged into another hallway, this one square instead of arched, and panelled in rich, dark wood. There were paintings on the walls – old ones, Claire thought – of pale people lit by candlelight, dressed in about a thousand pounds of costume and rice-white make-up and wigs.

She stopped and backed up, staring at one.

'What?' Hannah growled.

'That's her. Amelie.' It definitely was, only instead of the Princess Grace-style clothes she wore now, in the picture she was wearing an elaborate sky blue satin dress, cut way low over her breasts. She was wearing a big white wig, and staring out of the canvas in an eerily familiar way.

'Art appreciation later, Claire. We need to go.'

That was true, beyond any argument, but Claire kept throwing glances at the paintings as they passed. One looked like it could have been Oliver, from about four hundred years ago. One more modern one looked almost like Myrnin. *It's the vampire museum,* she realised. *It's their history.* There were glass cases lining the hall ahead, filled with books and papers and jewellery, clothing, and musical instruments. All the fine and fabulous things gathered through their long, long lives.

Ahead, the three vampires came to a sudden, motionless halt, and Hannah grabbed Claire by the arm to pull her out of the way, against the wall. 'What's happening?' Claire whispered.

'Sorting credentials.'

Claire didn't know what that meant, exactly, but when she risked moving out just a bit to see what was happening, she saw that there were lots of other vampires in here – about a hundred of them, some sitting down and obviously hurt. There were humans, too, mostly standing together and looking nervous, which seemed reasonable.

If these were Bishop's people, their little rescue party was in serious trouble.

Amelie exchanged some quiet words with the vampire who seemed to be in charge, and Gérard and his partner visibly relaxed. That settled the friend-or-foe question, apparently; Amelie turned and nodded to Claire, and she and Hannah edged out from behind the glass cases to join them.

Amelie made a gesture, and immediately several vampires peeled off from the group and joined her in a distant corner.

'What's going on?' Claire asked, and stared around her. Most of the vampires were still dressed in the costumes they'd worn to Bishop's welcome feast, but a few were in more military dress – black, mostly, but some in camouflage.

'It's a rally point,' Hannah said. 'She's talking strategy, probably. Those would be her captains. Notice there aren't any humans with her?'

Claire did. It wasn't exactly a pleasant sensation, the doubt that boiled up inside.

Whatever orders Amelie delivered, it didn't take long. One by one, the vampires nodded and peeled off from the meeting, gathered up followers – including humans this time – and departed. By the time Amelie had dispatched the last group, there were only about ten people left Claire didn't know, and they were all standing together.

Amelie came back to them, saw the group of humans and vamps, and nodded towards them.

'Claire, this is Theodosius Goldman,' Amelie said. 'Theo, he prefers to be called. These are his family.'

Family? That was a shock, because there were so many of them. Theo seemed to be kind of middle-aged, with greying, curly hair and a face that, except for its vampiric pallor, seemed kind of…nice.

'May I present my wife, Patience?' he said with the kind of old manners Claire had only seen on *Masterpiece Theatre*. 'Our sons, Virgil and Clarence. Their wives, Ida and Minnie.' There were more vampires bowing, or in the case of the one guy down on the floor, with his head held in the lap of a female vamp, waving. 'And their children.'

Evidently the grandchildren didn't merit individual introductions. There were four of them, two boys and two girls, all pale like their relatives. They seemed younger than Claire, at least physically; she guessed the littler girl was probably about twelve, the older boy around fifteen.

The older boy and girl glared at her, as if she were personally responsible for the mess they were in, but

Claire was too busy imagining how a whole family – down to grandchildren – could all be made vampires like this.

Theo, evidently, could see all that in her expression, because he said, 'We were made eternal a long time ago, my girl, by' – he cast a quick look at Amelie, who nodded – 'by her father, Bishop. It was a joke of his, you see, that we should all be together for all time.' He really did have a kind face, Claire thought, and his smile was kind of tragic. 'The joke turned on him, though. We refused to let it destroy us. Amelie showed us we did not have to kill to survive, and so we were able to keep our faith as well as our lives.'

'Your faith?'

'It's a very old faith,' Theo said. 'And today is our Sabbath.'

Claire blinked. 'Oh. You're Jewish?'

He nodded, eyes fixed on her. 'We found a refuge here, in Morganville. A place where we could live in peace, both with our nature and our God.'

Amelie said, softly, 'But will you fight for it now, Theo? This place that gave you refuge?'

He held out his hand. His wife's cool white fingers closed around it. She was a delicate china doll of a woman, with masses of sleek black hair piled on top of her head. 'Not today.'

'I'm sure God would understand if you broke the Sabbath under these circumstances.'

'I'm sure he would. God is forgiving, or we would not still be walking this world. But to be moral is not to need his divine forgiveness, I think.' He shook his head again, very regretfully. 'We cannot fight, Amelie. Not today. And I would prefer not to fight at all.'

'If you think you can stay neutral in this, you're wrong. I will respect your wishes. My father will not.'

Theo's face hardened. 'If your father threatens my family again, then we *will* fight. But until he comes for us, until he shows us the sword, we will not take up arms against him.'

Gérard snorted, which proved what he thought about it; Claire wasn't much surprised. He seemed like a practical sort of guy. Amelie simply nodded. 'I can't force you, and I wouldn't. But be careful. I cannot spare anyone to help you. You should be safe enough here, for a time. If any others come through, send them out to guard the power station and the campus.' She allowed her gaze to move beyond Theo, to touch the three humans huddled in the far corner of the room, under another painting, a big one. 'Are these under your Protection?'

Theo shrugged. 'They asked to join us.'

'Theo.'

'I will defend them if someone tries to harm them.' Theo pitched his voice lower. 'Also, we may need them, if we can't get supplies.'

Claire went cold. For all his kind face and smile, Theo was talking about using those people as portable blood banks.

'I don't want to do it,' Theo continued, 'but if things go against us, I have to think of my children. You understand.'

'I do,' Amelie said. Her face was back to a blank mask that gave away nothing of how she felt about it. 'I have never told you what to do, and I will not now. But by the laws of this town, if you place these humans under your Protection, you owe them certain duties. You know that.'

Another shrug, and Theo held out his hands to show he was helpless. 'Family comes first,' he said. 'I have always told you so.'

'Some of us,' Amelie said, 'are not so fortunate in our choice of families.'

She turned away from Theo without waiting for his response – if he'd been intending to give one – and without so much as a pause, slammed her fist into a glass-fronted wall box labelled EMERGENCY USE ONLY three steps to the right. It shattered in a loud clatter, and Amelie shook shards of glass from her skin.

She reached into the box and took out...Claire blinked. 'Is that a *paintball* gun?'

Amelie handed it to Hannah, who handled it like a

professional. 'It fires pellets loaded with silver powder,' she said. 'Very dangerous to us. Be careful where you aim.'

'Always am,' Hannah said. 'Extra magazines?'

Amelie retrieved them from the case and handed them over. Claire noticed that she protected herself even from a casual touch, with a fold of fabric over her fingers. 'There are ten shots per magazine,' she said. 'There is one already loaded, and six more here.'

'Well,' Hannah said, 'any problem I can't solve with seventy shots is probably going to kill us, anyway.'

'Claire,' Amelie said, and handed over a small, sealed vial. 'Silver powder, packed under pressure. It will explode on impact, so be very careful with it. If you throw it, there is a wide dispersal through the air. It can hurt your friends as much as your enemies.'

There were real uses for silver powder, like coating parts in computers; Claire supposed it wasn't exactly restricted, but she was surprised the vampires were progressive enough to lay in a supply. Amelie raised pale eyebrows at her.

'You've been expecting this,' Claire said.

'Not in detail. But I've learnt through my life that such preparations are never wasted, in the end. Sometime, somewhere, life always comes to a fight, and peace always comes to an end.'

Theo said, very quietly, 'Amen.'

CHAPTER FOUR

They left the museum by way of a side door. It was risky to go out into the night, but since the only other way to exit the museum was to go back into the darkness, nobody argued about the choice.

'Careful,' Amelie told them in a very soft voice that hardly reached past the shadows. 'I have gathered my forces. My father is doing the same. There will be patrols, especially here.'

The flames hadn't reached Founder's Square, which was where they came out – the heart of vamp territory. It didn't look like the calm, orderly place Claire remembered, though; the lights were all out, and the shops and restaurants that bordered it were closed and empty.

It looked afraid.

The only place she could see movement was on the marble steps of the Elders' Council building, where

Bishop's welcome feast had been held. Gérard hissed a warning, and they all froze, silent and still in the dark. Hannah's grip on Claire's arm felt like an iron band.

There were three vampires standing there, scanning the area.

Lookouts.

'Go,' Amelie said in a whisper so small it was like a ghost. 'Move, but be careful.'

They reached the edge of the shadows by the corner of the building, but just as Claire was starting to relax a little, Amelie, Gérard, and the other vampires moved in a blur, scattering in all directions.

This left Claire flat-footed for one horrible second, before Hannah tackled her facedown on the grass. Claire gasped, got a mouthful of crunchy dirt and bitter chlorophyll, and fought to get her breath. Hannah's heavy weight held her down, and the older woman braced her elbows on Claire's back.

She's firing the pistol, Claire thought, and tried to raise her head to see where Hannah was shooting.

'Head down!' Hannah snarled, and shoved Claire down with one hand while she continued to fire with the other. From the screams in the dark, she was hitting something. 'Get up! Run!'

Claire wasn't quick enough to suit either the marines or the vampires, and before she knew it, she was being half pulled, half dragged at a dead run through the night. It was all a confusing blur of shadows, dark buildings, pale faces, and the surly orange glow of flames in the distance.

'What is it?' she screamed.

'Patrols.' Hannah kept on firing behind them. She wasn't firing wildly, not at all; it seemed like she took a second or two between every shot, choosing her target. Most of the shots seemed to hit, from the shouts and snarls and screams. 'Amelie! We need an exit, *now*!'

Amelie looked back at them, a pale flash of face in the dark, and nodded.

They charged up the steps of another building on Founder's Square. Claire didn't have time to get more than a vague impression of it – some kind of official building, with columns in front and big stone lions snarling on the stairs – before their little party came to a halt at the top of the stairs, in front of a closed white door with no knob.

Gérard started to throw himself against it. Amelie stopped him with an outstretched hand. 'It will do no good,' she said. 'It can't be opened by force. Let me.'

The other vampire, facing away and down the

steps, said, 'Don't think we have time for sweet talk, ma'am. What you want us to do?' He had a drawling Texas accent, the first one Claire had heard from any vampire. She'd never heard him speak at all before.

He winked at her, which was even more of a shock. Until that moment, he hadn't even looked at her like a real person.

'A moment,' Amelie murmured.

The Texan nodded behind them. 'Don't think we've got one, ma'am.'

There were shadows converging in the dark at the foot of the steps – the patrol that Hannah had been shooting at. There were at least twenty of them. In the lead was Ysandre, the beautiful vampire Claire hated maybe more than she hated any other vampire in the entire world. She was Bishop's girl through and through – Amelie's vampire sister, if they thought in those kinds of terms.

Claire hated Ysandre for Shane's sake. She was glad the vamp was here, and not attacking Shane's Bloodmobile – one, because she wasn't so sure Shane could resist the evil witch, and two, she wanted to stake Ysandre herself.

Personally.

'No,' Hannah said, when Claire took a step out from behind her. 'Are you crazy? Get back!'

Hannah fired over her shoulder. It was at the outer extreme of the paintball gun's range, but the pellet hit one of the vampires – not Ysandre, Claire was disappointed to see – right in the chest. Silver dust puffed up in a lethal mist, and the close formation scattered. Ysandre might have had a few burns, but nothing that wouldn't heal.

The vampire Hannah had shot in the chest toppled over and hit the marble stairs, smoking and flailing.

Amelie slammed her palm flat against the door and closed her eyes, and deep inside the barrier something groaned and shifted with a scrape of metal. 'Inside,' Amelie murmured, still wicked controlled, and Claire spun and followed the three vampires across the threshold. Hannah backed in after, grabbed the door, and slammed it shut.

'No locks,' she said.

Amelie reached over and pushed Hannah's gun hand into an at-rest position at her side. 'None necessary. They won't get in.' She sounded sure of it, but from the look Hannah continued to give the door – as if she wished she could weld it shut with the force of her stare – she wasn't so certain. 'This way. We'll take the stairs.'

It was a library, full of books. Some – on this floor – were new, or at least newish, with colourful spines and crisp titles that Claire could read even in the low light. She slowed down a little, blinking. 'You guys have *vampire* stories in here?' None of the vampires answered. Amelie veered to the right, through the two-storey-tall shelves, and headed for a set of sweeping marble steps at the end. The books got older, the paper more yellow. Claire caught sight of a sign that read FOLKLORE, CA. 1870-1945, ENGLISH, and then another that identified a *German* section. Then *French*. Then script that might have been Chinese.

So many books, and from what she could tell, every single one of them had to do in some way with vampires. Was it history or fiction to them?

Claire didn't really have time to work it out. They were taking the stairs, moving around the curve up to the second level. Claire's legs burnt all along the calf muscles, and her breathing was getting raspy from the constant movement and adrenaline. Hannah flashed her a quick, sympathetic smile. 'Yeah,' she said. 'Consider it basic training. Can you keep up?'

Claire gave her a gasping nod.

More books here, old and crumbling, and the air tasted like dry leather and ancient paper. Towards the back of the room, there were things that looked like wine racks, the fancy X-shaped kind people put in cellars, only these held rolls of paper, each neatly tied with ribbon. They were scrolls, probably very old ones. Claire hoped they'd go that direction, but no, Amelie was turning them down another book aisle, towards a blank white wall.

No, not quite blank. It had a small painting on the wall, in a fussy gilt frame. Some bland-looking nature scene...and then, as Amelie stared at it, the painting *changed*.

It grew darker, as though clouds had come across the meadow and the drowsy sheep in the picture.

And then it was dark, just a dark canvas, then some pinpricks of light, like candle flames through smoke...

And then Claire saw Myrnin.

He was in chains, silver-coloured chains, kneeling on the floor, and his head was down. He was still wearing the blousy white pantaloons of his Pierrot costume, but no shirt. The wet points of his damp hair clung to his face and his marble-pale shoulders.

Amelie nodded sharply, and put a hand against the wall to the left of the picture, pressing what looked like a nail, and part of the wall swung out silently on oiled hinges.

Hidden doors: vampires sure seemed to love them.

There was darkness on the other side. 'Oh, *hell* no,' Claire heard Hannah mutter. 'Not again.'

Amelie sent her a glance, and there was a whisper of amusement in the look. 'It's a different darkness,' she said. 'And the dangers are very different, from this point on. Things may change quickly. You will have to adapt.'

Then she stepped through, and the vampires followed, and it was just Claire and Hannah.

Claire held out her hand. Hannah took it, still shaking her head, and the dark closed around them like a damp velvet curtain.

There was the hiss of a match dragging, and a flare of light from the corner. Amelie, her face turned ivory by the licking flame, set the match to a candle and left the light burning as she flicked on a small flashlight and played it around the room. Boxes. It was some kind of storeroom, dusty and disused. 'All right,' she said. 'Gérard, if you please.'

He swung another door open a crack, nodded, and widened it enough to slip through.

Another hallway. Claire was getting tired of hallways, and they were all starting to look the same. Where were they now, anyway? It looked like some kind of hotel, with polished heavy doors marked with brass plates, only instead of numbers, each door had one of the vampire markings, like the symbol on Claire's bracelet. Each vampire had one; at least she thought they did. So these would be – what? Rooms? Vaults? Claire thought she heard something behind one of the doors – muffled sounds, thumping, scratching. They didn't stop, though – and she wasn't sure she wanted to know, really.

Amelie brought them to a halt at the T-intersection of the hall. It was deserted in every direction, and disorienting, too; Claire couldn't tell one hallway from another. *Maybe we should drop crumbs,* she thought. *Or M&M's. Or blood.*

'Myrnin is in a room on this hall,' Amelie said. 'It is quite obviously a trap, and quite obviously meant for me. I will stay behind and ensure your escape route. Claire.' Her pale eyes fixed on Claire with merciless intensity. 'Whatever else happens, you must bring Myrnin out safely. Do you understand? Do not let Bishop have him.'

She meant, *Everybody else is expendable.* That made Claire feel sick, and she couldn't help but look at Hannah, and even at the two vampires. Gérard shrugged, so slightly she thought it might have been her imagination.

'We are soldiers,' Gérard said. 'Yes?'

Hannah smiled. 'Damn straight.'

'Excellent. You will follow my orders.'

Hannah saluted him, with just a little trace of irony. 'Yes sir, squad leader, sir.'

Gérard turned his attention to Claire. 'You will

stay behind us. Do you understand?'

She nodded. She felt cold and hot at the same time, and a little sick, and the wooden stake in her hand didn't seem like a heck of a lot, considering. But she didn't have any time for second thoughts, because Gérard had turned and was already heading down the hall, his wing man flanking him, and Hannah was beckoning Claire to follow.

Amelie's cool fingers brushed her shoulder. 'Careful.'

Claire nodded and went to rescue a crazy vampire from an evil one.

The door shattered under Gérard's kick. That wasn't an exaggeration; except for the wood around the door hinges, the rest of it broke into hand-sized pieces and splinters. Before that rain of wreckage hit the floor, Gérard was inside, moving to the left while his colleague went right. Hannah stepped in and swept the room from one side to the other, holding her air pistol ready to fire, then nodded sharply to Claire.

Myrnin was just as she'd seen him in the picture – kneeling in the centre of the room, anchored by tight-stretched silvery chains. The chains were double-strength, and threaded through massive steel bolts on the stone floor.

He was shaking all over, and where the chains

touched him, he had welts and burns.

Gérard swore softly under his breath and fiercely kicked the eyebolts in the floor. They bent, but didn't break.

Myrnin finally raised his head, and beneath the mass of sweaty dark hair, Claire saw wild dark eyes, and a smile that made her stomach twist.

'I knew you'd come,' he whispered. 'You fools. Where is she? Where's Amelie?'

'Behind us,' Claire said.

'*Fools.*'

'Nice way to talk to your rescuers,' Hannah said. She was nervous, Claire could see it, though the woman controlled it very well. 'Gérard? I don't like this. It's too easy.'

'I know.' He crouched down and looked at the chains. 'Silver coated. I can't break them.'

'What about the bolts in the floor?' Claire asked. In answer, Gérard grabbed the edge of the metal plate and twisted. The steel bent like aluminium foil, and, with a ripping shriek, tore free of the stones. Myrnin wavered as part of his restraints fell loose, and Gérard waved his partner to work on the other two plates while he focused on the second in front.

'Too easy, too easy,' Hannah kept on muttering. 'What's the point of doing this if Bishop is just going to let him go?'

The eyebolts were all ripped loose, and Gérard grabbed Myrnin's arm and helped him to his feet.

Myrnin's eyes sheeted over with blazing ruby, and he shook Gérard off and went straight for Hannah.

Hannah saw him coming and put the gun between them, but before she could fire, Gérard's partner knocked her hand out of line, and the shot went wild, impacting on the stone at the other side of the room. Silver flakes drifted on the air, igniting tiny burns where they landed on the vampires' skin. The two bodyguards backed off.

Myrnin grabbed Hannah by the neck.

'No!' Claire screamed, and ducked under Gerard's restraining hand. She raised her wooden stake.

Myrnin turned his head and grinned at her with wicked vampire fangs flashing. 'I thought you were here to save me, Claire, not kill me,' he purred, and whipped back towards his prey. Hannah was fumbling with her gun, trying to get it back into position. He stripped it away from her with contemptuous ease.

'I *am* here to save you,' Claire said, and before she could think what she was doing, she buried the stake in Myrnin's back, on the left side, right where she thought his heart would be.

He made a surprised sound, like a cough, and pitched forward into Hannah. His hand slid away from her throat, clutching blindly at her clothes, and then he fell limply to the floor.

Dead, apparently.

Gérard and his partner looked at Claire as if they'd never seen her before, and then Gérard roared, 'What do you think you're—'

'Pick him up,' Claire said. 'We can take the stake out later. He's old. He'll survive.'

That sounded cold, and scary, and she hoped it was true. Amelie had survived, after all, and she knew Myrnin was as old, or maybe even older. From the look he gave her, Gérard was reassessing everything he'd thought about the cute, fragile little human he'd been nurse-maiding. Too bad. Claire thought one of her strengths was that everybody always underestimated her.

She was cool on the outside, shaking on the inside, because although it was the only way to keep Myrnin calm right now without tranquillisers, or without letting him rip Hannah's throat out, she'd just killed her boss.

That didn't seem like a really good career move.

Amelie will help, she thought a bit desperately, and Gérard slung Myrnin over his shoulder in a fireman's carry, and then they were running, moving fast again back down the hall to where Amelie had stayed to secure their escape.

Gérard came to a fast halt, and Hannah and Claire almost skidded into him. 'What?' Hannah whispered, and looked past the two vampires in the lead.

Amelie was at the corner ahead of them, but ten feet past her was Mr Bishop.

They were standing motionless, facing each other. Amelie looked fragile and delicate, compared to her father in his bishop's robes. He looked ancient and angry, and the fire in his eyes was like something out of the story of Joan of Arc.

Neither of them moved. There was some struggle going on, but Claire couldn't tell what it was, or what it meant.

Gérard reached out and grabbed her arm, and Hannah's, and held them in place. 'No,' he said sharply. 'Don't go near them.'

'Problem, sir, that's the way out,' Hannah said. 'And the dude's alone.'

Gérard and the Texan sent her a wild look, almost identical in their disbelief. 'You think so?' the Texan said. 'Humans.'

Amelie took a step backward, just a small one, but a shudder went through her body, and Claire knew – just *knew* – it was a bad sign. Really bad.

Whatever confrontation had been going on, it broke.

Amelie whirled to them and screamed, 'Go!' There was fury and fear in her voice, and Gérard let go of both girls and dumped Myrnin off his shoulder, into their arms, and he and the Texan pelted not for the exit, but to Amelie's side.

They got there just in time to stop Bishop from ripping out her throat. They slammed the old man up against the wall, but then there were others coming out into the hall. Bishop's troops, Claire guessed.

There were a lot of them.

Amelie intercepted the first of Bishop's vampires to run in her direction. Claire recognised him, vaguely – one of the Morganville vamps, but he'd obviously switched sides, and he came for Amelie, fangs out.

She put him down on the floor with one twisting move, fast as a snake, and looked back at Hannah and Claire, with Myrnin's body sagging between them. 'Get him *out!*' she shouted. 'I'll hold the way!'

'Come on,' Hannah said, and shouldered the bulk of Myrnin's limp weight. 'We're leaving.'

Myrnin felt cold and heavy, like the dead man he was, and Claire swallowed a surge of nausea as she struggled to support his limp weight. Claire gritted her teeth and helped Hannah half carry, half drag Myrnin's staked body down the corridor.

Behind them, the sounds of fighting continued –
mainly bodies hitting the floor. No screaming, no
shouting.

Vampires fought in silence.

'Right,' Hannah gasped. 'We're on our own.'

That really wasn't good news – two humans stuck
God knew where, with a crazy vampire with a stake
in his heart in the middle of a war zone.

'Let's get back to the door,' Claire said.

'How are we going to get through it?'

'I can do it.'

Hannah threw her a look. 'You?'

It was no time to get annoyed; hadn't she just
been thinking that being underestimated was a gift?
Yeah, not so much, sometimes. 'Yes, really. I can do it.
But we'd better hurry.' The odds weren't in Amelie's
favour. She might be able to hang on and cover their
retreat, but Claire didn't think she could win.

She and Hannah dragged Myrnin past the symbol-
marked doorways. Hannah counted off, and nodded
to the one where they'd entered.

Not too surprisingly, it was marked with the
Founder's Symbol, the same one Claire wore on the
bracelet on her wrist.

Hannah tried to open it. 'Dammit! Locked.'

Not when Claire tried the knob. It opened at a
twist, and the single candle in the corner illuminated

very little. Claire caught her breath and rested her trembling muscles for a few seconds as Hannah checked the room and pronounced it safe before they entered.

Claire let Myrnin slide in a heap to the floor. 'I'm sorry,' she whispered to him. 'It was the only way. I hope it doesn't hurt too much.'

She had no idea if he could hear her when he was like this. She wanted to grab the stake and pull it out, but she remembered that with Amelie, and with Sam, it had been the other vampires who'd done it. Maybe they knew things she didn't. Besides, the disease weakened them – even Myrnin.

She couldn't take the risk. And besides, having him wake up wounded and crazy would be even worse, now that they didn't have any vampires who could help control him.

Hannah returned to her side. 'So,' she said, as she checked the clip on her paintball gun, frowned, and exchanged it for a new one, 'how do we do this? We got to go back to that museum first, right?'

Did they? Claire wasn't sure. She stepped up to the door, which currently featured nothing but darkness, and concentrated hard on Myrnin's lab, with all its clutter and debris. Light swam, flickered, shivered, and snapped into focus.

No problem at all.

'Guess it's only roundabout getting here,' Claire said. 'Maybe that's on purpose, to keep people out who shouldn't be here. But it makes sense that once Amelie got here, she'd want to take the express out.' She turned back. 'Shouldn't we wait?'

Hannah opened the door and looked out into the hall. Whatever she saw, it couldn't have been good news. She shook her head. 'We bug out, right now.'

With a grunt of effort, Hannah braced Myrnin's deadweight on one side and dragged him forward. Claire took his other arm.

'Did he just twitch?' Hannah asked. ''Cause if he twitches, I'm going to shoot him.'

'No! No, he didn't; he's fine,' Claire said, practically tripping over the words. 'Ready? One, two...'

And *three*, they were in Myrnin's lab. Claire twisted out from under Myrnin's cold body, slammed the door shut, and stared wildly at the broken lock. 'I need to fix that,' she said. But what about Amelie? No, she'd know all the exits. She didn't have to come here.

'Girl, you need to get us the hell out of here, is what you need to do,' Hannah said. 'You dial up the nearest Fort Knox or something on that thing. Damn, how'd you learn this, anyway?'

'I had a good teacher.' Claire didn't look at Myrnin. She couldn't. For all intents and purposes, she'd just killed him, after all. 'This way.'

There were two ways out of Myrnin's lab, besides the usually secured dimensional doorway: steps leading up to street level, which were probably the absolute worst idea ever right now, and a second, an even more hidden dimensional portal in a small room off to the side. That was the one Amelie had used to get them in.

But the problem was, Claire couldn't get it to work. She had the memories clear in her head – the Glass House, the portal to the university, the hospital, even the museum they'd visited on the way here. But nothing *worked*.

It just felt...dead, as if the whole system had been cut off.

They were lucky to have made it this far.

Amelie's trapped, Claire realised. *Back there. With Bishop. And she's outnumbered.*

Claire double-checked the other door, too, the one she'd blocked.

Nothing. It wasn't just a malfunctioning portal; the whole network was down.

'Well?' Hannah asked.

Claire couldn't worry about Amelie right now. She had a job to do – get Myrnin to safety. And that meant getting him to the only vampire she knew offhand who could help him: Oliver. 'I think we're walking,' she said.

'The hell we are,' Hannah said. 'I'm not hauling a dead vampire through the streets of Morganville. We'll get ourselves killed by just about *everybody*.'

'We can't leave him!'

'We can't take him, either!'

Claire felt her jaw lock into stubborn position. 'Well, fine, you go ahead. Because I'm not leaving him. I can't.'

She could tell that Hannah wanted to grab her by the hair and yank her out of there, but finally, the older woman nodded and stepped back. 'Third option,' she said. 'Call in the cavalry.'

CHAPTER FIVE

It wasn't quite the Third Armoured Division, but after about a dozen phone calls, they did manage to get a ride.

'I'm turning on the street – nobody in sight so far,' Eve's voice said from the speaker of Claire's cell phone. She'd been giving Claire a turn-by-turn description of her drive, and Claire had to admit, it sounded pretty frightening. 'Yeah, I can see the Day House. You're in the alley next to it?'

'We're on our way,' Claire said breathlessly. She was drenched with sweat, aching all over, from the effort of helping drag Myrnin out of the lab, up the steps, and down the narrow, seemingly endless dark alley. Next door, the Founder House belonging to Katherine Day and her granddaughter – a virtual copy of the house where Claire and her friends lived – was dark and closed, but Claire saw curtains moving at the upstairs windows.

'That's my great-aunt's house, Great-Aunt Kathy,' Hannah panted. 'Everybody calls her Granma, though. Always have, as far back as I can remember.'

Claire could see how Hannah was related to the Days; partly her features, but her attitude for sure. That was a family full of tough, smart, get-it-done women.

Eve's big, black car was idling at the end of the alley, and the back door kicked open as the two of them – three? Did Myrnin still count? – approached. Eve took a look at Myrnin, and the stake in his back, sent Claire a you've-got-to-be-kidding-me look, and reached out to drag him inside, facedown, on the backseat. 'Hurry!' she said, and slammed the back door on the way to the driver's side. 'Damn, he'd better not bleed all over the place. Claire, I thought you were supposed to—'

'I know,' Claire said, and climbed into the middle of the big, front bench seat. Hannah crammed in on the outside. 'Don't remind me. I was supposed to keep him safe.'

Eve put the car in gear and did a ponderous tank-heavy turn. 'So, who staked him?'

'I did.'

Eve blinked. 'OK, that's an interesting interpretation

of *safe*. Weren't you with Amelie?' Eve actually did a quick check of the backseat, as if she were afraid Amelie might have magically popped in back there, seated like a barbarian queen on top of Myrnin's prone body.

'Yeah. We were,' Hannah said.

'Do I have to ask? No, wait, do I *want* to ask?'

'We left her,' Claire said, miserable. 'Bishop set a trap. She was fighting when we had to go.'

'What about the other guys? I thought you went with a whole entourage!'

'We left most of them...' Her brain caught up with her, and she looked at Hannah, who looked back with the same thought in her expression. 'Oh, crap. The other guys. They were in Myrnin's lab, but not when we came back...'

'Gone,' Hannah said. 'Taken out.'

'Super. So, we're winning, then.' Eve's tone was wicked cynical, but her dark eyes looked scared. 'I talked to Michael. He's OK. They're at the university. Things are quiet there so far.'

'And Shane?' Claire realised, with a pure bolt of guilt, that she hadn't called him. If he'd called her, she wouldn't have known; she'd turned off the ringer, afraid of the noise when creeping around on a rescue mission.

But as she dug out her phone, she saw that she

hadn't missed any calls after all.

'Yeah, he's OK,' Eve said, and steered the car at semi-high speed around a corner. The town was dark, very dark, with a few houses lit up by lanterns or candles or flashlights. Most people were waiting in the dark, scared to death. 'They had some vamps try to board the bus, probably looking for a snack, but it wasn't even a real fight. So far they're cruising without too much trouble. He's fine, Claire.' She reached over and took Claire's hand to squeeze it. 'You, not so much. You look awful.'

'Thanks. I think I earned it.'

Eve took back her hand to haul the big wheel of the car around for a turn. Headlights swept over a group on the sidewalk – unnaturally pale. Unnaturally still. 'Oh, crap, we've got bogeys. Hang on, I'm going to floor it.'

That was, Claire thought, a pretty fantastic idea, because the vampires on the curb were now in the street, and following. There was a kind of manic glee to how they pursued the car, but not even a vamp could keep up with Eve's driving for long; they fell back into the dark, one by one. The last one was the fastest, and he nearly caught hold of the back bumper before he stumbled and was left behind in a black cloud of exhaust.

'Damn freaks,' Eve said, trying to sound tough but

not quite making it. 'Hey, Hannah. How's business?'

'Right now?' Hannah laughed softly. 'Not so fantastic, but I'm not bothered about it. Let's see if we can make it to the morning. Then I'll worry about making ends meet at the shop.'

'Oh, we'll make it,' Eve said, with a confidence Claire personally didn't feel. 'Look, it's already four a.m. Another couple of hours, and we're fine.'

Claire didn't say, *In a couple of hours, we could all be dead,* but she was thinking it. What about Amelie? What were they going to do to rescue her?

If she's even still alive.

Claire's head hurt, her eyes felt grainy from lack of sleep, and she just wanted to curl up in a warm bed, pull the pillow over her head, and not be so *responsible.*

Fat chance.

She wasn't paying attention to where Eve was going, and anyway, it was so dark and strange outside she wasn't sure she'd recognise things, anyway. Eve pulled to a halt at the curb, in front of a row of plate glass windows lit by candles and lanterns inside.

Just like that, they were at Common Grounds.

Eve jumped out of the driver's side, opened the back door, and grabbed Myrnin under the arms, all the while muttering, 'Ick, ick, ick!' Claire slid out to join her, and Hannah grabbed Myrnin's feet when they hit the pavement, and the three of them carried him into the coffee shop.

Claire found herself shoved immediately out of the way by two vampires: Oliver and some woman she didn't know. Oliver looked grim, but then, that wasn't new, either. 'Put him down,' Oliver said. 'No, not there, idiots, over there, on the sofa. You. Off.' That last was directed at the frightened humans who were seated on the indicated couch, and they scattered like quail. Eve continued her *ick* mantra as she and Hannah hauled Myrnin's deadweight over and settled him facedown on the couch cushions. He was about the colour of a fluorescent lightbulb now, blue-white and cold.

Oliver crouched next to him, looking at the stake in Myrnin's back. He steepled his fingers for a moment, and then looked up at Claire. 'What happened?'

She supposed he could tell, somehow, that it was *her* stake. Wonderful. 'I didn't have a choice. He came after us.' The *us* part might have been an exaggeration; he'd come after Hannah, really. But eventually he would have come after Claire, too; she knew that.

Oliver gave her a moment to squirm while he stared at her, and then looked back at Myrnin's still, very corpselike body. The area where the stake had gone in looked even paler than the surrounding

tissue, like the edge of a whirlpool draining all the
colour out of him. 'Do you have any of the drugs you
have been giving him?' Oliver asked. Claire nodded,
and fumbled in her pocket. She had some of the
powder form of the drug, and some of the liquid, but
she hadn't felt confident at all that she'd be able to
get it into Myrnin's mouth without a fight she was
bound to lose. When Myrnin was like this, you were
going to lose fingers, at the very least, if you got
anywhere near his mouth.

Not so much an issue now, she supposed. She
handed over the vials to Oliver, who turned them
over in his fingers, considering, and then handed
back the powder. 'The liquid absorbs into the body
more quickly, I expect.'

'Yes.' It also had some unpredictable side effects,
but this probably wasn't the time to worry about
that.

'And Amelie?' Oliver continued turning the bottle
over and over in his fingers.

'She's – we had to leave her. She was fighting
Bishop. I don't know where she is now.'

A deep silence filled the room, and Claire saw the
vampires all look at one another – all except Oliver,
who continued to stare down at Myrnin, no change
in his expression at all. 'All right, then. Helen, Karl,
watch the windows and doors. I doubt Bishop's

patrols will try storming the place, but they might, while I'm distracted. The rest of you' – he looked at the humans and shook his head – 'try to stay out of our way.'

He thumbed the top off the vial of clear liquid and held it in his right hand. 'Get ready to turn him face-up,' he said to Hannah and Claire. Claire took hold of Myrnin's shoulders, and Hannah his feet.

Oliver took the stake in his left hand and, in one smooth motion, pulled it out. It clattered to the floor, and he nodded sharply. 'Now.'

Once Myrnin was lying on his back, Oliver motioned her away and pried open Myrnin's bloodless lips. He poured the liquid into the other vampire's mouth, shut it, and placed a hand on his high forehead.

Myrnin's dark eyes were open. Wide-open. Claire shuddered, because they looked completely dead – like windows into a dark, dark room...and then he blinked.

He sucked in a very deep breath, and his back arched in silent agony. Oliver held his hand steady on Myrnin's forehead. His eyes were squeezed shut in concentration, and Myrnin writhed weakly, trying without much success to twist free. He collapsed limply back on the cushions, chest rising and falling. His skin still looked like polished marble, veined with cold blue, but his eyes were alive again.

And crazy. And hungry.

He swallowed, coughed, swallowed again, and gradually, the insane pilot light in his eyes went out. He looked tired and confused and in pain.

Oliver let out a long, moaning sigh, and tried to stand up. He couldn't. He made it about halfway up, then wavered and fell to his knees, one hand braced on the arm of the couch for support. His head went down, and his shoulders heaved, almost as if he were gasping or crying. Claire couldn't imagine Oliver – *Oliver* – doing either one of those things, really.

Nobody moved. Nobody touched him, although some of the other vampires exchanged unreadable glances.

He's sick, Claire thought. It was the disease. It made it harder and harder for them to concentrate, to do the things they'd always taken for granted, like make other vampires. Or revive them. Even Oliver, who hadn't believed anything about the sickness... even he was starting to fail.

And he knew it.

'Help me up,' Oliver finally whispered. His voice sounded faint and tattered. Claire grabbed his arm and helped him climb slowly, painfully up; he moved as if he were a thousand years old, and felt every year of it. One of the other vampires silently provided a chair, and Claire helped him into it.

Oliver braced his elbows on his thighs and hid his pale face in his hands. When she started to speak, he said, softly, 'Leave me.'

It didn't seem a good idea to argue. Claire backed off and returned to where Myrnin was, on the couch.

He blinked, still staring at the ceiling. He folded his hands slowly across his stomach, but didn't otherwise move.

'Myrnin?'

'Present,' he said, from what seemed like a very great distance away. He chuckled very softly, then winced. 'Hurts when I laugh.'

'Yeah, um – I'm sorry.'

'Sorry?' A very slight frown worked its way between Myrnin's eyebrows, made a slow V, and then went on its way. 'Ah. Staked me.'

'I...uh...yeah.' She knew what Oliver's reaction would have been, if she'd done that kind of thing to him, and the outcome wouldn't have been pretty. She wasn't sure what Myrnin might do. Just to be sure, she stayed out of easy-grabbing distance.

Myrnin simply closed his eyes for a moment and nodded. He looked old now, exhausted, like Oliver. 'I'm sure it was for the best,' he said. 'Perhaps you should have left the wood in place. Better for everyone, in the end. I would have just – faded away. It's not very painful, not comparatively.'

'No!' She took a step closer, then another. He just looked so – defeated. 'Myrnin, don't. We need you.'

He didn't open his eyes, but there was a tiny, tired smile curving his lips. 'I'm sure you think you do, but you have what you need now. I found the cure for you, Claire. Bishop's blood. It's time to let me go. It's too late for me to get better.'

'I don't believe that.'

This time, his great dark eyes opened and studied her with cool intensity. 'I see you don't,' he said. 'Whether or not that assumption is reasonable, that's another question entirely. Where is she?'

He was asking about Amelie. Claire glanced at Oliver, still hunched over, clearly in pain. No help. She bent closer to Myrnin. No way she wouldn't be overheard by the other vampires, though, she knew that. 'She's – I don't know. We got separated. The last I saw, she and Bishop were fighting it out.'

Myrnin sat up. It wasn't the kind of smooth, controlled motion vampires usually had, as though they'd been practicing it for three or four human lifetimes; he had to pull himself up, slowly and painfully, and it hurt Claire to watch. She put her hand against his shoulder blade to brace him. His skin still felt marble-cold, but not *dead*. It was hard to figure out what the difference was – maybe it was the muscles, underneath, tensed and alive again.

'We have to find her,' he said. 'Bishop will stop at nothing to get her, if he hasn't already. Once you were safely away, she'd have retreated. Amelie is a guerrilla fighter. It's not like her to fight in the open, not against her father.'

'We're not going anywhere,' Oliver said, without taking his head out of his hands. 'And neither are you, Myrnin.'

'You owe her your fealty.'

'I owe nothing to the dead,' Oliver said. 'And until I see proof of her survival, I will not sacrifice my life, or anyone else's, in a futile attempt at rescue.'

Myrnin's face twisted in contempt. 'You haven't changed,' he said.

'Neither have you, fool,' Oliver murmured. 'Now shut up. My head aches.'

Eve was pulling shots behind the counter, wearing a formal black apron that went below her knees. Claire slid wearily onto a barstool on the other side. 'Wow,' she said. 'Flashback to the good times, huh?'

Eve made a sour face as she thumped a mocha

down in front of her friend. 'Yeah, don't remind me,' she said. 'Although I have to say, I missed the Monster.'

'The Monster?'

Eve patted the giant, shiny espresso machine beside her affectionately. 'Monster, meet Claire. Claire, meet the Monster. He's a sweetie, really, but you have to know his moods.'

Claire reached out and patted the machine, too. 'Nice to meet you, Monster.'

'Hey.' Eve caught her wrist when she tried to pull back. 'Bruises? What gives?'

Amelie's grip on her really had raised a crop of faint blue smudges on her upper arm, like a primitive tattoo. 'Don't freak. I don't have any bite marks or anything.'

'I'll freak if I wanna. As long as Michael isn't here, I'm kind of—'

'What, my mom?' Claire snapped, and was instantly sorry. And guilty, for an entirely different reason. 'I didn't mean—'

Eve waved it away. 'Hey, if you can't spark a 'tude on a day like this, when can you? Your mother's OK, by the way, because I know that's your next question. So far, Bishop's freaks haven't managed to shut down the cell network, so I've been keeping in touch, since nothing's happening here except for some serious caffeine production. Landlines are dead, though. So is the Internet. Radio and TV are both off the air, too.'

Claire looked at the clock. Five a.m. Two hours until dawn, more or less – probably less. It felt like an eternity.

'What are we going to do in the morning?' she asked.

'Good question.' Eve wiped down the counter. Claire sipped the sweet, chocolatey comfort of the mocha. 'When you think of something, let us know, because right now, I don't think anybody's got a clue.'

'You'd be wrong, thankfully,' Oliver said. He seemed to come out of nowhere – *God*, didn't Claire hate that! – as he settled on the stool next to her. He seemed almost back to normal now, but very tired. There was a shadow in his eyes that Claire didn't remember seeing before. 'There is a plan in place. Amelie's removal from the field of battle is a blow, but not a defeat. We continue as she would want.'

'Yeah? You want to tell us?' Eve asked. That earned her a cool stare. 'Yeah, I didn't think so. Vampires really aren't all about the sharing, unless it benefits them first.'

'I will tell you what you need to know, when you

need to know it,' Oliver said. 'Get me one of the bags from the walk-in refrigerator.'

Eve looked down at the top of her apron. 'Oh, I'm sorry, where does it say *servant* on here? Because I'm so very not.'

For a second, Claire held her breath, because the expression on Oliver's face was murderous, and she saw a red light, like the embers of a banked fire, glowing in the back of his eyes.

Then he blinked and said, simply, 'Please, Eve.'

Eve hadn't been expecting that. She blinked, stared back at him for a second, then silently nodded and walked away, behind a curtained doorway.

'You're wondering if that hurt,' Oliver said, not looking at Claire at all, but staring after Eve. 'It did, most assuredly.'

'Good,' she said. 'I hear suffering's good for the soul, or something.'

'Then we shall all be right with our God by morning.' Oliver swivelled on the stool to look her full in the face. 'I should kill you for what you did.'

'Staking Myrnin?' She sighed. 'I know. I didn't think I had a choice. He'd have bitten my hand off if I'd tried to give him the medicine, and by the time it took effect, me and Hannah would have been dog food, anyway. It seemed like the quickest, quietest way to get him out.'

'Even so,' Oliver said, his voice low in his throat, 'as an Elder, I have the power to sentence you, right now, to death, for attempted murder of a vampire. You do understand?'

Claire held up her hand and pointed to the gold bracelet on her wrist – the symbol of the Founder. Amelie's symbol. 'What about this?'

'I would pay reparations,' he said. 'I imagine I could afford it. Amelie would be tolerably upset with me, for a while, always assuming she is still alive. We'd reach an accommodation. We always do.'

Claire didn't say anything else in her defence, just waited. And after a moment, he nodded. 'All right,' he said. 'You were right to take the action you did. You have been right about a good deal that I was unwilling to admit, including the fact that some of us are' – he cast a quick look around, and dropped his voice so low she could make out the word only from the shape his lips gave it – 'unwell.'

Unwell. Yeah, that was one way to put it. She resisted an urge to roll her eyes. *How about dying? Ever heard the word* pandemic?

Oliver continued without waiting for her response. 'Myrnin's mind was...very disordered,' he said. 'I didn't think I could get him back. I wouldn't have, without that dose of medication.'

'Does that mean you believe us now?' She meant, *about the vampire disease*, but she couldn't say that out loud. Even the roundabout way they were speaking was dangerous; too many vampire ears with too little to do, and once they knew about the sickness, there was no predicting what they might do. Run, probably. Go off to rampage through the human world, sicken, and die alone, very slowly. It'd take years, maybe decades, but eventually, they'd all fall, one by one. Oliver's case was less advanced than many of the others, but age seemed to slow down the disease's progress; he might last for a long time, losing himself slowly.

Becoming nothing more than a hungry shell.

Oliver said, 'It means what it means,' and he said it with an impatient edge to it, but Claire wondered if he really did know. 'I am talking about Myrnin. Your drugs may not be enough to hold him for long, and that means we will need to take precautions.'

Eve emerged from the curtain carrying a plastic blood bag, filled with dark cherry syrup. That was what Claire told herself, anyway. Dark cherry syrup. Eve looked shaken, and she dumped the bag on the counter in front of Oliver like a dead rat.

'You've been planning this,' she said. 'Planning for a siege.'

Oliver smiled slowly. 'Have I?'

'You've got enough blood in there to feed half the vampires in town for a month, *and* enough of those heat-and-eat meals campers use to feed the rest of us even longer. Medicines, too. Pretty much anything we'd need to hold out here, including generators, batteries, bottled water...'

'Let's say I am cautious,' he said. 'It's a trait many of us have picked up during our travels.' He took the blood bag and motioned for a cup; when Eve set it in front of him, he punctured the bag with a fingernail, very neatly, and squeezed part of the contents into the cup. 'Save the rest,' he said, and handed it back to Eve, who looked even queasier than before. 'Don't look so disgusted. Blood in bags means none taken unwillingly from your veins, after all.'

Eve held it at arm's length, opened the smaller refrigerator behind the bar, and put it in an empty spot on the door rack inside. 'Ugh,' she said. 'Why am I behind the bar again?'

'Because you put on the apron.'

'Oh, you're just *loving* this, aren't you?'

'Guys,' Claire said, drawing both of their stares. 'Myrnin. Where are we going to put him?'

Before Oliver could answer, Myrnin pushed

through the crowd in the table-and-chairs area of
Common Grounds and walked towards them. He
seemed normal again, or as normal as Myrnin ever
got, anyway. He'd begged, borrowed, or outright
stolen a long, black velvet coat, and under it he was
still wearing the poofy white Pierrot pants from his
costume, dark boots, and no shirt. Long, black, glossy
hair and decadently shining eyes.

Oliver took in the outfit, and raised a brow. 'You
look like you escaped from a Victorian brothel,' he
said. 'One that...specialised.'

In answer, Myrnin skinned up the sleeves of
the coat. The wound in his back might have healed
– or might be healing, anyway – but the burns
on his wrists and hands were still livid red, with
an unhealthy silver tint to them. 'Not the sort of
brothel I'd normally frequent, by choice,' he said,
'though of course you might be more adventurous,
Oliver.' Their gazes locked, and Claire resisted the
urge to take a step back. She thought, just for a
second, that they were going to bare fangs at each
other...and then Myrnin smiled. 'I suppose I should
say thank you.'

'It would be customary,' Oliver agreed.

Myrnin turned to Claire. 'Thank you.'

Somehow, she guessed that wasn't what Oliver
had expected; she certainly hadn't. It was the kind

of snub that got most people hurt in Morganville, but then again, she guessed Myrnin wasn't most people, even to Oliver.

Oliver didn't react. If there was a small red glow in the depths of his eyes, it could have been a reflection from the lights.

'Um – for what?' Claire asked.

'I remember what you did.' Myrnin shrugged. 'It was the right choice at the moment. I couldn't control myself. The pain...the pain was extremely difficult to contain.'

She cast a nervous glance at his wrists. 'How is it now?'

'Tolerable.' His tone dismissed any further discussion. 'We need to get to a portal and locate Amelie. The closest is at the university. We will need a car, I suppose, and a driver. Some sturdy escorts wouldn't go amiss.' Myrnin sounded casual, but utterly certain that his slightest wish would be obeyed, and again, she felt that flare of tension between him and Oliver.

'Perhaps you've missed the announcement,' Oliver said. 'You're no longer a king, or a prince, or whatever you were before you disappeared into your filthy hole. You're Amelie's exotic pet alchemist, and you don't give me orders. Not in *my* town.'

'Your town,' Myrnin repeated, staring at him

intently. His face had set into pleasant, rigid lines, but those eyes – not pleasant at all. Claire moved herself prudently out of the way. 'What a surprise! I thought it was the Founder's town.'

Oliver looked around. 'Oddly, she seems unavailable, and that makes it my town, little man. So go and sit down. You're not going anywhere. If she's in trouble – which I do not yet believe – and if there's rescuing to be done, we will consider all the risks.'

'And the benefits of not acting at all?' Myrnin asked. His voice was wound as tight as a clock spring. 'Tell me, Old Ironsides, how you plan to win this campaign. I do hope you don't plan to re-enact Drogheda.'

Claire had no idea what that meant, but it meant something to Oliver, something bitter and deep, and his whole face twisted for a moment.

'We're not fighting the Irish campaigns, and whatever errors I made once, I'll not be making them again,' Oliver said. 'And I don't need advice from a blue-faced hedge witch.'

'There's the old Puritan spirit!'

Eve slapped the bar hard. 'Hey! Whatever musty old prejudices the two of you have rattling around in your heads, *stop*. We're here, twenty-first century, USA, and we've got problems that don't include your ancient history!'

Myrnin blinked, looked at Eve, and smiled. It was his seductive smile, and it came with a lowering of his thick eyelashes. 'Sweet lady,' he said, 'could you get me one of those delicious drinks you prepared for my friend, here?' He gracefully indicated Oliver, who remembered the cup of blood still sitting in front of him, and angrily choked it down. 'Perhaps warm the bag a bit in hot water first? It's a bit disgusting, cold.'

'Yeah, sure,' Eve sighed. 'Want a shot of espresso with that?'

Myrnin seemed to be honestly considering it. Claire urgently shook her head *no*. The last thing she – any of them – needed just now was Myrnin on caffeine.

As Eve walked away to prepare Myrnin's drink, Oliver shook himself out of his anger with a physical twitch, took a deep breath, and said, 'It's less than two hours to dawn. Even if something has happened to Amelie – which again, I dispute – it's too risky to launch a search just now. If Bishop has Amelie, he'll have her some place that'll hold against an assault in any case. Two hours isn't enough time, and I won't risk our people in the dawn.'

Myrnin flicked a glance towards Claire. 'Some of those here aren't affected by the dawn.'

'Some of them are also highly vulnerable,' Oliver

said. 'I wouldn't send a human out after Bishop. I wouldn't send a human *army* out after Bishop, unless you're planning to deduce his location from the corpses he leaves behind.'

For a horrified second, Myrnin actually mulled that over, and then he shook his head. 'He'd hide the bodies,' he said regretfully. 'A useful suggestion, though.'

Claire couldn't tell if he was mocking Oliver, or if he really meant it. Oliver couldn't tell, either, from the long, considering look he gave him.

Oliver turned his attention to her. 'Tell me everything.'

CHAPTER SIX

In an hour, the blush of dawn was already on the horizon, bringing an eerie blue glow to the night world. Somewhere out there, vampires all over town would be getting ready for it, finding secure places to stay the day – whatever side they were fighting on.

The ones in Common Grounds seemed content to stay on, which made sense; it was kind of a secured location anyway, from what Oliver and Amelie had said before – one of the key places in town to hold if they intended to keep control of Morganville.

But Claire wasn't entirely happy with the way some of those vampires – strangers, mostly, though all from Morganville, according to Eve – seemed to be whispering in the corners. 'How do we know they're on our side?' she asked Eve, in a whisper she hoped would escape vampire notice.

No such luck. 'You don't,' Oliver said, from several feet away. 'Nor is that your concern, but I will reassure you in any case. They are all loyal to me, and through me, to Amelie. If any of them "turn coats", you may be assured that they'll regret it.' He said it in a normal tone of voice, to carry to all parts of the room.

The vampires stopped whispering.

'All right,' Oliver said to Claire and Eve. The light of dawn was creeping up like a warning outside the windows. 'You understand what I want you to do?'

Eve nodded and gave him a sloppy, insolent kind of salute. 'Sir, yes *sir*, General sir!'

'Eve.' His patience, what little there was, was worn to the bone. 'Repeat my instructions.'

Eve didn't like taking orders under the best of circumstances, which these weren't. Claire quickly said, 'We take these walkie-talkies to each of the Founder Houses, to the university, and to anybody else on the list. We tell them all strategic orders come through these, not through cell phone or police band.'

'Be sure to give them the code,' he said. Each one of the tiny little radios had a keypad, like a cell phone, but the difference was that you had to enter the code into it to access the emergency communication channel he'd established. Pretty high tech, but then, Oliver didn't really seem the type to lag much behind on the latest cool stuff. 'All right. I'm sending Hannah with you as your escort. I'd send one of my own, but—'

'Dawn, yeah, I know,' Eve said. She offered a high five to Hannah, who took it. 'Damn, girl, love the Rambo look.'

'Rambo was a Green Beret,' Hannah said. 'Please. We eat those army boys for breakfast.'

Which was maybe not such a comfortable thing to say in a room full of maybe-hungry vampires. Claire cleared her throat. 'We should—'

Hannah nodded, picked up the backpack (Claire's, now filled with handheld radios instead of books), and handed it to her. 'I need both hands free,' she said. 'Eve's driving. You're the supply master. There's a checklist inside, so you can mark off deliveries as we go.'

Myrnin was sitting off to the side, ominously quiet. His eyes still looked sane, but Claire had warned Oliver in the strongest possible terms that he couldn't trust him. Not really.

As if I would, Oliver had said with a snort. *I've known the man for many human lifetimes, and I've never trusted him yet.*

The vampires in the coffee shop had mostly

retreated out of the big, front area, into the better-protected, light-proofed interior. Outside of the plate glass windows, there was little to be seen. The fires had gone out, or been extinguished. They'd seen some cars speeding about, mostly official police or fire, but the few figures they'd spotted had been quick and kept to the shadows.

'What are they doing?' Claire asked as she hitched her backpack to a more comfortable position on her shoulder. She didn't really expect Oliver to reply; he wasn't much on the sharing.

He surprised her. 'They're consolidating positions,' he said. 'This is not a war that will be fought in daylight, Claire. Or in the open. We have our positions; they have theirs. They may send patrols of humans they've recruited, but they won't come themselves. Not after dawn.'

'Recruited,' Hannah repeated. 'Don't you mean strong-armed? Most folks just want to be left alone.'

'Not necessarily. Morganville is full of humans who don't love us, or the system under which they labour,' Oliver replied. 'Some will believe Bishop is the answer. Some will act out of fear, to protect their loved ones. He will know how to appeal to them, and how to pressure. He'll find his human cannon fodder.'

'Like you've found yours,' Hannah said.

They locked stares for a few seconds, and then

Oliver inclined his head just a bit. 'If you like.'

'I don't,' she said, 'but I'm used to the front lines. You got to know, others won't be.'

Claire couldn't tell anything from Oliver's expression. 'Perhaps not,' he said. 'But for now, we can count on our enemies regrouping. We should do the same.'

Hannah nodded. 'I'm out first, then you, Eve. Have your keys in your hand. Don't hesitate, run like hell for the car, and get it unlocked. I'll get Claire to the passenger side.'

Eve nodded, clearly jittery. She took the car keys out of her pocket and held them in her hand, sorting through until she had the right key pointing out.

'One more thing,' Hannah said. 'You got a flashlight?'

Eve fumbled in her other pocket and came up with a tiny little penlight. When she twisted it, it gave a surprisingly bright glow.

'Good.' Hannah nodded. 'Before you get in the car, you shine that in the front and backseats. Make sure you can see all the way down to the carpet. I'll cover you from the door.'

The three of them moved to the exit, and Hannah put her left hand on the knob.

'Be careful,' Oliver said from the back of the room, which was kind of warmly surprising. He spoilt it by continuing, 'We need those radios delivered.'

Should have known it wasn't personal. Claire resisted the urge to flip him off.

Eve didn't bother to resist hers.

Then Hannah was swinging open the door and stepping outside. She didn't do it like in the movies; no drama, she just stepped right out, turned in a slow half circle as she scanned the street with the paintball gun held at rest. She finally motioned for Eve. Eve darted out and headed around the hood of the big, black car. Claire saw the glow of her penlight as she checked the inside, and then Eve was in the driver's seat and the car growled to a start, and Hannah pushed her towards the passenger door.

Behind them, the Common Grounds door slammed shut and locked. When she looked back, Claire saw that they were pulling down some kind of steel shutters inside the glass.

Locking up for dawn.

Claire and Hannah made it to the car without any problems. Even so, Claire was breathing hard, her heart racing.

'You OK?' Eve asked her. Claire nodded, still gasping. 'Yeah, I know. Terror Aerobics. Just wait until they get it at the gym. It'll be bigger than Pilates.'

Claire choked on her fear, laughed, and felt better.

'That's my girl. Locks,' Eve said. 'Also, seat belts,

please. We may be making some sudden stops along the way. Don't want anybody saying hello to Mr Windshield at speed.'

The drive through predawn Morganville was eerie. It was very...quiet. They'd mapped out a route, planning to avoid the most dangerous areas, but they almost had to divert immediately, because of a couple of cars parked in the middle of the street.

The doors were hanging open, interior lights were still shining.

Eve slowed down and crawled past on the right side, two wheels up on the curb. 'See anything?' she asked anxiously. 'Any bodies or anything?'

The cars were completely empty. They were still running, and the keys were in the ignition. One strange thing nagged at Claire, but she couldn't think what it was...

'Those are vampire cars,' Hannah said. 'Why would they leave them here like that?' Oh. That was the odd thing. The tinting on the windows.

'They needed to pee?' Eve asked. 'When you've gotta go...'

Hannah said nothing. She was watching out the windows with even more focus than before.

'Yeah, that is weird,' Eve said more quietly. 'Maybe they went to help somebody.' Or hunt somebody. Claire shivered.

They made their first radio delivery to one of the Founder Houses; Claire didn't know the people who answered the door, but Eve did, of course. She quickly explained about the radio and the code, and they were back in the car and rolling in about two minutes flat. 'Outstanding,' Hannah said. 'You girls could give some of my buddies in the marines a run for their money.'

'Hey, you know how it is, Hannah: living in Morganville really is combat training.' Eve and Hannah awkwardly slapped palms – awkwardly, because Eve kept facing front, and Hannah didn't turn away from her post at the car's back window. She had the window rolled down halfway, and the paintball gun at the ready, but so far she hadn't fired a single shot.

'More cars,' Claire said softly. 'You see?'

It wasn't just a couple of cars, it was a bunch of them, scattered on both sides of the street now, engines running, lights on, doors open.

Empty.

They cruised past slowly, and Claire took note of the heavy tinting on the windows. They were all the same type of car, the same type Michael had been issued on his official conversion to vampire.

'What the hell is going on?' Eve asked. She sounded tense and anxious, and Claire couldn't blame her. She felt pretty tense herself. 'This close to dawn, they wouldn't be doing this. They shouldn't even be outside. He said both sides would regroup, but this looks like some kind of full-on panic.'

Claire had to agree, but she also had no explanation. She dug one of the radios out of her backpack, typed in the code that Oliver had given her, and pressed the TALK button. 'Oliver? Come in.'

After a short delay, his voice came back. 'Go.'

'Something strange is happening. We're seeing lots of vampire cars, but they're all abandoned. Empty. Still running.' Static on the other end. 'Oliver?'

'Keep me informed,' he finally said. 'Count the number of cars. Make a list of licence numbers, if you can.'

'Er – anything else? Should we come back?'

'No. Deliver the radios.'

That was it. Claire tried again, but he'd shut off or he was ignoring her. She pressed the RESET button to scramble the code, and looked at Eve, who shrugged. They pulled to a halt in front of the second Founder House. 'Let's just get it done,' Eve said. 'Let the vamps worry about the vamps.'

It seemed reasonable, but Claire was afraid that somehow...it wasn't.

* * *

Three of the Founder Houses were piles of smoking wood and ash, and the Morganville Fire Department was still pouring water on one of them. Eve cruised by, but didn't stop. The horizon was getting lighter and lighter, and they still had a couple of stops to make.

'You OK back there?' Eve asked Hannah, as they turned another corner, heading into an area Claire actually recognised.

'Fine,' Hannah said. 'We going to the Day House?'

'Yeah, next on my list.'

'Good. I want to talk to Cousin Lisa.'

Eve pulled up outside of the big Founder House; it was lit up in every window, a stark contrast to its dark, shuttered neighbouring residences. As she put the car in park, the front door opened and spilt a wedge of lemon-coloured light across the immaculately kept front porch. Granma Day's rocker was empty, nodding in the slight wind.

The person at the door was Lisa Day – tall, strong, with more than a slight resemblance to Hannah. She watched them get out of the car. Upstairs windows opened, and gun barrels came out.

'They're all right,' she called, but she didn't step outside. 'Claire, right? And Eve? Hey, Hannah.'

'Hey.' Hannah nodded. 'Let's get in. I don't like this quiet out here.'

As soon as they were in the front door, in a familiar-looking hallway, Lisa slammed down locks and bolts, including a recently installed iron bar that slotted into place on either side of the frame. Hannah watched this with bemused approval. 'You knew this was coming?' she asked.

'I figured it'd come sooner or later,' Lisa said. 'Had the hardware in the basement. All we had to do was put it in. Granma didn't like it, but I did it, anyway. She keeps yelling about me putting holes in the wood.'

'Yeah, that's Granma.' Hannah grinned. 'God forbid we should mess up her house while the war's going on.'

'Speaking of that,' Lisa said, 'y'all need to stay here, if you want to stay safe.'

Eve exchanged a quick glance with Claire. 'Yeah, well, we can't, really. But thanks.'

'You sure?' Lisa's eyes were very bright, very focused. 'Because we're thinking maybe these vamps will kill each other off this time, and maybe we should all stick together. All the humans. Never mind the bracelets and the contracts.'

Eve blinked. 'Seriously? Just let them fight it out on their own?'

'Why not? What's it to us, anyway, who wins?' Lisa's smile was bitter and brief. 'We get screwed no matter what. Maybe it's time to put a human in charge of this town, and let the vampires find someplace else to live.'

Dangerous, Claire thought. Really dangerous. Hannah stared at her cousin, her expression tight and controlled, and then nodded. 'OK,' she said. 'You do what you want, Lisa, but you be careful, all right?'

'We're being real damn careful,' Lisa said. 'You'll see.'

They came to the end of the hallway, where the area opened up into the big living room, and Eve and Claire both stopped cold.

'Oh, *shit*,' Eve muttered.

The humans were all armed – guns, knives, stakes, blunt objects. The vampires who'd been assigned to guard the house were all sitting tied to chairs with so many turns of rope it reminded Claire of hangman's loops. She supposed if you were going to restrain vamps, it made sense, but—

'What the hell are you doing?' Eve blurted. At least some of the vampires sitting there, tied and gagged, were ones who'd been at Michael's house, or who'd fought on Amelie's side at the banquet. Some of them were struggling, but most seemed quiet.

Some looked *unconscious*.

'They're not hurt,' Lisa said. 'I just want 'em out of the way, in case things go bad.'

'You're making one hell of a move, Lisa,' Hannah said. 'I hope you know what the hell you're about.'

'I'm about protecting my own. You ought to be, too.'

Hannah nodded slowly. 'Let's go,' she said to Claire and Eve.

'What about—'

'No,' Hannah said. 'No radio. Not here.'

Lisa moved into their path, a shotgun cradled in her arms. 'Going so soon?'

Claire forgot to breathe. There was a feeling here, a darkness in the air. The vampires, those who were still awake, were staring at them. Expecting rescue, maybe?

'You don't want to do this,' Hannah said. 'We're not your enemies.'

'You're standing with the vamps, aren't you?'

There it was, out in the open. Claire swallowed hard. 'We're trying to get everybody out of this alive,' she said. 'Humans and vampires.'

Lisa didn't look away from her cousin's face. 'Not going to happen,' she said. 'So you'd better pick a side.'

Hannah stepped right up into her face. After a cold second, Lisa moved aside. 'Already have,'

Hannah said. She jerked her head at Claire and Eve. 'Let's move.'

Outside in the car, they all sat in silence for a few seconds. Hannah's face was grim and closed off, not inviting any conversation.

Eve finally said, 'You'd better tell Oliver. He needs to know about this.'

Claire plugged in the code and tried. 'Oliver, come in. Oliver, it's Claire. I have an update. Oliver!'

Static hissed. There was no response.

'Maybe he's ignoring you,' Eve said. 'He seemed pretty annoyed before.'

'You try.' Claire handed it over, but it was no use. Oliver wasn't responding. They tried calling for anyone at Common Grounds instead, and got another voice, one Claire didn't recognise.

'Hello?'

Eve squeezed her eyes shut in relief. 'Excellent. Who's this?'

'Quentin Barnes.'

'Tin-Tin! Hey man, how are you?'

'Ah – good, I guess.' Tin-Tin, whoever he was, sounded nervous. 'Oliver's kind of busy right now. He's trying to keep some people from taking off.'

'Taking off?' Eve's eyes widened. 'What do you mean?'

'Some of the vamps, they're just trying to leave.

It's too close to dawn. He's had to lock some of them up.'

Things were getting weird all over. Eve keyed the mike and said, 'There's trouble at the Day House. Lisa's tied up the vamps. She's going to sit this thing out. I think – I think maybe she's working with some other people, trying to put together a third side. All humans.'

'Dude,' Tin-Tin sighed, 'that's just what we need, getting the vampire slayers all in the mix. OK, I'll tell Oliver. Anything else?'

'More empty vampire cars. You think they're like those guys who were trying to leave? Maybe, I don't know, getting drawn off somewhere?'

'Probably. Look, just watch yourself, OK?'

'Will do. Eve out.'

Hannah stirred in the back. 'Let's move out to the next location.'

'I'm sorry,' Claire said. 'I know they're your family and all.'

'Lisa always was preaching about how we could take the town if we stuck together. Maybe she's thinking it's the right time to make a move.' Hannah shook her head. 'She's an idiot. All she's going to do is get people killed.'

Claire was no general, but she knew that fighting a war on two fronts and dividing their forces wasn't a great idea. 'We have to find Amelie.'

'Wherever she's taken herself off to,' Eve snorted. 'If she's even still—'

'Don't,' Claire whispered. She restlessly rubbed the gold bracelet on her wrist until it dug into her skin. 'We need her.'

More than ever, she was guessing.

By the time they'd dropped off the next to last radio, at their own home, which was currently inhabited by a bunch of freaked-out humans and a few vampires who hadn't yet felt whatever was pulling some of them off, the dawn was starting to really set in. The horizon was Caribbean blue, with touches of gold and red just flaring up like footlights at a show. Claire delivered the radio, the code, and a warning to the humans and vampires alike. 'You have to watch the vamps,' she pleaded. 'Don't let them leave. Not in the daylight.'

Monica Morrell, who was clutching the walkie-talkie in her red-taloned fingers, frowned at her. 'How are we supposed to do that, freak? Give them a written warning and scold them really hard? Come on!'

'If you let them go, they may not get wherever it is they're being called before sunrise,' Hannah said. She shrugged, a fluid flow that emphasised her muscles, and smiled. 'Hey, no skin off my nose or anything, but we may need 'em later. And you could get blamed for not stepping up.'

Monica kept on frowning, but she didn't seem inclined to argue with Hannah. Nobody did, Claire noticed. The former marine had an air about her, a confidence that somehow didn't come off at all like arrogance.

'Great,' Monica finally said. 'Wonderful. Like I needed another problem. By the way, Claire, your house really sucks ass. I hate it here.'

It was Claire's turn to smile this time. 'It probably hates you right back. I'm sure you'll figure it out,' she said. 'You're a natural leader, right?'

'Oh, bite it. Someday, your boyfriend won't be around to—' Monica widened her eyes. 'Oh, snap! He's *isn't* around, is he? Won't be back, ever. Remind me to send flowers for the funeral.'

Eve grabbed the back of Claire's shirt. 'Whoa, Mini-Me, chill out. We've got to get moving. Much as I'd like to see the cage match, we're kind of on a schedule.'

The hot crimson haze disappeared from Claire's eyes, and she took in a breath and nodded. Her muscles were aching. She realised she'd managed to clench just about every muscle, iron-hard, and tried to relax. Her hands twinged when she stretched them out of fists.

'See you soon,' Monica said, and shut the door on them. 'Wait, probably not, loser. And your clothes are pathetic, by the way!'

That last part came muffled, but clear – as clear as the sound of the locks snapping into place.

'Let's go,' Hannah said, and herded them off the porch and down the walk towards the white picket fence.

Walking on the street, heading vaguely north, was a vampire. 'Oh, crap,' Eve said, alarmed, but the vamp didn't seem to care about them, or even know they were there. He was wearing a police uniform, and Claire remembered him; he'd been riding with Richard Morrell, from time to time. Didn't seem like a bad guy, apart from the whole vampire thing. 'That's Officer O'Malley. Hey! Hey, Officer! Wait up!'

He ignored them and kept walking.

Claire looked east. The sun's golden glow was heating up the sky, fast. It wasn't over the horizon yet, but it would be in a matter of seconds, minutes at most. 'We've got to get him,' she said. 'Get him inside somewhere.'

'And do what, babysit him the rest of the day? O'Malley's not like Myrnin,' Eve said. 'You can't stake him. He's not that old. Seventy, eighty, something like that. He's only a little older than Sam.'

'We could run him over,' Hannah said. 'It wouldn't kill him.'

Eve sent her a wide-eyed look. 'Excuse me? With my *car*?'

'You're asking for something non-lethal. That's all I've got right now. The three of us aren't any kind of match for a vampire who wants to get somewhere, if he fights us.'

Claire took off running towards the vampire, ignoring their shouts. She looked back. Hannah was after her, and gaining.

She still got to Officer O'Malley first, and skidded into his path.

He paused for a second, his green eyes focusing on her, and then he reached out and moved her aside. Gently, but firmly.

And he kept on walking.

'You have to get inside!' Claire yelled, and got in front of him again. 'Sir, you have to! Right now! Please!'

He moved her again, this time without as much care. He didn't say a word.

'Oh, God,' Hannah said. 'Too late.'

The sun came up in a fiery burst, and the first rays of sunlight hit the parked cars, Eve's standing figure, the houses...and Officer O'Malley's back.

'Get a blanket!' Claire screamed. She could see

the smoke curling off him, like morning mist. 'Do something!'

Eve ran to get something from the car. Hannah grabbed Claire and pulled her out of his way.

Officer O'Malley kept walking. The sun kept rising, brighter and brighter, and within three or four steps, the smoke rising up from him turned to flames.

In ten more steps, he fell down.

Eve ran up breathlessly, a blanket clutched in both hands. 'Help me get it over him!'

They threw the fabric over Officer O'Malley, but instead of smothering the flames, it just caught fire, too.

Hannah pulled Claire back as she tried to pat out the flames. 'Don't,' she said. 'It's too late.'

Claire turned towards Hannah in a raw fury, struggling to get free. 'We can still—'

'No, we can't,' Hannah said. 'There's not a damn thing we can do for him. He's dying, Claire. You tried your best, but he's dying. And he's not going to take our help. Look, he's still trying to crawl. He's not stopping.'

She was right, but it hurt, and in the end, Claire wrapped her arms around Hannah for comfort and turned away.

When she finally looked back, Officer O'Malley was a pile of ash and smoke and burnt blanket.

'Michael,' Claire whispered. She looked at the sun. 'We have to find Michael!'

Hannah went very still for a second, and then nodded. 'Let's go.'

CHAPTER SEVEN

The gates of the university were shut, locked, and there were paramilitary-style men posted at the gates, all in black. Armed. Eve coasted the big car slowly up to them and rolled down the window.

'Delivery for Michael Glass,' she called. 'Or Richard Morrell.'

The guard who leant in was huge, tough, and intimidating – until he saw Hannah in the backseat, and then he grinned like a kid with a new puppy. 'Hannah Montana!'

She looked deeply pained. 'Don't *ever* call me that again, Jessup, or I *will* gut you.'

'Get out and make me stop, Smiley. Yeah, I heard you were back. How were the marines?'

'Better than the damn rangers.'

'Don't you just wish?' He lost the smile and got serious again. 'Sorry, H, orders are orders.

Who sent you? Who's with you?'

'Oliver sent me. You probably know Eve Rosser –
that's Claire Danvers.'

'Really? Huh. Thought she'd be bigger. Hey, Eve.
Sorry, didn't recognise you right off. Long time, no
see.' Jessup nodded to the other guard, who slung his
rifle and pressed in a key code at the panel on the
stone fence. The big iron gates slowly parted. 'You be
careful, Hannah. This town's the Af-Pak border all
over again right now.'

Inside, except for the guards patrolling the fence,
Texas Prairie University seemed eerily normal.
The birds sang to the rising sun, and there were
students out – *students!* – to class as if there were
nothing wrong at all. They were chatting, laughing,
running to make the cross-campus early-morning
bell.

'What the *hell*?' Eve said. Claire was glad she
wasn't the only one freaked out by it. 'I know they
had orders to keep things low profile, but damn,
this is ridiculous. Where's the dean's office?'

Claire pointed. Eve steered the car around the
winding curves, past dorms and lecture halls, and
pulled it to a stop on the nearly deserted lot in
front of the Administration Building. There were
two police cruisers there, and a bunch of black
Jeeps. Not a lot of civilian cars in the lot.

As they walked up the steps to the building, Claire realised there were two more guards outside of the main door. Hannah didn't know these guys, but she repeated their names and credentials, and after a brief, impersonal search, they were allowed inside.

The last time Claire had been here she'd been adding and dropping classes, and the building had been full of grumpy bureaucrats and anxious students, all moving at a hectic pace. Now it was very quiet. A few people were at their desks, but there were no students Claire could see, and the TPU employees looked either bored or nervous. Most of the activity seemed cantered down the carpeted hall, which was hung with formal portraits of the former university deans and notables.

One or two of the former deans, Claire was just now realising, might have been vampires, from the pallor of their skins. Or maybe they were just old white guys. Hard to say.

At the end of the hallway they found not a guard, but a secretary – just as tough as any of the armed men outside, though. She sat behind an expensive-looking antique desk that had not a speck of dust on it, and nothing else except a piece of paper cantered exactly in the middle, a pen at right angles to it, and a fancy, black multi-line telephone. No computer that Claire could spot – no, there it was, hidden away in a roll-out credenza to the side.

The room was lushly carpeted, so much so that Claire's feet sank into the depth at least an inch; it was like walking on foam. Solid, dark wood panelling. Paintings and dim lights. The windows were covered with fancy velvet curtains, and there was music playing – classical, of course. Claire couldn't imagine anybody would ever switch the station to rock. Not here.

'I'm Ms Nance,' the woman said, and stood to offer her hand to each of them in turn; she didn't even hesitate with Eve, who intimidated most people. She was a tall, thin, grey woman dressed in a tailored grey suit with a lighter grey blouse under the jacket. Gray hair curled into exact waves. Claire couldn't see her shoes, but she bet they were fashionable, grey, and yet somehow sensible. 'I'm the secretary to Dean Wallace. Do you have an appointment?'

Eve said, 'I need to see Michael.'

'I'm sorry? I don't think I know that person.'

Eve's expression froze, and Claire could see the horrible dread in her eyes.

Hannah, seeing it too, said, 'Let's cut the crap, Ms Nance. Where's Michael Glass?'

Ms Nance's eyes narrowed. They were pale blue, not as pale as Amelie's, but kind of faded, like jeans left in the sun. 'Mr Glass is in conference with the dean,' she said. 'I'm afraid you'll have to—'

The door at the far end of her office opened, and Michael came out. Claire's heart practically melted with relief. *He's OK. Michael's OK.*

Except that he closed the door and walked straight past them, a man on a mission.

He walked right past Eve, who stood there flat-footed, mouth open, fear dawning in her expression.

'Michael!' Claire yelped. He didn't even pause. 'We have to stop him!'

'Great,' Hannah said, and the three of them took off in pursuit.

It helped that Michael wasn't actually *running*, just moving with a purpose. Claire and Eve edged by him in the hall and blocked his path.

His blue eyes were wide-open, but he just didn't *see*. He sensed an obstacle, at least, and paused.

'Michael,' Claire said. *Dammit, why couldn't I have tranquillisers? Why?* 'Michael, you can't go out there. It's already morning. You'll die.'

'He's not listening,' Hannah said. And she was right; he wasn't. He tried to push between them, but Eve put a hand in the centre of his chest and held him back.

'Michael? It's me. You know me, don't you? Please?'

He stared at her with utterly blank eyes, and then shoved her out of his way. Hard.

Hannah sent Claire a quick, commanding look. 'Get help. *Now*. I'll try to hold him.'

Claire hesitated, but Hannah was without any doubt better equipped to handle a potentially hostile Michael than she was. She turned and ran, past startled desk jockeys and coffee-bearing civil servants, and slid to a stop in front of one of the black-uniformed soldiers. 'Richard Morrell,' she blurted. 'I need him. Right *now*.'

The soldier didn't hesitate. He grabbed the radio clipped to his shoulder and said, 'Admin to Morrell.'

'Morrell, go.'

The soldier unclipped the radio and silently offered it to Claire. She took it – it was heavier than the walkie-talkies – and pressed the button to talk. 'Richard? It's Claire. We have a big problem. We need to stop Michael and anybody else...' How could she say *vampire* without actually saying it? 'Anybody else with a sun allergy from going outside.'

'Why the hell would they be—'

'I don't know! They just *are*!' The image of Officer O'Malley on fire leapt into her mind, and she caught her breath on a sob. 'Help us. They're going out in the sun.'

'Give the radio back,' he ordered. She handed it to the black-uniformed man. 'I need you to go with this girl and help her. No questions.'

'Yes sir.' He clicked off the radio and looked down at Claire. 'After you.'

She led the way back towards the hallway. As they reached it, there was a crash of glass, and Hannah came flying out to land flat on her back, blinking.

Michael walked over her. Eve was hauling on his arm, trying to hold him back, but he shook her off.

'We can't let him get outside!' Claire said. She tried to grab him, but it was like grabbing a freight train. She'd forgotten how strong he was now.

'Out of the way,' the soldier said, and pulled a handgun from a holster at his side.

'No, don't—'

The bureaucrats scattered, hiding under their desks, dropping their coffee to hug the carpet.

The soldier sighted on Michael's chest, and fired three times in quick succession. Instead of the loud bangs Claire had been expecting, there were soft compressed-air coughs.

And three darts feathered Michael's chest, clustered above his heart.

He *still* took three steps towards the soldier before

collapsing in slow motion to his knees, and then onto his face.

'All clear,' the soldier said. He took hold of Michael, turned him over, and yanked out the darts. 'He'll be under for about an hour, probably no longer than that. Let's get him to the dean's office.'

Hannah wiped a trickle of blood from her mouth, coughed, and rolled to her feet. She and Eve helped Claire grab Michael's shoulders and feet, and they carried him down the hallway, past paintings that were going to need some major repair and reframing, past splintered panels and broken glass, into Ms Nance's office.

Ms Nance took one look at them and moved smartly to the door marked with a discreet brass plaque that said DEAN WALLACE. She rapped and opened the door for them to carry Michael through.

Dean Wallace was a woman, which was kind of a surprise to Claire. She'd been expecting a pudgy, middle-aged man; *this* Dean Wallace was tall, graceful, thin, and a whole lot younger than Claire would have imagined. She had straight brown hair worn long around her shoulders, and a simple black suit that was almost the negative image of Ms Nance's, only somehow less formal. It looked…lived in.

Dean Wallace's lips parted, but she didn't ask a question. She checked herself, then nodded at the leather couch on the far side of the room, across from her massive desk. 'Right, put him there.' She had a British accent, too. Definitely not a Texas girl. 'What happened?'

'Whatever it is, it's happening all over,' Hannah said as they arranged Michael's unconscious body on the sofa. 'They're just taking off. It's like they don't even know or care the sun's up. Some kind of homing signal just gets switched on.'

Dean Wallace thought for a second, then pressed a button on her desk. 'Ms Nance? I need a bulletin to go out through the emergency communication system. All vampires on campus should be immediately restrained or tranquillised. No exceptions. This is priority one.' She frowned as she got the acknowledgment, and looked up at their little group. 'Michael seemed very rational, and there was no warning this would happen. I just thought he had somewhere to go. He didn't seem odd, at least at first.'

'How many other vampires on campus?' Hannah asked.

'Some professors of course, but they're mostly not here at the moment, since they teach at night. No students, obviously. Apart from the ones Michael and

Richard brought in, we have perhaps five in total on the grounds. More were here earlier, but they headed for shelter before sunrise, off campus.' Dean Wallace seemed calm, even in the face of all this. 'You're Claire Danvers?'

'Yes ma'am,' she said, and shook the hand Dean Wallace offered her.

'I had a talk with your Patron recently regarding your progress. Despite your – challenges, you have done excellent course work.'

It was stupid to feel pleased about that, but Claire couldn't help it. She felt herself blush, and shook her head. 'I don't think that matters very much right now.'

'On the contrary, it matters a great deal, I believe.'

Eve settled herself down next to the sofa, holding Michael's limp hand. She looked shattered. Hannah leant against the wall and nodded to the soldier as he exited the office. 'So,' she said, 'want to explain to me how you can have half the US Army walking the perimeter and not have massive student panic?'

'We've told all students and their parents that the university is cooperating in a government emergency drill, and of course that all weapons are non-lethal. Which is quite true, so far as it goes.

The issue of keeping students on campus is a bit trickier, but we've managed so far by linking it to the emergency drills. Can't go on for long, though. The local kids are already well informed, and it's only a matter of time before the out-of-town students begin to realise that we're having them on when they can't get word out to their friends and relatives. We're filtering all Internet and phone access, of course.' Dean Wallace shook her head. 'But that's my problem, not yours, and yours is much more pressing. We can't knock out every vampire in town, and we can't *keep* them knocked out in any case.'

'Not enough happy juice in the world,' Hannah agreed. 'We need to either stop this at its source, or get the heck out of their way.'

There was a soft knock on the door, and Ms Nance stepped in. 'Richard Morrell,' she announced, and moved aside for him.

Claire stared. Monica's brother looked like about fifty miles of bad road – exhausted, red-eyed, pale, running on caffeine and adrenaline. Just like the rest of them, she supposed. As Ms Nance quietly closed the door behind him, Richard strode forward, staring at Michael's limp body. 'Is he out?' His voice sounded rough, too, as if he'd been yelling. A *lot*.

'Sleeping the sleep of the just,' Hannah said. 'Or the just drugged, anyway. Claire. Radio.'

Oh. She'd forgotten about the backpack still slung over her shoulder. She quickly took out the last radio and handed it over, explaining what it was for. Richard nodded.

'I think this calls for a strategy meeting,' he said, and pulled up a chair next to the couch. Hannah and Claire took seats as well, but Eve stayed where she was, by Michael, as if she didn't want to leave him even for a moment.

Dean Wallace sat behind her desk, fingers steepled, watching with interested calm.

'I put in the code, right?' He was already doing it, so Claire just nodded. A signal bleeped to show he was logged on the network. 'Richard Morrell, University, checking in.'

After a few seconds, a voice answered. 'Check, Richard, you're the last station to report. Stand by for a bulletin.'

There were a few clicks, and then another voice came over the radio.

This is Oliver. I am broadcasting to all on the network with emergency orders. Restrain every vampire allied to us that you can find, by whatever means necessary. Locked rooms, chains, tranquillisers, cells, use what you have. Until we know how and why this is happening, we must take every precaution during the day. It seems that some of us have resistance to the call, and others have immunity, but this could change at any time. Be on your guard. From this point forward, we will conduct hourly calls, and each location will report status. University station, report.

Richard clicked the TALK button. 'Michael Glass and all the other vampires in our group are being restrained. We've got student containment here, but it won't last. We'll have to open the gates no later than tomorrow morning, if we can keep it together until then. Even with the phone and Internet blackout, somebody's going to get word out.'

'We're following the plan,' Oliver said. 'We're taking the cell towers down in ten minutes, until further notice. Phone lines are already cut. The only communication from this point forward will be strategic, using the radios. What else do you need?'

'Whip and a chair? Nothing. We're fine here for now. I don't think anybody will try a daylight assault, not with as many guards as we have here.' Richard hesitated, then keyed the mike again. 'Oliver, I've been hearing things. I think there are some factions out there forming. Human factions. Could complicate things.'

Oliver was silent for a moment, then said, 'Yes, I understand. We'll deal with that as it arises.'

Oliver moved on to the next station on his list, which was the Glass House. Monica reported in, which was annoying. Claire resisted the urge to grind her teeth. It was a quick summary, at least, and as more Founder Houses reported in, the situation seemed the same: some vampires were responding to the homing signal, and some weren't. At least, not yet.

Richard Morrell was staring thoughtfully into the distance, and finally, when all the reports were finished, he clicked the button again. 'Oliver, it's Richard. What happens if *you* start going zombie on us?'

'I won't,' Oliver said.

'If you do. Humour me. Who takes over?'

Oliver obviously didn't want to think about this, and Claire could hear the barely suppressed fury in his voice when he replied. 'You do,' he said. 'I don't care how you organise it. If we have to hand the defence of Morganville over to mere humans, we've already lost. Oliver signing out. Next check-in, one hour from now.'

The walkie-talkie clicked off.

'That went well,' Dean Wallace observed. 'He's named you heir apparent to the Apocalypse. Congratulations.'

'Yeah, it's one hell of a field promotion.' Richard stood up. 'Let's find a place for Michael.'

'We have some storage areas in the basement – steel doors, no windows. That's where they'll take the others.'

'That'll do for now. I want to move him to the jail as soon as we can, centralise the containment.'

Claire looked at Eve, and then at Michael's sleeping face, and thought about him alone in a cell – because what else could you call it? Locked away like Myrnin.

Myrnin. She wondered if he'd felt this weird pull, too, and if he had, whether or not they'd been able to stop him from taking off. Probably not, if he'd been determined to go running off. Myrnin was one of those unstoppable forces, and unless he met an immovable object...

She sighed and helped carry Michael down the hall, past the stunned bureaucrats, to his temporary holding cell.

Life went on, weirdly enough – human life, anyway. People began to venture out, clean up the streets, retrieve things from burnt and trashed houses. The police began to establish order again.

But there were things happening. People gathering in groups on street corners. Talking. Arguing.

Claire didn't like what she saw, and she could tell that Hannah and Eve didn't, either.

Hours passed. They cruised around for a while, and passed bulletins back to Oliver on the groups they saw. The largest one was almost a hundred people, forming up in the park. Some guy Claire didn't know had a loudspeaker.

'Sal Manetti,' Hannah said. 'Always was a troublemaker. I think he was one of Captain Obvious's guys for a while, but they had a falling-out. Sal wanted a lot more killing and a lot less talking.'

That wasn't good. It really wasn't good how many people were out there listening to him.

Eve went back to Common Grounds to report in, and that was just when things started to go wrong.

Hannah was driving Claire back home, after dropping off a trunk full of blood bags from the university storage vaults, when the radio Claire had in her pocket began to chime for attention. She logged in with the code. As soon as she did, a blast of noise tumbled out of the speaker.

She thought she heard something about Oliver, but she wasn't sure. Her shouted questions weren't answered. It was as if someone had pressed the button by accident, in the middle of a fight, and everybody was too busy to answer.

Then the broadcast went dead.

Claire exchanged a look with Hannah. 'Better—'

'Go to Common Grounds? Yeah. Copy that.'

When they arrived, the first thing Claire saw was the broken glass. The shutters were up, and two front windows had been shattered out, not in; there were sprays of broken pieces all the way to the curb.

It seemed very, very quiet.

'Eve?' Claire blurted, and bailed before Hannah could tell her to stay put. She hit the front door of the coffee shop at a run, but it didn't open, and she banged into it hard enough to bruise.

Locked.

'Will you *wait?*' Hannah snapped, and grabbed her arm as she tried to duck in through one of the broken windows. 'You're going to get yourself cut. Hang on.'

She used the paintball gun she carried to break out some of the hanging sharp edges, and before Claire could dart ahead, she blocked the path and stepped over the low wooden sill. Claire followed. Hannah didn't try to stop her, probably because she knew better.

'Oh man,' Hannah said. As Claire climbed in after

her, she saw that most of the tables and chairs were overturned or shoved out of place. Broken crockery littered the floor.

And people were down, lying motionless among the wreckage. Hannah went from one to the other, quickly assessing their conditions. There were five down that Claire could see. Two of them made Hannah shake her head in regret; the other three were still alive, though wounded.

There were no vampires in the coffee bar, and there was no sign of Eve.

Claire ducked behind the curtain. More signs of a struggle. Nobody left behind, alive or dead. She sucked in a deep breath and opened up the giant commercial refrigerator.

It was full of blood bags, but no bodies.

'Anything?' Hannah asked at the curtain.

'Nobody here,' Claire said. 'They left the blood, though.'

'Huh. Weird. You'd think they'd need that more than anything. Why attack the place if you're not taking the good stuff?' Hannah stared out into the coffee shop, her expression blank and distant. 'Glass is broken out, not in. No sign anybody got in the doors, either front or back. I don't think anybody attacked from the outside, Claire.'

With a black, heavy feeling gathering in her

stomach, Claire swung the refrigerator door shut. 'You think the vampires fought to get *out*.'

'Yeah. Yeah, I do.'

'Oliver, too.'

'Oliver, Myrnin, all of them. Whatever bat signal was calling them got turned up to eleven, I think.'

'Then where's Eve?' Claire asked.

Hannah shook her head. 'We don't know anything. It's all guesswork. Let's get some boots on the ground and figure this thing out.' She continued to stare outside. 'If they went out there, most of them could make it for a while in the sun, but they'd be hurt. Some couldn't make it far at all.'

Some, like the policeman Claire had seen burn up in front of her, would already be gone. 'You think it's Mr Bishop?' she asked, in a very small voice.

'I hope so.'

Claire blinked. 'Why?'

'Because if it's not, that's got to be a whole lot worse.'

CHAPTER EIGHT

Three hours later, they didn't know much more, except that nothing they tried to do to keep the vampires from leaving seemed to work, apart from tranquillising them and locking them up in sturdy cells. Tracking those who did leave wasn't much good, either. Claire and Hannah ended up at the Glass House, which seemed like the best place to gather – central to most things, and close to City Hall in an emergency.

Richard Morrell arrived, along with a few others, and set up shop in the kitchen. Claire was trying to figure out what to do to feed everybody, when there was another knock at the door.

It was Granma Day. The old woman, straight-backed and proud, leant on her cane and stared at Claire from age-faded eyes. 'I ain't staying with my daughter,' she said. 'I don't want any part of that.'

Claire quickly moved aside to let her in, and the
old lady shuffled inside. As Claire locked the door
behind her, she asked, 'How did you get here?'

'Walked,' Granma said. 'I know how to use my
feet just fine. Nobody bothered me.' Nobody would
dare, Claire thought. 'Young Mr Richard! Are you in
here?'

'Ma'am?' Richard Morrell came out of the kitchen,
looking very much younger than Claire had ever seen
him. Granma Day had that effect on people. 'What
are you doing here?'

'My fool daughter's off her head,' Granma said.
'I'm not having any of it. Move out of the way, boy.
I'm making you some lunch.' And she tapped her
cane right past him, into the kitchen, and clucked
and fretted over the state of the kitchen while
Claire stood by, caught between giggles and horror.
She was just a pair of hands, getting ordered
around, but at the end of it there was a plate full of
sandwiches and a big jug of iced tea, and everybody
was seated around the kitchen table, except for
Granma, who'd gone off into the other room to rest.
Claire had hesitantly taken a chair, at Richard's
nod. Detectives Joe Hess and Travis Lowe were also
present, and they were gratefully scoffing down food
and drink. Claire felt exhausted, but they looked a
whole lot worse. Tall, thin Joe Hess had his left arm

in a sling – broken, apparently, from the brace on it – and both he and his rounder, heavier partner had cuts and bruises to prove they'd been in a fight or two.

'So,' Hess said, 'any word on where the vampires are heading when they take off?'

'Not so far,' Richard said. 'Once we started tracking them, we could keep up only for a while, and then they lost us.'

'Aren't they hurt by the sun?' Claire asked. 'I mean—'

'They start smoking, not in the Marlboro way, and then they start crisping,' Travis Lowe said around a mouthful of turkey and Swiss. 'The older ones, they can handle it OK, and anyway, they're not just charging out there anymore. They're putting on hats and coats and blankets. I saw one wrapped up in a Sponge-Bob rug from some kid's bedroom, if you can believe that. It's the younger vamps that are in trouble. Some of them won't make it to the shade if they're not careful.'

Claire thought about Michael, and her stomach lurched. Before she even formed the question, Richard saw her expression and shook his head. 'Michael's OK,' he said. 'Saw to it myself. He's got himself a nice, secure jail cell, along with the other vampires we could catch before it was too late. He's not as strong as some of the others. He can't bend steel with his bare hands. Yet, anyway.'

'Any word on—' Claire was wearing out the question, and Richard didn't even let her finish it.

'No sign of Eve,' he said. 'No word from her. I'd try to put a GPS track on her phone, but we'd have to bring the cell network up, and that's too dangerous right now. I've asked the guys on the street to keep an eye out for her, but we've got a lot of things going on, Claire.'

'I know. But—' She couldn't put it into words, exactly. She just knew that somewhere, somehow, Eve was in trouble, and they needed to find her.

'So,' Joe Hess said, and stood up to look at a blown-up map of Morganville taped to the wall. 'This still accurate?' The map was covered in coloured dots: blue for locations held by those loyal to Amelie; red for those loyal to Bishop; black for those burnt or otherwise put out of commission, which accounted for three Founder Houses, the hospital, and the blood bank.

'Pretty much,' Richard said. 'We don't know if the vampires are leaving Bishop's locations, but we know they're digging in, just like Amelie's folks. We can verify locations only where Amelie's people were supposed to be, and they're gone from just about every location we've got up in blue.'

'Where were they last seen?'

Richard consulted notes, and began to add yellow dots to the map. Claire saw the pattern almost immediately. 'It's the portals,' she said. 'Myrnin got the portals working again, somehow. That's what they're using.'

Hess and Lowe looked blank, but Richard nodded. 'Yeah, I know about that. Makes sense. But where are they *going*?'

She shrugged helplessly. 'Could be anywhere. I don't know all the places the portals go; maybe Myrnin and Amelie do, but I don't think anybody else does.' But she felt unreasonably cheered by the idea that the vampires weren't out wandering out in the daylight, spontaneously combusting all over the place. She didn't want to see that happen to them... not even to Oliver.

Well, maybe to Oliver, sometimes. But not today.

The three men stared at her for a few seconds, then went back to studying the map, talking about perimeters and strategies for patrols, all kinds of things that Claire didn't figure really involved her. She finished her sandwich and walked into the living room, where tiny, wizened little Granma Day was sitting in an overstuffed wing chair with her feet up, talking to Hannah. 'Hey, little girl,' Granma Day said. 'Sit yourself.'

Claire perched, looking around the room. Most of the vampires were gone, either confined to cells or locked away for safety; some, they hadn't been able to stop. She couldn't seem to stop anxiously rubbing her hands together. *Shane.* Shane was supposed to be here. Richard Morrell had said that they'd arranged for the Bloodmobile to switch drivers, and that meant Shane would be coming soon for his rest period.

She needed him right now.

Granma Day was looking at her with distant sympathy in her faded eyes. 'You worried?' she asked, and smiled. 'You got cause, I expect.'

'I do?' Claire was surprised. Most adults tried to pretend it was all going to be OK.

'Sure thing, sugar. Morganville's been ruled by the vampires a long time, and they ain't always been the gentlest of folks. Been people hurt, people killed without reason. Builds up some resentment.' Granma nodded towards the bookcase. 'Fetch me that red book right there, the one that starts with *N*.'

It was an encyclopaedia. Claire got it and set it in her lap. Granma's weathered, sinewy fingers opened it and flipped pages, then handed it back. The heading said, *New York Draft Riots, 1863.*

The pictures showed chaos – mobs, buildings on fire. And worse things. Much, much worse.

'People forget,' Granma said. 'They forget what can happen, if anger builds up. Those New York folks, they were angry because their men were being drafted to fight the Civil War. Who you think they took it out on? Mostly black folks, of all things. Folks who couldn't fight back. They even burnt up an orphanage, and they'd have killed every one of those children if they'd caught them.' She shook her head, clicking her tongue in disgust. 'Same thing happened in Tulsa in 1921. Called it the Greenwood Riot, said black folks were taking away their business and jobs. Back in France, they had a revolution where they took all those fancy aristocrat folks and cut their heads off. Maybe it was their fault, and maybe not. It's all the same thing: you get angry, you blame it on some folks, and you make them pay, guilty or not. Happens all the time.'

Claire felt a chill. 'What do you mean?'

'I mean, you think about France, girl. Vampires been holding us all down a long time, just like those aristocrats, or that's how people around here think of it. Now, you think about all those folks out there with generations of grudges, and nobody really in charge right now. You think it won't go bad on us?'

There weren't enough shudders in the world.

Claire remembered Shane's father, the fanatical light in his eyes. He'd be one of those leading a riot, she thought. One of those pulling people out of their houses as collaborators and turncoats and hanging them up from lampposts.

Hannah patted the shotgun in her lap. She'd put the paintball gun aside – honestly, it wasn't much use now, with the vampires missing in action. 'They're not getting in here, Granma. We won't be having any Greenwood in Morganville.'

'I ain't so much worried about you and me,' Granma said. 'But I'd be worried for the Morrells. They're gonna be coming for them, sooner or later. That family's the poster children for the old guard.'

Claire wondered if Richard knew that. She thought about Monica, too. Not that she liked Monica – God, no – but still.

She thanked Granma Day and walked back into the kitchen, where the policemen were still talking. 'Granma Day thinks there's going to be trouble,' she said. 'Not the vampires. Regular people, like those people in the park. Maybe Lisa Day, too. And she thinks you ought to look after your family, Richard.'

Richard nodded. 'Already done,' he said. 'My mom and dad are at City Hall. Monica's headed there, too.' He paused, thinking about it. 'You're right. I should make sure she gets there all right, before she becomes another statistic.' His face had tightened, and there was a look in his eyes that didn't match the way he said it. He was worried.

Given what Claire had just heard from Granma Day, she thought he probably ought to be. Joe Hess and Travis Lowe sent each other looks, too, and she thought they were probably thinking the same thing. *She deserves it,* Claire told herself. *Whatever happens to Monica Morrell, she earned it.*

Except the pictures from Granma Day's book kept coming back to haunt her.

The front door banged shut, and she heard Hannah's voice – not an alarm, just a welcome. She spun around and went to the door of the kitchen... and ran directly into Shane, who grabbed her and folded his arms around her.

'You're here,' he said, and hugged her so tightly that she felt ribs creak. 'Man, you don't make it easy, Claire. I've been freaking out all damn day. First I hear you're off in the middle of Vamptown; then you're running around like bait with Eve—'

'You're one to talk about bait,' Claire said, and pushed back to look up into his face. 'You OK?'

'Not a scratch,' he said, and grinned. 'Ironic, because I'm usually the one with the battle scars, right? The worst thing that happened to me was that I had to pull over and let a bunch of vampires off the bus, or they'd have ripped right through the walls. You'd be proud. I even let them off in the shade.' His smile faded, but not the warmth in his eyes. 'You look tired.'

'Yeah, you think?' She caught herself on a yawn. 'Sorry.'

'We should get you home and catch some rest while we can.' He looked around. 'Where's Eve?'

Nobody had told him. Claire opened her mouth and found her throat clenching tight around the words. Her eyes filled with tears. *She's gone*, she wanted to say. *She's missing. Nobody knows where she is.*

But saying it out loud, saying it to Shane, that would make it real, somehow.

'Hey,' he said, and smoothed her hair. 'Hey, what's wrong? Where is she?'

'She was at Common Grounds,' Claire finally choked out. 'She—'

His hands went still, and his eyes widened.

'She's missing,' Claire finally said, and a wave of utter misery broke over her. 'She's out there somewhere. That's all I know.'

'Her car's outside.'

'We drove it here.' Claire nodded at Hannah, who'd come in behind Shane and was silently watching. He acknowledged her with a glance; that was all.

'OK,' Shane said. 'Michael's safe, you're safe, I'm safe. Now we're going to go find Eve.'

Richard Morrell stirred. 'That's not a good idea.'

Shane spun on him, and the look on his face was hard enough to scare a vampire. 'Want to try and stop me, *Dick*?'

Richard stared at him for a moment, then turned back to the map. 'You want to go, go. We've got things to do. There's a whole town of people out there to serve and protect. Eve's one girl.'

'Yeah, well, she's our girl,' Shane said. He took Claire's hand. 'Let's go.'

Hannah leant against the wall. 'Mind if I call shotgun?'

'Since you're carrying one? Feel free.'

Outside, things were odd – quiet, but with a suppressed feeling of excitement in the air. People were still outside, talking in groups on the streets. The stores were shut down, for the most part, but Claire noticed with a stir of unease that the bars were open, and so was Morganville's gun shop.

Not good.

The gates of the university had opened, and they were issuing some kind of passes to people to leave – still sticking to the emergency drill story, Claire assumed.

'Oh, man,' Shane muttered, as they turned down one of the streets that led to the heart of town, and Founder's Square – Vamptown. There were more people here, more groups. 'I don't like this. There's Sal Manetti up there. He was one of my dad's drinking buddies, back in the day.'

'The cops don't like it much, either,' Hannah said, and pointed at the police cars ahead. They were blocking off access at the end of the street, and when Claire squinted, she could see they were out of their cruisers and arranged in a line, ready for anything. 'This could turn bad, any time. All they need is somebody to strike a match out there, and we're all on fire.'

Claire thought about Shane saying his father was coming to town, and she knew he was thinking about that, too. He shook his head. 'We've got to figure out where Eve might be. Ideas?'

'Maybe she left us some clues,' Claire said. 'Back at Common Grounds. We should probably start there.'

Common Grounds, however, was deserted, and the steel shutters were down. The front door was locked. They drove around back, to the alley. Nothing was there but trash cans, and—

'What the hell is that?' Shane asked. He hit the brakes and put the car in park, then jumped out and picked up something small on the ground. He got back in and showed it to Claire.

It was a small white candy in the shape of a skull. Claire blinked at it, then looked down the alley. 'She left a trail of breath mints?'

'Looks like. We'll have to go on foot to follow it.'

Hannah didn't seem to like that idea much, but Shane wasn't taking votes. They parked and locked Eve's car in the alley behind Common Grounds and began hunting for skull candies.

'Over here!' Hannah yelled, at the end of the alley. 'Looks like she's dropping them when she makes a turn. Smart. She went this way.'

After that, they went faster. The skull candies were in plain sight, easy to spot. Claire noticed that they were mostly in the shadows, which would have made sense, if Eve was with Myrnin or the other vampires. *Why didn't she stay?* Maybe she hadn't had a choice.

They ran out of candy trail after a few blocks. It led them into an area where Claire hadn't really been before – abandoned old buildings, mostly, falling to pieces under the relentless pressure of years and sun. It looked and felt deserted.

'Where now?' Claire asked, looking around. She didn't see anything obvious, but then she spotted something shiny, tucked in behind a tipped-over rusty trash can. She reached behind and came up with a black leather collar, studded with silver spikes.

The same collar Eve had been wearing. She wordlessly showed it to Shane, who turned in a slow circle, looking at the blank buildings. 'Come on, Eve,' he said. 'Give us something. Anything.' He froze. 'You hear that?'

Hannah cocked her head. She was standing at the end of the alley, shotgun held in her arms in a way that was both casual and scarily competent. 'What?'

'You don't hear it?'

Claire did. Somebody's phone was ringing. A cell phone, with an ultrasonic ringtone – she'd heard that older people couldn't hear those frequencies, and kids in school had used them all the time to sneak phone calls and texts in class. It was faint, but it was definitely there. 'I thought the networks were down,' she said, and pulled her own phone out.

Nope. The network was back up. She wondered if Richard had done it, or they'd lost control of the cell phone towers. Either one was possible.

They found the phone before the ringing stopped. It was Eve's – a red phone, with silver skull cell phone charms on it – discarded in the shadow of a broken, leaning doorway. 'Who was calling?' Claire asked, and Shane paged through the menu.

'Richard,' he said. 'I guess he really was looking for her after all.'

Claire's phone buzzed – just once. A text message. She opened it and checked.

It was from Eve, and it had been sent hours ago; the backlog of messages was just now being delivered, apparently.

It read, 911 @ GERMANS. Claire showed it to Shane. 'What is this?'

'Nine one one. Emergency message. German's—' He looked over at Hannah, who pushed away from the wall and came towards them.

'German's Tyre Plant,' she said. 'Damn, I don't like that; it's the size of a couple of football fields, at least.'

'We should let Richard know,' Claire said. She dialled, but the network was busy, and then the bars failed again.

'I'm not waiting,' Shane said. 'Let's get the car.'

CHAPTER NINE

The tyre plant was near the old hospital, which made Claire shudder; she remembered the deserted building way too well. It had been incredibly creepy, and then of course it had also nearly got her and Shane killed, too, so again, not fond.

She was mildly shocked to see the hulking old edifice still standing, as Shane turned the car down the street.

'Didn't they tear that place down?' It had been scheduled for demolition, and boy, if any place had ever needed it...

'I heard it was delayed,' Shane said. He didn't seem any happier about it than Claire was. 'Something about historic preservation. Although anybody wanting to preserve that thing has never been inside it running for their life, I'll bet.'

Claire stared out the window. On her side of the

car was the brooding monstrosity of a hospital. The cracked stones and tilted columns in front made it look like something straight out of one of Shane's favourite zombie-killing video games. 'Don't be hiding in there,' she whispered. 'Please don't be hiding in there.' Because if Eve and Myrnin *had* taken refuge there, she wasn't sure she'd have the courage to go charging in after them.

'There's German's,' Hannah said, and nodded towards the other side of the street. Claire hadn't really noticed it the last time she'd been out here – preoccupied with the whole not-dying issue – but there it was, a four-storey square building in that faded tan colour that everybody had used back in the sixties. Even the windows – those that weren't broken out – were painted over. It was plain, big, and blocky, and there was absolutely nothing special about it except its size – it covered at least three city blocks, all blind windows and blank concrete.

'You ever been inside there?' Shane asked Hannah, who was studying the building carefully.

'Not for a whole lot of years,' she said. 'Yeah, we used to hide up in there sometimes, when we cut class or something. I guess everybody did, once in a while. It's a mess in there, a real junkyard. Stuff everywhere, walls falling apart, ceilings none too stable, either. If you go up to the second level, you watch yourself. Make sure you don't trust the floors, and watch those iron stairs. They were shaky even back then.'

'Are we going in there?' Claire asked.

'No,' Shane said. '*You're* not going anywhere. You're staying here and getting Richard on the phone and telling him where we are. Me and Hannah will check it out.'

There didn't seem to be much room for argument, because Shane didn't give her time; he and Hannah bailed out of the car, made lock-the-door motions, and sprinted towards a gap in the rusted, sagging fence.

Claire watched until they disappeared around the corner of the building, and realised her fingers were going numb from clutching her cell phone. She took a deep breath and flipped it open to try Richard Morrell again.

Nothing. No signal again. The network was going up and down like a yo-yo.

The walkie-talkie signal was low, but she tried it anyway. There was some kind of response, but it was swallowed by static. She gave their position, on the off chance that someone on the network would be able to hear her over the noise.

She screamed and dropped the device when the

light at the car window was suddenly blocked out, and someone battered frantically on the glass.

Claire recognised the silk shirt – *her* silk shirt – before she recognised Monica Morrell, because Monica definitely didn't look like herself. She was out of breath, sweating, her hair was tangled, and what make-up she had on was smeared and running.

She'd been crying. There was a cut on her right cheek, and a forming bruise, and dirt on the silk blouse as well as bloodstains. She was holding her left arm as though it was hurt.

'Open the door!' she screamed, and pounded on the glass again. 'Let me in!'

Claire looked behind the car.

There was a mob coming down the street: thirty, forty people, some running, some following at a walk. Some were waving baseball bats, boards, pipes.

They saw Monica and let out a yell. Claire gasped, because that sound didn't seem human at all – more the roar of a beast, something mindless and hungry.

Monica's expression was, for the first time, absolutely open and vulnerable. She put her palm flat against the window glass. 'Please help me,' she said.

But even as Claire clawed at the lock to open it, Monica flinched, turned, and ran on, limping.

Claire slid over the front seat and dropped into the driver's seat. Shane had left the keys in the ignition. She started it up and put the big car in gear, gave it too much gas, and nearly wrecked it on the curb before she straightened the wheel. She rapidly gained on Monica. She passed her, squealed to a stop, and reached over to throw open the passenger door.

'Get in!' she yelled. Monica slid inside and banged the door shut, and Claire hit the gas as something impacted loudly against the back of the car – a brick, maybe. A hail of smaller stones hit a second later. Claire swerved wildly again, then straightened the wheel and got the car moving more smoothly. Her heart pounded hard, and her hands felt sweaty on the steering wheel. 'You all right?'

Monica was panting, and she threw Claire a filthy look. 'No, of *course* I'm not all right!' she snapped, and tried to fix her hair with trembling hands. 'Unbelievable. What a stupid question. I guess I shouldn't expect much more from someone like you, though—'

Claire stopped the car and stared at her.

Monica shut up.

'Here's how this is going to go,' Claire said. 'You're going to act like an actual human being for a change, or else you're on your own. Clear?'

Monica glanced behind them. 'They're coming!'

'Yes, they are. So, are we clear?'

'OK, OK, yes! Fine, whatever!' Monica cast a clearly terrified look at the approaching mob. More stones peppered the paint job, and one hit the back glass with enough force to make Claire wince. 'Get me out of here! Please!'

'Hold on, I'm not a very good driver.'

That was kind of an understatement. Eve's car was huge and heavy and had a mind of its own, and Claire hadn't taken the time to readjust the bench seat to make it possible for her to reach the pedals easily. The only good thing about her driving, as they pulled away from the mob and the falling bricks, was that it was approximately straight, and pretty fast.

She scraped the curb only twice.

Once the fittest of their pursuers had fallen behind, obviously discouraged, Claire finally remembered to breathe, and pulled the car around the next right turn. This section of town seemed deserted, but then, so had the other street, before Monica and her fan club had shown up. The big, imposing hulk of the tyre plant glided by on the passenger side – it seemed like miles of featureless brick and blank windows.

Claire braked the car on the other side of the street, in front of a deserted, rusting warehouse complex. 'Come on,' she said.

'What?' Monica watched her get out of the car and take the keys with uncomprehending shock. 'Where are you going? We have to get out of here! They were going to *kill* me!'

'They probably still are,' Claire said. 'So you should probably get out of the car now, unless you want to wait around for them.'

Monica said something Claire pretended not to hear – it wasn't exactly complimentary – and limped her way out of the passenger side. Claire locked the car. She hoped it wouldn't get banged up, but that mob had looked pretty excitable, and just the fact that Monica *had* been in it might be enough to ensure its destruction.

With any luck, though, they'd assume the girls had run into the warehouse complex, which was what Claire wanted.

Claire led them in the opposite direction, to the fence around German's Tyre. There was a split in the wire by one of the posts, an ancient curling gap half hidden by a tangle of tumbleweeds. She pushed through and held the steel aside for Monica. 'Coming?'

she asked when Monica hesitated. 'Because, you know what? Don't really care all that much. Just so you know.'

Monica came through without any comment. The fence snapped back into place. Unless someone was looking for an entrance, it ought to do.

The plant threw a large, black shadow on the weed-choked parking lot. There were a few rusted-out trucks still parked here and there; Claire used them for cover from the street as they approached the main building, though she didn't think the mob was close enough to really spot them at this point. Monica seemed to get the point without much in the way of instruction; Claire supposed that running for her life had humbled her a little. Maybe.

'Wait,' Monica said, as Claire prepared to bolt for a broken-out bottom-floor window into the tyre plant. 'What are you doing?'

'Looking for my friends,' she said. 'They're inside.'

'Well, *I'm* not going in there,' Monica declared, and tried to look haughty. It would have been more effective if she hadn't been so frazzled and sweaty. 'I was on my way to City Hall, but those losers got in my way. They slashed my tyres. I need to get to my parents.' She said it as though she expected Claire to salute and hop like a toad.

Claire raised her eyebrows. 'Better start walking,

I guess. It's kind of a long way.'

'But – but—'

Claire didn't wait for the sputtering to die; she turned and ran for the building. The window opened into total darkness, as far as she could tell, but at least it was accessible. She pulled herself up on the sash and started to swing her legs inside.

'Wait!' Monica dashed across to join her. 'You can't leave me here alone! You saw those jerks out there!'

'Absolutely.'

'Oh, you're just loving this, aren't you?'

'Kinda.' Claire hopped down inside the building, and her shoes slapped bare concrete floor. It was bare except for a layer of dirt, anyway – undisturbed for as far as the light penetrated, which wasn't very far. 'Coming?'

Monica stared through the window at her, just boiling with fury; Claire smiled at her and started to walk into the dark.

Monica, cursing, climbed inside.

'I'm not a bad person,' Monica was saying – whining, actually. Claire wished she could find a two-by-four to whack her with, but the tyre plant, although full of wreckage and trash, didn't seem to be big on wooden planks. Some nice pipes, though. She might use one of those.

Except she really didn't want to hit anybody, deep down. Claire supposed that was a character flaw, or something.

'Yes, you really are a bad person,' she told Monica, and ducked underneath a low-hanging loop of wire that looked horror-movie ready, the sort of thing that dropped around your neck and hauled you up to be dispatched by the psycho-killer villain. Speaking of which, this whole place was decorated in Early Psycho-Killer Villain, from the vast soaring darkness overhead to the lumpy, skeletal shapes of rusting equipment and abandoned junk. The spray painting – decades of it, in layered styles from Early Tagger to cutting-edge gang sign – gleamed in the random shafts of light like blood. Some particularly unpleasant spray-paint artist had done an enormous, terrifying clown face, with windows for the eyes and a giant, open doorway for a mouth. *Yeah, really not going in there*, Claire thought. Although the way these things went, she probably would have to.

'Why do you say that?'

'Say what?' Claire asked absently. She was listening for any sound of movement, but this place was enormous and confusing – just as Hannah had warned.

'Say that I'm a bad person!'

'Oh, I don't know – you tried to kill me? *And* get me raped at a party? Not to mention—'

'That was payback,' Monica said. 'And I didn't mean it or anything.'

'Which makes it all so much better. Look, can we not bond? I'm busy. Seriously. *Shhhh.*' That last was to forestall Monica from blurting out yet another injured defence of her character. Claire squeezed past a barricade of piled-up boxes and metal, into another shaft of light that arrowed down from a high-up broken window. The clown painting felt like it was watching her, which was beyond creepy. She tried not to look too closely at what was on the floor. Some of it was animal carcasses, birds, and things that had got inside and died over the years. Some of it was old cans, plastic wrappers, all kinds of junk left behind by adventurous kids looking for a hideout. She didn't imagine any of them stayed for long.

This place just felt...haunted.

Monica's hand grabbed her arm, just on the bruise that Amelie's grip had given her earlier. Claire winced.

'Did you hear that?' Monica's whisper was fierce and hushed. She needed mouthwash, and she smelt like sweat more than powder and perfume. 'Oh my *God*. Something's in here with us!'

'Could be a vampire,' Claire said. Monica sniffed.

'Not afraid of those,' she said, and dangled her fancy, silver Protection bracelet in front of Claire's face. 'Nobody's going to cross Oliver.'

'You want to tell that to the mob of people chasing you back there? I don't think they got the memo or something.'

'I mean, no vampire would. I'm Protected.' Monica said it like there was simply no possibility anything else could be true. The earth was round, the sun was hot, and a vampire would never hurt her because she'd sold herself to Oliver, body and soul.

Yeah, right.

'News flash,' Claire whispered. 'Oliver's missing in action from Common Grounds. Amelie's disappeared. In fact, most of the vampires all over town have dropped out of sight, which makes these bracelets cute fashion accessories, but not exactly bulletproof vests or anything.'

Monica started to speak, but Claire frowned angrily at her and pointed off into the darkness, where she'd heard the noise. It had sounded odd – kind of a sigh, echoing from the steel and concrete, bouncing and amplifying.

It sounded as if it had come out of the clown's dark mouth.

Of course.

Claire reached into her pocket. She still had the vial of silver powder that Amelie had given her, but she was well aware that it might not do her any good. If her friend-vampires were mixed in with enemy-vamps, she was out of luck. Likewise, if what was waiting for her out there was trouble of a human variety, instead of bloodsuckers...

Shane and Hannah were in here. Somewhere. And so – hopefully – was Eve.

Claire eased around a tattered sofa that smelt like old cats and mould, and sidestepped a truly impressive rat that didn't bother to move out of her way. It sat there watching her with weird, alert eyes.

Monica looked down, saw it, and shrieked, stumbling backward. She fell into a stack of ancient cartons that collapsed on her, raining down random junk. Claire grabbed her and pulled her to her feet, but Monica kept on whimpering and squirming, slapping at her hair and upper body.

'Oh my *God*, are they on me? Spiders? Are there spiders?'

If there were, Claire hoped they bit her. 'No,' she said shortly. Well, there were, but they were little ones. She brushed them off Monica's back. 'Shut *up* already!'

'Are you kidding me? Did you see that rat? It was the size of freaking Godzilla!'

That was it, Claire decided. Monica could just wander around on her own, screaming about rats and spiders, until someone came and ate her. What. *Ever.*

She got only about ten feet away when Monica's very small whisper stopped her dead in her tracks.

'Please don't leave me.' That didn't sound like Monica, not at all. It sounded scared, and very young. 'Claire, please.'

It was probably too late for being quiet, anyway, and if there were vampires hiding in German's Tyre Plant, they all knew exactly where they were, and for that matter, could tell what blood type they were. So stealth didn't seem a priority.

Claire cupped her hands over her mouth and yelled, very loudly, 'Shane! Eve! Hannah! Anybody!'

The echoes woke invisible birds or bats high overhead, which flapped madly around; her voice rang from every flat surface, mocking Claire with her own ghost.

In the whispering silence afterward, Monica murmured, 'Wow, I thought we were being subtle or something. My mistake.'

Claire was about to hiss something really unpleasant at her, but froze as another voice came bouncing through the vast room – Shane's voice. 'Claire?'

'Here!'

'Stay there! And shut up!'

He sounded frantic enough to make Claire wish she'd stuck with the whole quiet-time policy, and then Monica stopped breathing and went very, very still next to her. Her hands closed around Claire's arm, squeezing bruises again.

Claire froze, too, because something was coming out of the mouth of that painted clown – something white, ghostly, drifting like smoke...

It had a face. Several faces, because it was a group of what looked like vampires, all very pale, all very quiet, all heading their way.

Staying put was not such a great plan, Claire decided. She was going to go *with run away*.

Which, grabbing Monica's wrist, she did.

The vampires did make sounds then, as their quarry started to flee – little whispering laughs, strange hisses, all kinds of creepy noises that made the skin on the back of Claire's neck tighten up. She held the glass vial in one hand, running faster, leaping over junk when she could see it coming and stumbling across it when she couldn't. Monica kept up, somehow, although Claire could hear the tortured, steady moaning of her breath. Whatever she'd done to her right leg must have hurt pretty badly.

Something pale landed ahead of her, with a silent leap like a spider pouncing. Claire had a wild impression of a white face, red eyes, a wide-open mouth, and gleaming fangs. She drew back to throw the vial...and realised it was Myrnin facing her.

The hesitation cost her. Something hit her from the back, sending her stumbling forward across a fallen iron beam. She dropped the vial as she fell, trying to catch herself, and heard the glass break on the edge of the girder. Silver dust puffed out. Monica shrieked, a wild cry that made the birds panic again high up in heaven; Claire saw her stumble away, trying to put distance between herself and Myrnin.

Myrnin was just outside of the range of the drifting silver powder, but it wasn't Myrnin who was the problem. The other vampires, the ones who'd come out of the clown's mouth, leapt over stacks of trash, running for the smell of fresh, flowing blood.

They were coming up behind them, fast.

Claire raked her hand across the ground and came up with a palm full of silver powder and glass shards as she rolled up to her knees. She turned and threw the powder into the air between her, Monica, and the rest of the vampires. It dispersed into a fine, glittering mist, and when the vampires hit it, every tiny grain of silver caught fire.

It was beautiful, and horrible, and Claire flinched at the sound of their cries. There was so much silver, and it clung to their skin, eating in. Claire didn't know if it would kill them, but it definitely stopped them cold.

She grabbed Monica's arm and pulled her close.

Myrnin was still in front of them, crouched on top of a stack of wooden pallets. He didn't look at all human, not at *all*.

And then he blinked, and the red light went out in his eyes. His fangs folded neatly backward, and he ran his tongue over pale lips before he said, puzzled, 'Claire?'

She felt a sense of relief so strong it was like falling. 'Yeah, it's me.'

'Oh.' He slithered down off the stacked wood, and she realised he was still dressed the way she'd seen him back at Common Grounds – a long, black velvet coat, no shirt, white pantaloons left over from his costume. He should have looked ridiculous, but somehow, he looked...right. 'You shouldn't be here, Claire. It's very dangerous.'

'I know—'

Something cold brushed the back of her neck, and she heard Monica make a muffled sound like a choked cry. Claire whirled and found herself face-to-face with a red-eyed, angry vampire with part of his skin still smoking from the silver she'd thrown.

Myrnin let out a roar that ripped the air, full of menace and fury, and the vampire stumbled backward, clearly shocked.

Then the five who'd chased them silently withdrew into the darkness.

Claire turned to face Myrnin. He was staring thoughtfully at the departing vamps.

'Thanks,' she said. He shrugged.

'I was raised to believe in the concept of noblesse oblige,' he said. 'And I do owe you, you know. Do you have any more of my medication?'

She handed him her last dose of the drug that kept him sane – mostly sane, anyway. It was the older version, red crystals rather than clear liquid, and he poured out a dollop into his palm and licked the crystals up, then sighed in deep satisfaction.

'Much better,' he said, and pocketed the rest of the bottle. 'Now. Why are you here?'

Claire licked her lips. She could hear Shane – or someone – coming towards them through the darkness, and she saw someone in the shadows behind Myrnin. Not vampires, she thought, so it was probably Hannah, flanking Shane. 'We're looking for my friend Eve. You remember her, right?'

'Eve,' Myrnin repeated, and slowly smiled. 'Ah. The girl who followed me. Yes, of course.'

Claire felt a flush of excitement, quickly damped by dread. 'What happened to her?'

'Nothing. She's asleep,' he said. 'It was too dangerous out here for her. I put her in a safe place, for now.'

Shane pushed through the last of the barriers and stepped into a shaft of light about fifty feet away. He paused at the sight of Myrnin, but he didn't look alarmed.

'This is your friend as well,' Myrnin said, glancing back at Shane. 'The one you care so much for.' She'd never discussed Shane with Myrnin – not in detail, anyway. The question must have shown in her face, because his smile broadened. 'You carry his scent on your clothes,' he said. 'And he carries yours.'

'Ewww,' Monica sighed.

Myrnin's eyes focused in on her like laser sights. 'And who is this lovely child?'

Claire almost rolled her eyes. 'Monica. The mayor's daughter.'

'Monica Morrell.' She offered her hand, which Myrnin accepted and bent over in an old-fashioned way. Claire assumed he was also inspecting the bracelet on her wrist.

'Oliver's,' he said, straightening. 'I see. I am charmed, my dear, simply charmed.' He hadn't let go of her hand. 'I don't suppose you would be willing to donate a pint for a poor, starving stranger?'

Monica's smile froze in place. 'I – well, I—'

He pulled her into his arms with one quick jerk. Monica yelped and tried to pull away, but for all his relatively small size, Myrnin had strength to burn.

Claire pulled in a deep breath. 'Myrnin. Please.'

He looked annoyed. 'Please *what*?'

'She's not free range or anything. You can't just munch her. Let go.' He didn't look convinced. 'Seriously. *Let go.*'

'Fine.' He opened his arms, and Monica retreated as she clapped both hands around her neck. She sat down on a nearby girder, breathing hard. 'You know, in my youth, women lined up to grant me their favours. I believe I'm a bit offended.'

'It's a strange day for everybody,' Claire said. 'Shane, Hannah, this is Myrnin. He's sort of my boss.'

Shane moved closer, but his expression stayed cool and distant. 'Yeah? This the guy who took you to the ball? The one who dumped you and left you to die?'

'Well...uh...yes.'

'Thought so.'

Shane punched him right in the face. Myrnin, surprised, stumbled back against the tower of crates, and snarled; Shane took a stake from his back pocket and held it at the ready.

'No!' Claire jumped between them, waving her hands. 'No, honest, it's not like that. Calm down, everybody, please.'

'Yes,' Myrnin said. 'I've been staked quite enough today, thank you. I respect your need to avenge her, boy, but Claire remains quite capable of defending her own honour.'

'Couldn't have said it better myself,' she said. 'Please, Shane. Don't. We need him.'

'Yeah? Why?'

'Because he may know what's going on with the vampires.'

'Oh, that,' Myrnin said, in a tone that implied they were all idiots for not knowing already. 'They're being called. It's a signal that draws all vampires who have sworn allegiance to you with a blood exchange – it's the way wars were fought, once upon a time. It's how you gather your army.'

'Oh,' Claire said. 'So...why not you? Or the rest of the vampires here?'

'It seems as though your serum offers me some

portion of immunity against it. Oh, I feel the draw, most certainly, but in an entirely academic way. Rather curious. I remember how it felt before, like an overwhelming panic. As for those others, well. They're not of the blood.'

'They're not?'

'No. Lesser creatures. Failed experiments, if you will.' He looked away, and Claire had a horrible suspicion.

'Are they *people*? I mean, regular humans?'

'A failed experiment,' he repeated. 'You're a scientist, Claire. Not all experiments work the way they're intended.'

Myrnin had done this to them, in his search for the cure to the vampire disease. He had turned them into something that wasn't vampire, wasn't human, wasn't – well, wasn't anything, exactly. They didn't fit in either society.

No wonder they were hiding here.

'Don't look at me that way,' Myrnin said. 'It's not my fault the process was imperfect, you know. I'm not a monster.'

Claire shook her head.

'Sometimes, you really are.'

Eve was fine – tired, shaking, and tear-streaked, but OK. 'He didn't, you know,' she said, and made two-finger pointy motions towards her throat. 'He's kind of sweet, actually, once you get past all the crazy. Although there's a lot of the crazy.'

There was, as Claire well knew, no way of getting past the crazy. Not really. But she had to admit that at least Myrnin had behaved more like a gentleman than expected.

Noblesse oblige. Maybe he'd felt obligated.

The place he'd kept Eve had once been some kind of storage locker within the plant, all solid walls and a single door that he'd locked off with a bent pipe. Shane hadn't been all that happy about it. 'What if something had happened to you?' he'd asked, as Myrnin untwisted the metal as though it were solder instead of iron. 'She'd have been locked in there, all alone, no way out. She'd have starved.'

'Actually,' Myrnin had answered, 'that's not very likely. Thirst would have killed her within four days, I imagine. She'd never have had a chance to starve.' Claire stared at him. He raised his eyebrows. 'What?'

She just shook her head. 'I think you missed the point.'

Monica tagged along with Claire, which was annoying; she kept casting Shane nervous glances, and she was now outright terrified of Myrnin, which was probably how it should have been, really. At the very least, she'd shut up, and even the sight of another rat, this one big and kind of albino, hadn't set off her screams this time.

Eve, however, was less than thrilled to see Monica. 'You're kidding,' she said flatly, staring first at her, then at Shane. 'You're OK with this?'

'OK would be a stretch. Resigned, that's closer,' Shane said. Hannah, standing next to him with her shotgun at port arms, snorted out a laugh. 'As long as she doesn't talk, I can pretend she isn't here.'

'Yeah? Well *I* can't,' Eve said. She glared at Monica, who glared right back. 'Claire, you have to stop picking up strays. You don't know where they've been.'

'You're one to talk about diseases,' Monica shot back, 'seeing as how you're one big, walking social one.'

'That's not pot, kettle – that's more like cauldron, kettle. Witch.'

'Whore!'

'You want to go play with your new friends back there?' Shane snapped. 'The really pale ones with the taste for plasma? Because believe me, I'll drop your skanky butt right in their nest if you don't shut up, Monica.'

'You don't scare me, Collins!'

Hannah rolled her eyes and racked her shotgun. 'How about me?'

That ended the entire argument.

Myrnin, leaning against the wall with his arms folded over his chest, watched the proceedings with great interest. 'Your friends,' he said to Claire. 'They're quite...colourful. So full of energy.'

'Hands off my friends.' Not that that statement exactly included Monica, but whatever.

'Oh, absolutely. I would never.' Hand to his heart, Myrnin managed to look angelic, which was a bit of a trick considering his Lord-Byron-on-a-bender outfit. 'I've just been away from normal human society for so long. Tell me, is it usually this...spirited?'

'Not usually,' she sighed. 'Monica's special.' Yeah, in the short-bus sense, because Monica was a head case. Not that Claire had time or inclination to explain all the dynamics of the Monica-Shane-Eve relationship to Myrnin right now. 'When you said that someone was calling the vampires together for some kind of fight – was that Bishop?'

'Bishop?' Myrnin looked startled. 'No, of course not. It's Amelie. Amelie is sending the call. She's consolidating her forces, putting up lines of defence. Things are rapidly moving towards a confrontation, I believe.'

That was exactly what Claire was afraid he was going to say. 'Do you know who answered?'

'Anyone in Morganville with a blood tie to her,' he said. 'Except me, of course. But that would include almost every vampire in town, save those who were sworn through Oliver. Even then, Oliver's tie would bind them in some sense, because he swore fealty to her when he came to live here. They might feel the pull less strongly, but they would still feel it.'

'Then how is Bishop getting an army? Isn't everybody in town, you know, Amelie's?'

'He bit those he wished to keep on his side.' Myrnin shrugged. 'Claimed them from her, in a sense. Some of them went willingly, some not, but all owe him allegiance now. All those he was able to turn, which is a considerable number, I believe.' He looked sharply at her. 'The call continued in the daytime. Michael?'

'Michael's fine. They put him in a cell.'

'And Sam?'

Claire shook her head in response. Next to Michael, his grandfather Sam was the youngest vampire in town, and Claire hadn't seen him at all, not since he'd left the Glass House, well before any of the other vamps. He'd gone off on some mission for Amelie; she trusted him more than most of the others, even those she'd known for hundreds of years. That was, Claire thought, because Amelie knew how Sam felt about her. It was the storybook kind of love, the kind that ignored things like practicality and danger, and never changed or died.

She found herself looking at Shane. He turned his head and smiled back.

The storybook kind of love.

She was probably too young to have that, but this felt so strong, so real...

And Shane wouldn't even man up and tell her he loved her.

She took a deep breath and forced her mind off that. 'What do we do now?' Claire asked. 'Myrnin?'

He was silent for a long moment, then moved to one of the painted-over first-floor windows and pulled it open. The sun was setting again. It would be down completely soon.

'You should get home,' he said. 'The humans are in charge for now, at least, but there are factions out there. There will be power struggles tonight, and not just between the two vampire sides.'

Shane glanced at Monica – whose bruises were living proof that trouble was already under way – and then back at Myrnin. 'What are you going to do?'

'Stay here,' Myrnin said. 'With my friends.'

'*Friends?* Who, the – uh – failed experiments?'

'Exactly so.' Myrnin shrugged. 'They look upon me as a kind of father figure. Besides, their blood is as good as anyone else's, in a pinch.'

'So much more than I wanted to know,' Shane said, and nodded to Hannah. 'Let's go.'

'Got your back, Shane.'

'Watch Claire's and Eve's. I'll take the lead.'

'What about me?' Monica whined.

'Do you really want to know?' Shane gave her a glare that should have scorched her hair off. 'Be grateful I'm not leaving you as an after-dinner mint on his pillow.'

Myrnin leant close to Claire's ear and said, 'I think I like your young man.' When she reacted in pure confusion, he held up his hands, smiling. 'Not in that way, my dear. He just seems quite trustworthy.'

She swallowed and put all that aside. 'Are you going to be OK here? Really?'

'Really?' He locked gazes with her. 'For now, yes. But we have work to do, Claire. Much work, and very little time. I can't hide for long. You do realise that stress accelerates the disease, and this is a great deal of stress for us all. More will fall ill, become confused. It's vital we begin work on the serum as quickly as possible.'

'I'll try to get you back to the lab tomorrow.'

They left him standing in a fading shaft of sunlight, next to a giant rusting crane that lifted its head three stories into the dark, with pale birds flitting and diving overhead.

And wounded, angry failed experiments lurking in the shadows, maybe waiting to attack their vampire creator.

Claire felt sorry for them, if they did.

The mobs were gone, but they'd given Eve's car a good battering while they were at it. She choked when she saw the dents and cracked glass, but at least it was still on all four tyres, and the damage was cosmetic. The engine started right up.

'Poor baby,' Eve said, and patted the big steering wheel affectionately as she settled into the driver's seat. 'We'll get you all fixed up. Right, Hannah?'

'And here I was wondering what I was going to do tomorrow,' Hannah said, taking – of course – the shotgun seat. 'Guess now I know. I'll be hammering dents out of the Queen Mary and putting in new safety glass.'

In the backseat, Claire was the human equivalent of Switzerland between the warring nations of Shane and Monica, who sat next to the windows. It was tense, but nobody spoke.

The sun was going down in a blaze of glory in the west, which normally would have made Morganville a vampire-friendly place. Not so much tonight, as became evident when Eve left the dilapidated warehouse district and cruised closer to Vamptown.

There were people out on the streets, *at sunset*.

And they were angry, too.

'Shouty,' Eve said, as they passed a big group clustered around a guy standing on a wooden box, yelling at the crowd. He had a pile of wooden stakes, and people were picking them up. 'OK, this is looking less than great.'

'You think?' Monica slumped down in her seat, trying not to be noticed. 'They tried to kill me! And I'm not even a vampire!'

'Yeah, but you're you, so there's that explained.' Eve slowed down. 'Traffic.'

Traffic? In Morganville? Claire leant forward and saw that there were about six cars in the street ahead. The first one was turned sideways, blocking the second – a big van, which was trying to back up but was handicapped by the third car.

The trapped passenger van was vampire-dark. The two cars blocking it in were old, battered sedans, the kind humans drove.

'That's Lex Perry's car, the one turned sideways,'

Hannah said. 'I think that's the Nunally brothers in the third one. They're drinking buddies with Sal Manetti.'

'Sal, as in, the guy out there rabble-rousing?'

'You got it.'

And now people were closing in around the van, pushing against it, rocking it on its tyres.

Nobody in their car spoke a word.

The van rocked harder. The tyres spun, trying to pull away, but it tipped and slammed over on its side, helpless. With a roar, the crowd climbed on top of it and started battering the windows.

'We should do something,' Claire finally said.

'Yeah?' Hannah's voice was very soft. 'What, exactly?'

'Call the police?' Only the police were already here. There were two cars of them, and they couldn't stop what was happening. In fact, they didn't even look inclined to try.

'Let's go,' Shane said quietly. 'There's nothing we can do here.'

Eve silently put the car in reverse and burnt rubber backing up.

Claire broke out of her trance. 'What are you doing? We can't just leave—'

'Take a good look,' Eve said grimly. 'If anybody out there sees Princess Morrell in this car, we've all had it. We're all collaborators if we're protecting her, and *you're* wearing the Founder bracelet. We can't risk it.'

Claire sank back in her seat as Eve shifted gears again and turned the wheel. They took a different street, this one unblocked so far.

'What's happening?' Monica asked. 'What's happening to our town?'

'France,' Claire said, thinking about Granma Day. 'Welcome to the revolution.'

Eve drove through a maze of streets. Lights were flickering on in houses, and the few streetlamps were coming on as well. Cars – and there were a lot of them out now – turned on their headlights and honked, as if the local high school had just won a big football game.

As if it were one big, loud party.

'I want to go home,' Monica said. Her voice sounded muffled. 'Please.'

Eve looked at her in the rear-view mirror, and finally nodded.

But when they turned down the street where the Morrell family home was located, Eve slammed on the brakes and put the car into reverse, instantly.

The Morrell home looked like the site of another of Monica's infamous, unsupervised parties... only this one really was unsupervised, and those uninvited guests, they weren't just there for the free booze.

'What are they doing?' Monica asked, and let out a strangled yell as a couple of guys carried a big plasma television out the front door. 'They're stealing it! They're stealing our stuff!'

Pretty much everything was being looted – mattresses, furniture, art. Claire even saw people upstairs tossing linens and clothing out the windows to people waiting on the ground.

And then, somebody ran up with a bottle full of liquid, stuffed with a burning rag, and threw it into the front window.

The flames flickered, caught, and gained strength.

'No!' Monica panted and clawed at the door handle, but Eve had locked it up. Claire grabbed Monica's arms and held them down.

'Get us out of here!' she yelled.

'My parents could be in there!'

'No, they're not. Richard told me they're at City Hall.'

Monica kept fighting, even as Eve steered the car away from the burning house, and then suddenly just...stopped.

Claire heard her crying. She wanted to think, *Good, you deserve it,* but somehow she just couldn't force herself to be that cold.

Shane, however, could. 'Hey, look on the bright side,' he said. 'At least your little sister isn't inside.'

Monica caught her breath, then kept crying.

By the time they'd turned on Lot Street, Monica seemed to be pulling herself together, wiping her face with trembling hands and asking for a tissue, which Eve provided out of the glove box in the front.

'What do you think?' Eve asked Shane. Their street seemed quiet. Most of the houses had lights on, including the Glass House, and although there were some folks outside, talking, it didn't look like mobs were forming. Not here, anyway.

'Looks good. Let's get inside.'

They agreed that Monica needed to go in the middle, covered by Hannah. Eve went first, racing up the walk to the front door and using her keys to open it up.

They made it in without attracting too much attention or anybody pointing fingers at Monica – but then, Claire thought, Monica definitely didn't look much like herself right now. More like a bad Monica impersonator. Maybe even one who was a guy.

Shane would laugh himself sick over that if she mentioned it. After seeing the puffy redness around

Monica's eyes, and the shattered expression, Claire kept it to herself.

As Shane slammed, locked, and dead bolted the front door, Claire felt the house come alive around them, almost tingling with warmth and welcome. She heard people in the living room exclaim at the same time, so it wasn't just her; the house really had reacted, and reacted strongly, to three out of four of its residents coming home.

Claire stretched out against the wall and kissed it. 'Glad to see you, too,' she whispered, and pressed her cheek against the smooth surface.

It almost felt like it hugged her back.

'Dude, it's a *house*,' Shane said from behind her. 'Hug somebody who cares.'

She did, throwing herself into his arms. It felt like he'd never let her go, not even for a second, and he lifted her completely off the ground and rested his head on her shoulder for a long, precious moment before setting her gently back on her feet.

'Better see who's here,' he said, and kissed her very lightly. 'Down payment for later, OK?'

Claire let go, but held his hand as they walked down the hallway and into the living room of the Glass House, which was filled with people.

Not vampires.

Just people.

Some of them were familiar, at least by sight –
people from town: the owner of the music store where
Michael worked; a couple of nurses she'd seen at the
hospital, who still wore brightly coloured medical
scrubs and comfortable shoes. The rest, Claire barely
knew at all, but they had one thing in common – they
were all scared.

An older, hard-looking woman grabbed Claire by
the shoulders. 'Thank God you're home,' she said, and
hugged her. Claire, rigid with surprise, cast Shane a
what-the-hell look, and he shrugged helplessly. 'This
damn house won't do *anything* for us. The lights keep
going out, the doors won't open, food goes bad in the
fridge – it's as if it doesn't want us here!'

And it probably didn't. The house could have
ejected them at any time, but obviously it had been a
bit uncertain about exactly what its residents might
want, so it had just made life uncomfortable for the
intruders instead.

Claire could now feel the air-conditioning
switching on to cool the overheated air, hear doors
swinging open upstairs, see lights coming on in
darkened areas.

'Hey, Celia,' Shane said, as the woman let go of
Claire at last. 'So, what brings you here? I figured
the Barfly would be doing good business tonight.'

'Well, it would be, except that some jerks came in

and said that because I was wearing a bracelet I had to serve them for free, on account of being some kind of sympathiser. "What kind of sympathiser?" I said, and one of them tried to hit me.'

Shane lifted his eyebrows. Celia wasn't a young woman. 'What did you do?'

'Used the Regulator.' Celia lifted a baseball bat propped against the wall. It was old hardwood, lovingly polished. 'Got myself a couple of home runs, too. But I decided maybe I wouldn't stay for the extra innings, if you know what I mean. I figure they're drinking me dry over there right now. Makes me want to rip my bracelet off, I'll tell ya. Where are the damn vampires when you need them, after all that?'

'You didn't take your bracelet off? Even when they gave you the chance?' Shane seemed surprised. Celia gave him a glare.

'No, I didn't. I ain't breaking my word, not unless I have to. Right now, I don't have to.'

'If you take it off now, you may never need to put it on again.'

Celia levelled a wrinkled finger at. him. 'Look, Collins, I know all about you and your dad. I don't hold with any of that. Morganville's an all-right place. You follow the rules and stay out of trouble – about like anyplace, I guess. You people wanted chaos. Well, this is what it looks like – people getting beaten, shops looted, houses burnt. Sure, it'll settle down sometime, but into what? Maybe no place I'd want to live.'

She turned away from him, shouldered her baseball bat, and marched away to talk with a group of adults her own age.

Shane caught Claire looking at him, and shrugged. 'Yeah,' he sighed. 'I know. She's got a point. But how do we know it won't be better if the vamps just—'

'Just what, Shane? *Die?* What about Michael, have you thought about him? Or Sam?' She stomped off.

'Where are you going?'

'To get a Coke!'

'Would you—'

'No!'

She twisted the cap off the Coke she'd retrieved from the fridge – which was stocked up again, although she knew it hadn't been when they'd left. Another favour from the house, she guessed, although how it went shopping on its own she had no idea.

The cold syrupy goodness hit her like a brick wall, but instead of energising her, it made her feel weak and a little sick. Claire sank down in a chair at the kitchen table and put her head in her hands, suddenly overwhelmed.

It was all falling apart.

Amelie was calling the vampires, probably going to fight Bishop to the death. Morganville was ripping itself in pieces. And there was nothing she could *do*.

Well, there was one thing.

She retrieved and opened four more bottles of Coke, and delivered them to Hannah, Eve, Shane, and – because it felt mean to leave her out at a time like this – Monica.

Monica stared at the sweating bottle as if she suspected Claire had put rat poison in it. 'What's this?'

'What does it look like? Take it or don't, I don't really care.' Claire put it down on the table next to where Monica sat, and went to curl up on the couch next to Shane. She checked her cell phone. The network was back up again, at least for the moment, and she had a ton of voicemails. Most were from Shane, so she saved them to listen to later; two more were from Eve, which she deleted, since they were instructions on where to find her.

The last one was from her mother. Claire caught her breath, tears pricking in her eyes at the sound of Mom's voice. Her mother sounded calm, at least – mostly, anyway.

Claire, sweetie, I know I shouldn't be worrying but I am. Honey, call us. I've been hearing some terrible

things about what's happening out there. Some of
the people with us here are talking about fights and
looting. If I don't hear from you soon – well, I don't
know what we'll do, but your father's going crazy. So
please, call us. We love you, honey. Bye.

Claire got her breathing back under control,
mainly by sternly telling herself that she needed to
sound together and completely in control to keep her
parents from charging out there into the craziness.
She had it more or less managed by the time the
phone rang on the other end, and when her mother
picked it up, she was able to say, 'Hi, Mom,' without
making it sound like she was about to burst into
tears. 'I got your message. Is everything OK there?'

'Here? Claire, don't you be worrying about us!
We're just fine! Oh, honey, are you OK? Really?'

'Honestly, yes, I'm OK. Everything's—' She
couldn't say that everything was OK, because of
course it wasn't. It was, at best, kind of temporarily
stable. 'It's quiet here. Shane's here, and Eve.'
Claire remembered that Mom had liked Monica
Morrell, and rolled her eyes. Anything to calm her
fears. 'That girl from the dorm, Monica, she's here,
too.'

'Oh, yes, Monica. I liked her.' It really did seem
to help, which was not exactly an endorsement of
Mom's character-judging ability. 'Her brother came

by here to check on us about an hour ago. He's a nice boy.'

Claire couldn't quite imagine referring to Richard Morrell as a *boy*, but she let it go. 'He's kind of in charge of the town right now,' she said. 'You have the radio, right? The one we dropped off earlier?'

'Yes. We've been doing everything they say, of course. But, honey, I'd really like it if you could come here. We want to have you home, with us.'

'I know. I know, Mom. But I think I'd better stay here. It's important. I'll try to come by tomorrow, OK?'

They talked a little more, about nothing much, just chatter to make life seem kind of normal for a change. Mom was holding it together, but only barely; Claire could hear the manic quaver in her voice, could almost see the bright tears in her eyes. She was going on about how they'd had to move most of the boxes into the basement to make room for all the company – *company?* – and how she was afraid that Claire's stuff would get damp, and then she talked about all the toys in the boxes and how much Claire had enjoyed them when she was younger.

Normal Mom stuff.

Claire didn't interrupt, except to make soothing noises and acknowledgments when Mom paused. It helped, hearing Mom's voice, and she knew it was helping her to talk. But finally, when her mother ran down like a spring-wound clock, Claire agreed to all the parental requirements to be careful and watch out and wear warm clothes.

Goodbye seemed very final, and once Claire hung up, she sat in silence for a few minutes, staring at the screen of her cell phone.

On impulse, she tried to call Amelie. It rang and rang. No voicemail.

In the living room, Shane was organising some kind of sentry duty. A lot of people had already crashed out in piles of pillows, blankets, sometimes just on a spare rug. Claire edged around the prone bodies and motioned to Shane that she was going upstairs. He nodded and kept talking to the two guys he was with, but his gaze followed her all the way.

Eve was in her bedroom, and there was a note on the door that said DO NOT KNOCK OR I WILL KILL YOU. THIS MEANS YOU, SHANE. Claire considered knocking, but she was too tired to run away.

Her bedroom was dark. When she'd left in the morning, Eve's kind-of-friend Miranda had been sleeping here, but she was gone, and the bed was neatly made again. Claire sat down on the edge, staring out the windows, and then pulled out clean underwear and her last pair of blue jeans from the closet, plus a tight black shirt Eve had lent her last week.

The shower felt like heaven. There was even enough hot water for a change. Claire dried off, fussed with her hair a bit, and got dressed. When she came out, she listened at the stairs, but didn't hear Shane talking anymore. Either he was being quiet, or he'd gone to bed. She paused next to his door, wishing she had the guts to knock, but she went on to her own room instead.

Shane was inside, sitting on her bed. He looked up when she opened the door, and his lips parted, but he was silent for a long few seconds.

'I should go,' he finally said, but he didn't get up.

Claire settled in next to him. It was all perfectly correct, the two of them sitting fully dressed like this, but somehow she felt like they were on the edge of a cliff, both in danger of falling off.

It was exciting, and terrifying, and all kinds of wrong.

'So what happened to you today?' she asked. 'In the Bloodmobile, I mean?'

'Nothing really. We drove to the edge of town and parked outside the border, where we'd be able to see anybody coming. A couple of vamps showed, trying to make a withdrawal, but we sent them packing.

Bishop never made an appearance. Once we lost contact with the vampires, we figured we'd cruise around and see what was going on. We nearly got boxed in by a bunch of drunk idiots in pickup trucks, and then the vampires in the Bloodmobile went nuts – that call thing going off, I guess. I dropped them at the grain elevator – that was the biggest, darkest place I could find, and it casts a lot of shadows. I handed off the driving to Cesar Mercado. He's supposed to drive it all the way to Midland tonight, provided the barriers are down. Best we can do.'

'What about the book? Did you leave it on board?'

In answer, Shane reached into his waistband and pulled out the small leather-bound volume. Amelie had added a lock on it, like a diary lock. Claire tried pressing the small, metal catch. It didn't open, of course.

'You think you should be fooling with that thing?' Shane asked.

'Probably not.' She tried prying a couple of pages apart to peek at the script. All she could tell was that it was handwritten, and the paper looked relatively old. Oddly, when she sniffed it, the paper smelt like chemicals.

'What are you doing?' Shane looked like he couldn't decide whether to be repulsed or fascinated.

'I think somebody restored the paper,' she said.

'Like they do with really expensive old books and stuff. Comics, sometimes. They put chemicals on the paper to slow down the aging process, make the paper whiter again.'

'Fascinating,' Shane lied. 'Gimme.' He plucked the book from her hands and put it aside, on the other side of the bed. When she grabbed for it, he got in her way; they tangled, and somehow, he was lying prone on the bed and she was stretched awkwardly on top of him. His hands steadied her when she started to slide off.

'Oh,' she murmured. 'We shouldn't—'

'Definitely not.'

'Then you should—'

'Yeah, I should.'

But he didn't move, and neither did she. They just looked at each other, and then, very slowly, she lowered her lips to his.

It was a warm, sweet, wonderful kiss, and it seemed to go on for ever. It also felt like it didn't last nearly long enough. Shane's hands skimmed up her sides, up her back, and cupped her damp hair as he kissed her more deeply. There were promises in that kiss.

'OK, red flag,' he said. He hadn't let her go, but there was about a half an inch of air between their lips. Claire's whole body felt alive and tingling, pulse pounding in her wrists and temples, warmth pooling like light in the centre of her body.

'It's OK,' she said. 'I swear. Trust me.'

'Hey, isn't that my line?'

'Not now.'

Kissing Shane was the reward for surviving a long, hard, terrifying day. Being enfolded in his warmth felt like going to heaven on moonbeams. She kicked off her shoes, and, still fully dressed, crawled under the blankets. Shane hesitated.

'Trust me,' she said again. 'And you can keep your clothes on if you don't.'

They'd done this before, but somehow it hadn't felt so...intimate. Claire pressed against him, back to front under the covers, and his arms went around her. Instant heat.

She swallowed and tried to remember all those good intentions she'd had as she felt Shane's breath whisper on the back of her neck, and then his lips brushed her skin. 'So wrong,' he murmured. 'You're killing me, you know.'

'Am not.'

'On this, you'll have to trust *me*.' His sigh made her shiver all the way to her bones. 'I can't believe you brought Monica back here.'

'Oh, come on. You wouldn't have left her out there, all alone. I know you better than that, Shane. Even as bad as she is—'

'The satanic incarnation of evil?'

'Maybe so, but I can't see you letting them get her and...hurt her.' Claire turned around to face him, a squirming motion that made them wrestle for the covers. 'What's going to happen? Do you know?'

'What am I, Miranda the teen screwed-up psychic? No, I don't know. All I know is that when we get up tomorrow, either the vampires will be back, or they won't. And then we'll have to make a choice about how we're going to go forward.'

'Maybe we don't go forward. Maybe we wait.'

'One thing I do know, Claire: you can't stay in the same place, not even for a day. You keep on moving. Maybe it's the right direction, maybe not, but you still move. Every second things change, like it or not.'

She studied his face intently. 'Is your dad here? Now?'

He grimaced. 'Truthfully? No idea. I wouldn't be surprised. He'd know that it was time to move in and take command, if he could. And Manetti's a running buddy from way back. This kind of feels like Dad's behind it.'

'But if he does take over, what happens to Michael? To Myrnin? To any other vampires out there?'

'Do you really need me to tell you?'

Claire shook her head. 'He'll tell people they have

204   Rachel Caine

to kill all the vampires, and then, he'll come after the Morrells, and anybody else he thinks is responsible for what happened to your family. Right?'

'Probably,' Shane sighed.

'And you're going to let all that happen.'

'I didn't say that.'

'You didn't say you weren't, either. Don't tell me it's complicated, because it isn't. Either you stand up for something, or you lie down for it. You said that to me one time, and you were right.' Claire burrowed closer into his arms. 'Shane, you were *right* then. Be right now.'

He touched her face. His fingers traced down her cheek, across her lips, and his eyes – she'd never seen that look in his eyes. In anyone's, really.

'In this whole screwed-up town, you're the only thing that's always been right to me,' he whispered. 'I love you, Claire.' She saw something that might have been just a flash of panic go across his expression, but then he steadied again. 'I can't believe I'm saying this, but I do. I love you.'

He said something else, but the world had narrowed around her. Shane's lips kept moving, but all she heard were the same words echoing over and over inside her head like the tolling of a giant brass bell: *I love you.*

He sounded like it had taken him completely by

surprise – not in a bad way, but more as if he hadn't really understood what he was feeling until that instant.

She blinked. It was as if she'd never really seen him before, and he was *beautiful*. More beautiful than any man she'd ever seen in her entire life, ever.

Whatever he was saying, she stopped it by kissing him. A lot. And for a very long time. When he finally backed up, he didn't go far, and this look in his eyes, this intense and overwhelming *need* – that was new, too.

And she liked it.

'I love you,' he said, and kissed her so hard he took her breath away. There was more to it than before – more passion, more urgency, more...everything. It was as if she were caught in a tide, carried away, and she thought that if she never touched the shore again, it would be good to drown like this, just swim for ever in all this richness.

Red flag, some part of her screamed, *come on, red flag. What are you doing?*

She wished it would just shut up.

'I love you, too,' she whispered to him. Her voice was shaking, and so were her hands where they rested on his chest. Under the soft T-shirt, his muscles were tensed, and she could feel every deep breath he took. 'I'd do anything for you.'

She meant it to be an invitation, but that was the thing that shocked sense back into him. He blinked. 'Anything,' he repeated, and squeezed his eyes shut. 'Yeah. I'm getting that. Bad idea, Claire. Very, very bad.'

'Today?' She laughed a little wildly. 'Everything's crazy today. Why can't we be? Just once?'

'Because I made promises,' he said. He wrapped his arms around her and pulled her close, and she felt a groan shake his whole body. 'To your parents, to myself, to Michael. To you, Claire. I can't break my word. It's pretty much all I've got these days.'

'But...what if—'

'Don't,' he whispered in her ear. 'Please don't. This is tough enough already.'

He kissed her again, long and sweetly, and somehow, it tasted like tears this time. Like some kind of goodbye.

'I really do love you,' he said, and smoothed away the damp streaks on her cheeks. 'But I can't do this. Not now.'

Before she could stop him, he slid out of bed, put on his shoes, and walked quickly to the door. She sat up, holding the covers close as if she were naked underneath, instead of fully clothed, and he hesitated there, one hand gripping the doorknob.

'Please stay,' she said. 'Shane—'

He shook his head. 'If I stay, things are going to

happen. You know it, and I know it, and we just can't do this. I know things are falling apart, but—' He hitched in a deep, painful breath. 'No.'

The sound of the door softly closing behind him went through her like a knife.

Claire rolled over, wretchedly hugging the pillow that smelt of his hair, sharing the warm place in the bed where his body had been, and thought about crying herself to sleep.

And then she thought of the dawning wonder in his eyes when he'd said, *I love you.*

No. It was no time to be crying.

When she did finally sleep, she felt safe.

CHAPTER TEN

The next day, there was no sign of the vampires, none at all. Claire checked the portal networks, but as far as she could tell, they were down. With nothing concrete to do, she helped around the house – cleaning, straightening, running errands. Richard Morrell came around to check on them. He looked a little better for having slept, which didn't mean he looked good, exactly.

When Eve wandered down, she looked almost as bad. She hadn't bothered with her Goth make-up, and her black hair was down in a lank, uncombed mess. She poured Richard some coffee from the ever-brewing pot, handed it over, and said, 'How's Michael?'

Richard blew on the hot surface in the cup without looking at her. 'He's at City Hall. We moved all the vampires we still had into the jail, for safekeeping.'

Eve's face crumpled in anguish. Shane put a hand on her shoulder, and she pulled in a damp breath and got control of herself.

'Right,' she said. 'That's probably for the best, you're right.' She sipped from her own battered coffee mug. 'What's it like out there?' *Out there* meant beyond Lot Street, which remained eerily quiet.

'Not so good,' Richard said. His voice sounded hoarse and dull, as if he'd yelled all the edges off it. 'About half the stores are shut down, and some of those are burnt or looted. We don't have enough police and volunteers to be everywhere. Some of the store owners armed up and are guarding their own places – I don't like it, but it's probably the best option until everybody settles down and sobers up. The problem isn't everybody, but it's a good portion of the town who's been down and angry a long time. You heard they raided the Barfly?'

'Yeah, we heard,' Shane said.

'Well, that was just the beginning. Dolores Thompson's place got broken into, and then they went to the warehouses and found the bonded liquor storage. Those who were inclined to deal with all this by getting drunk and mean have had a real holiday.'

'We saw the mobs,' Eve said, and glanced at Claire. 'Um, about your sister—'

'Yeah, thanks for taking care of her. Trust my idiot sister to go running around in her red convertible during a riot. She's damn lucky they didn't kill her.'

They would have, Claire was certain of that. 'I guess you're taking her with you...?'

Richard gave her a thin smile. 'Not the greatest houseguest?'

Actually, Monica had been very quiet. Claire had found her curled up on the couch, wrapped in a blanket, sound asleep. She'd looked pale and tired and bruised, and much younger than Claire had ever seen her. 'She's been OK.' She shrugged. 'But I'll bet she'd rather be with her family.'

'Her *family's* under protective custody downtown. My dad nearly got dragged off by a bunch of yahoos yelling about taxes or something. My mom—' Richard shook his head, as if he wanted to drive the pictures right out of his mind. 'Anyway. Unless she likes four walls and a locked door, I don't think she's going to be very happy. And you know Monica: if she's not happy—'

'Nobody is,' Shane finished for him. 'Well, I want her out of our house. Sorry, man, but we did our duty and all. Past this point, she'd have to be a friend to keep crashing here. Which, you know, she isn't. Ever.'

'Then I'll take her off your hands.' Richard set the cup down and stood. 'Thanks for the coffee. Seems like that's all that's keeping me going right now.'

'Richard...' Eve rose, too. 'Seriously, what's it like out there? What's going to happen?'

'With any luck, the drunks will sober up or pass out, and those who've been running around looking for people to punish will get sore feet and aching muscles and go home to get some sleep.'

'Not like we've had a lot of luck so far, though,' Shane said.

'No,' Richard agreed. 'That we haven't. But I have to say, we can't keep things locked down. People have to work, the schools have to open, and for that, we need something like normal life around here. So we're working on that. Power and water's on, phone lines are back up. TV and radio are broadcasting. I'm hoping that calms people down. We've got police patrols overlapping all through town, and we can be anywhere in under two minutes. One thing, though: we're getting word that there's bad weather in the forecast. Some kind of real big front heading towards us tonight. I'm not too happy about that, but maybe it'll keep the crazies off the streets for a while. Even riots don't like rain.'

'What about the university?' Claire asked. 'Is it open?'

'Open and classes are running, believe it or not. We passed off some of the disturbances as role-playing in the disaster drill, and said that the looting and burning was part of the exercise. Some of them believed us.'

'But...no word about the vampires?'

Richard was silent for a moment, and then he said, 'No. Not exactly.'

'Then what?'

'We found some bodies, before dawn,' he said. 'All vamps. All killed with silver or decapitation. Some of them – I knew some of them. Thing is, I don't think they were killed by Bishop. From the looks of things, they were caught by a mob.'

Claire caught her breath. Eve covered her mouth. 'Who—?'

'Bernard Temple, Sally Christien, Tien Ma, and Charles Effords.'

Eve lowered her hand to say, 'Charles Effords? Like, Miranda's Charles? Her Protector?'

'Yeah. From the state of the bodies, I'd guess he was the primary target. Nobody loves a paedophile.'

'Nobody except Miranda,' Eve said. 'She's going to be really scared now.'

'Yeah, about that...' Richard hesitated, then plunged forward. 'Miranda's gone.'

'Gone?'

'Disappeared. We've been looking for her. Her parents reported her missing early last night. I'm hoping she wasn't with Charles when the mob caught up to him. You see her, you call me, OK?'

Eve's lips shaped the agreement, but no sound came out.

Richard checked his watch. 'Got to go,' he said. 'Usual drill: lock the doors, check IDs on anybody you're not expecting who shows up. If you hear from any vampire, or hear anything *about* the vampires, you call immediately. Use the coded radios, not the phone lines. And be careful.'

Eve swallowed hard, and nodded. 'Can I see Michael?'

He paused, as if that hadn't occurred to him, then shrugged. 'Come on.'

'We're all going,' Shane said.

It was an uncomfortable ride to City Hall, where the jail was located, mainly because although the police cruiser was large, it wasn't big enough to have Richard, Monica, Eve, Shane, and Claire all sharing the ride. Monica had taken the front seat, sliding close to her brother, and Claire had squeezed in with her friends in the back.

They didn't talk, not even when they cruised past burnt-out, broken hulks of homes and stores. There weren't any fires today, or any mobs that Claire spotted. It all seemed quiet.

Richard drove past a police barricade around City Hall and parked in the underground garage. 'I'm taking Monica to my parents',' he said. 'You guys go on down to the cells. I'll be there in a minute.'

It took a lot more than a minute for them to gain access to Michael; the vampires – all five of those the humans still had in custody – were housed in a special section, away from daylight and in reinforced cells. It reminded Claire, with an unpleasant lurch, of the vampires in the cells where Myrnin was usually locked up, for his own protection. Had anyone fed them? Had anyone even tried?

She didn't know three of the vampires, but she knew the last two. 'Sam!' she blurted, and rushed to the bars. Michael's grandfather was lying on the bunk, one pale hand over his eyes, but he sat up when she called his name. Claire could definitely see the resemblance between Michael and Sam – the same basic bone structure, only Michael's hair was a bright gold, and Sam's was red.

'Get me out,' Sam said, and lunged for the door. He rattled the cage with unexpected violence. Claire fell back, open-mouthed. 'Open the door and get me out, Claire! *Now!*'

'Don't listen to him,' Michael said. He was

standing at the bars of his own cell, leaning against them, and he looked tired. 'Hey, guys. Did you bring me a lockpick in a cupcake or something?'

'I had the cupcake, but I ate it. Hard times, man.' Shane extended his hand. Michael reached through the bars and took it, shook solemnly, and then Eve threw herself against the metal to try to hug him. It was awkward, but Claire saw the relief spread over Michael, no matter how odd it was with the bars between the two of them. He kissed Eve, and Claire had to look away from that, because it seemed like such a private kind of moment.

Sam rattled his cage again. 'Claire, open the door! I need to get to Amelie!'

The policeman who'd escorted them down to the cells pushed off from the wall and said, 'Calm down, Mr Glass. You're not going anywhere; you know that.' He shifted his attention to Shane and Claire. 'He's been like that since the beginning. We had to trank him twice; he was hurting himself trying to get out. He's worse than all the others. They seem to have calmed down. Not him.'

No, Sam definitely hadn't calmed down. As Claire watched, he tensed his muscles and tried to force the lock, but subsided in panting frustration and stumbled back to his bunk. 'I have to go,' he muttered. 'Please, I need to go. She needs me. Amelie—'

Claire looked at Michael, who didn't seem to be nearly as distressed. 'Um...sorry to ask, but...are you feeling like that? Like Sam?'

'No,' Michael said. His eyes were still closed. 'For a while there was this...call, but it stopped about three hours ago.'

'Then why is Sam—'

'It's not the call,' Michael said. 'It's Sam. It's killing him, knowing she's out there in trouble and he can't help her.'

Sam put his head in his hands, the picture of misery. Claire exchanged a look with Shane. 'Sam,' she said. 'What's happening? Do you know?'

'People are dying, that's what's happening,' he said. 'Amelie's in trouble. I need to go to her. I can't just sit here!'

He threw himself at the bars again, kicking hard enough to make the metal ring like a bell.

'Well, that's where you're going to stay,' the policeman said, not exactly unsympathetically. 'The way you're acting, you'd go running out into the sunlight, and that wouldn't do her or you a bit of good, now, would it?'

'I could have gone hours ago before sunrise,' Sam snapped. *Hours ago.*

'And now you have to wait for dark.'

That earned the policeman a full-out vicious snarl,

and Sam's eyes flared into bright crimson. Everybody stayed back, and when Sam subsided this time, it seemed to be for good. He withdrew to his bunk, lay down, and turned his back to them.

'Man,' Shane breathed softly. 'He's a little intense, huh?'

From what the policeman told them – and Richard, when he rejoined them – all the captured vampires had been at about the same level of violence, at first. Now it was just Sam, and as Michael said, it didn't seem to be Amelie's summons that was driving him... It was fear for Amelie herself.

It was love.

'Step back, please,' the policeman said to Eve. She looked over her shoulder at him, then at Michael. He kissed her, and let go.

She did take a step back, but it was a tiny one. 'So – are you OK? Really?'

'Sure. It's not exactly the Ritz, but it's not bad. They're not keeping us here to hurt us, I know that.' Michael stretched out a finger and touched her lips. 'I'll be back soon.'

'Better be,' Eve said. She mock-bit at his finger. 'I could totally date somebody else, you know.'

'And I could rent out your room.'

'And I could put your game console on eBay.'

'Hey,' Shane protested. 'Now you're just being mean.'

'See what I mean? You need to come home, or it's total chaos. Dogs and cats, living together.' Eve's voice dropped, but not quite to a whisper. 'And I miss you. I miss seeing you. I miss you all the time.'

'I miss you, too,' Michael murmured, then blinked and looked at Claire and Shane. 'I mean, I miss all of you.'

'Sure you do,' Shane agreed. 'But not in that way, I hope.'

'Shut up, dude. Don't make me come out there.'

Shane turned to the policeman. 'See? He's fine.'

'I was more worried about you guys,' Michael confessed. 'Everything OK at the house?'

'I have to burn a blouse Monica borrowed,' Claire said. 'Otherwise, we're good.'

They tried to talk a while longer, but somehow, Sam's silent, rigid back turned towards them made conversation seem more desperate than fun. He was really hurting, and Claire didn't know – short of letting him go for a jog in the noontime sun – how to make it any better. She didn't know where Amelie was, and with the portals shut, she doubted she could even know where to start looking.

Amelie had gathered up an army – whatever Bishop hadn't grabbed first – but what she was doing with it was anybody's guess. Claire didn't have a clue.

So in the end, she hugged Michael and told Sam it would all be OK, and they left.

'If they stay calm through the day, I'll let them out tonight,' Richard said. 'But I'm worried about letting them roam around on their own. What happened to Charles and the others could keep on happening. Captain Obvious used to be our biggest threat, but now we don't know who's out there, or what they're planning. And we can't count on the vampires to be able to protect themselves right now.'

'My dad would say that it's about time the tables turned,' Shane said.

Richard fixed him with a long stare. 'Is that what you say, too?'

Shane looked at Michael, and at Sam. 'No,' he said. 'Not anymore.'

The day went on quietly. Claire got out her books and spent part of the day trying to study, but she couldn't get her brain to stop spinning. Every few minutes, she checked her e-mail and her phone, hoping for something, anything, from Amelie. *You can't just leave us like this. We don't know what to do.*

Except keep moving forward. Like Shane had said, they couldn't stay still. The world kept on turning.

Eve drove Claire to her parents' house in the

afternoon, where she had cake and iced tea and listened to her mother's frantic flow of good cheer. Her dad looked sallow and unwell, and she worried about his heart, as always. But he seemed OK when he told her he loved her, and that he worried, and that he wanted her to move back home.

Just when she thought they'd got past that...

Claire exchanged a quick look with Eve. 'Maybe we should talk about that when things get back to normal?' As if they ever were normal in Morganville. 'Next week?'

Dad nodded. 'Fine, but I'm not going to change my mind, Claire. You're better off here, at home.' Whatever spell Mr Bishop had cast over her father, it was still working great; he was single-minded about wanting her out of the Glass House. And maybe it hadn't been a spell at all; maybe it was just normal parental instinct.

Claire crammed her mouth with cake and pretended not to hear, and asked her mom about the new curtains. That filled another twenty minutes, and then Eve was able to make excuses about needing to get home, and then they were in the car.

'Wow,' Eve said, and started the engine. 'So. Are you going to do it? Move in with them?'

Claire shrugged helplessly. 'I don't know. I don't know if we're going to get through the day! It's kind

222   Rachel Caine

of hard to make plans.' She wasn't going to say anything, truly, she wasn't, but the words had been boiling and bubbling inside her all day, and as Eve put the car in drive, Claire said, 'Shane said he loved me.'

Eve hit the brakes, hard enough to make their seat belts click in place. 'Shane *what*? Said *what*?'

'Shane said he loved me.'

'OK, first impressions – fantastic, good, that's what I was hoping you'd said.' Eve took a deep breath and let up on the brake, steering out into the deserted street. 'Second impressions, well, I hope that you two…um…how can I put this? Watch yourselves?'

'You mean, don't have sex? We won't.' Claire said it with a little bit of an edge. 'Even if we wanted to. I mean, he promised, and he's not going to break that promise, not even if I say it's OK.'

'Oh. *Oh.*' Eve stared at her, wide-eyed, for way too long for road safety. 'You're kidding! Wait, you're not. He said he loved you, and then he said—'

'No,' Claire said. 'He said no.'

'Oh.' Funny, how many meanings that word could have. This time it was full of sympathy. 'You know, that makes him—'

'Great? Superbly awesome? Yeah, I know. I just—' Claire threw up her hands. 'I just *want* him, OK?'

'He'll still be there in a couple of months, Claire.

At seventeen, you're not a kid, at least in Texas.'

'You've put some thought into this.'

'Not me,' Eve said, and gave her an apologetic look.

'*Shane?* You mean – you mean you talked about this? With Shane?"

'He needed some girl guidance. I mean, he's taking this really seriously – a lot more seriously than I expected. He wants to do the right thing. That's cool, right? I think that's cool. Most guys, it's just, whatever.'

Claire clenched her jaw so hard she felt her teeth grinding. 'I can't believe he talked to you about it!'

'Well, you're talking to me about it.'

'He's a guy!'

'Guys occasionally talk, believe it or not. Something more than *pass the beer* or *where's the porn?*' Eve turned the corner, and they cruised past a couple of slow blocks of houses, some people out walking, an elementary school with a TEMPORARILY CLOSED sign out front. 'You didn't exactly ask for advice, but I'm going to give it: don't rush this. You may think you're good to go, but give it some time. It's not like you have a sell-by date or anything.'

Despite her annoyance, Claire had to laugh. 'Feels like it right now.'

'Well, duh. Hormones!'

'So how old were you when—'

'Too young. I speak from experience, grasshopper.' Eve's expression went distant for a second. 'I wish I'd waited for Michael.'

That was, for some reason, kind of a shock, and Claire blinked. She remembered some things, and felt deeply uncomfortable. 'Uh...did Brandon...?' Because Brandon had been her family's Protector vampire, and he'd been a complete creep. She couldn't imagine much worse than having Brandon be your first.

'No. Not that he didn't want to, but no, it wasn't Brandon.'

'Who?'

'Sorry. Off-limits.'

Claire blinked. There wasn't much Eve considered off-limits. 'Really?'

'Really.' Eve pulled the car up to the curb. 'Bottom line? If Shane says he loves you, he does, full stop. He wouldn't say it if he didn't mean it, all the way. He's not the kind of guy to tell you what you want to hear. That makes you really, really lucky. You should remember that.'

Claire was trying, really, but from time to time that moment came back to her, that blinding, searing moment when he'd looked into her face and said those words, and she'd seen that amazing light in his eyes. She'd wanted to see it again, over and over. Instead, she'd seen him walk away.

It felt romantic. It also felt frustrating, on some level she didn't even remember feeling before. And now there was something new: doubt. *Maybe that was my fault. Maybe I was supposed to do something I didn't do. Some signal I didn't give him.*

Eve read her expression just fine. 'You'll be OK,' she said, and laughed just a little. 'Give the guy a break. He's only the second actual gentleman I've ever met. It doesn't mean he doesn't want to throw you on the bed and go. Just means he won't, right now. Which you have to admit is kinda hot.'

Put in those terms, it kind of was.

As it got closer to nightfall, Richard called to say he was letting Michael go. For the second time, the three of them piled into the car and went racing to City Hall. The barricades had mostly come down. According to the radio and television, it had been a very quiet day, with no reports of violence. Store owners – the human ones, anyway – were planning on reopening in the morning. Schools would be in session.

Life was going on, and Mayor Morrell was expected to come out with some kind of a speech. Not that anybody would listen.

'Are they letting Sam out, too?' Claire asked, as Eve parked in the underground lot.

'Apparently. Richard doesn't think he can really keep anybody much longer. Some kind of town ordinance, which means law and order really is back in fashion. Plus, I think he's really afraid Sam's going to hurt himself if this goes on. And also, maybe he thinks he can follow Sam to find Amelie.' Eve scanned the dark structure – there were a few dark-tinted cars in the lot, but then, there always were. The rest of the vehicles looked like they were human-owned. 'You guys see anything?'

'Like what? A big sign saying This Is a Trap?' Shane opened his door and got out, taking Claire's hand to help her. He didn't drop it once she was standing beside him. 'Not that I wouldn't put it past some of our finer citizens. But no, I don't see anything.'

Michael was being let out of his cell when they arrived, and there were hugs and handshakes. The other vampires didn't have anyone to help them, and looked a little confused about what they were supposed to do.

Not Sam.

'Sam, wait!' Michael grabbed his arm on the way past, dragging his grandfather to a stop. Looking at them standing together, Claire was struck again by how alike they were. And always would be, she supposed, given that neither one of them was going to age any more. 'You can't go charging off by yourself. You don't even know where she is. Running around town on your white horse will get you really, truly killed.'

'Doing nothing will get *her* killed. I can't have that, Michael. None of this means anything to me if she dies.' Sam shook Michael's hand away. 'I'm not asking you to come with me. I'm just telling you not to get in my way.'

'Grandpa—'

'Exactly. Do as you're told.' Sam could move vampire-quick when he wanted to, and he was gone almost before the words hit Claire's ears – a blur, heading for the exit.

'So much for trying to figure out where she is from where he goes,' Shane said. 'Unless you've got light speed under the hood of that car, Eve.'

Michael looked after him with a strange expression on his face – anger, regret, sorrow. Then he hugged Eve closer and kissed the top of her head.

'Well, I guess my family's no more screwed up than anybody else's,' he said.

Eve nodded. 'Let's recap. My dad was an abusive jerk—'

'Mine, too.' Shane raised his hand.

'Thank you. My brother's a psycho backstabber—'

Shane said, 'You don't even want to talk about my dad.'

'Point. So, in short, Michael, your family is *awesome* by comparison. Bloodsucking, maybe. But kind of awesome.'

Michael sighed. 'Doesn't really feel like it at the moment.'

'It will.' Eve was suddenly very serious. 'But Shane and I don't have that to look forward to, you know. You're our only real family now.'

'I know,' Michael said. 'Let's go home.'

CHAPTER ELEVEN

Home was theirs again. The refugees were all out now, leaving a house that badly needed picking up and cleaning – not that anybody had gone out of their way to trash the place, but with that many people coming and going, things happened. Claire grabbed a trash bag and began clearing away paper plates, old Styrofoam cups half full of stale coffee, crumpled wrappers, and papers. Shane fired up the video game, apparently back in the mood to kill zombies. Michael took his guitar out of its case and tuned it, but he kept getting up to stare out the windows, restless and worried.

'What?' Eve asked. She'd heated up leftover spaghetti out of the refrigerator, and tried to hand Michael a plate first. 'Do you see something?'

'Nothing,' he said, and gave her a quick, strained smile as he waved away the food. 'Not really hungry, though. Sorry.'

'More for me,' Shane said, and grabbed the plate. He propped it on his lap and forked spaghetti into his mouth. 'Seriously. You all right? Because you never turn down food.'

Michael didn't answer. He stared out into the dark.

'You're worried,' Eve said. 'About Sam?'

'Sam and everybody else. This is nuts. What's going on here—?' Michael checked the locks on the window, but as a kind of automatic motion, as though his mind wasn't really on it. 'Why hasn't Bishop taken over? What's he *doing* out there? Why aren't we seeing the fight?'

'Maybe Amelie's kicking his ass out there in the shadows somewhere.' Shane shovelled in more spaghetti.

'No. She's not. I can feel that. I think – I think she's in hiding. With the rest of her followers, the vampires, anyway.'

Shane stopped chewing. 'You know where they are?'

'Not really. I just feel—' Michael shook his head. 'It's gone. Sorry. But I feel like things are changing. Coming to a head.'

Claire had just taken a plate of warm pasta when they all heard the thump of footsteps overhead. They looked up, and then at each other, in silence.

Michael pointed to himself and the stairs, and they all nodded. Eve opened a drawer in the end table and took out three sharpened stakes; she tossed one to Shane, one to Claire, and kept one in a white-knuckled grip.

Michael ascended the stairs without a sound, and disappeared.

He didn't come back down. Instead, there was a swirl of black coat and stained white balloon pants tucked into black boots; then Myrnin leant over the railing to say, 'Upstairs, all of you. I need you.'

'Um...' Eve looked at Shane. Shane looked at Claire.

Claire followed Myrnin. 'Trust me,' she said. 'It won't do any good to say no.'

Michael was waiting in the hallway, next to the open, secret door. He led the way up.

Whatever Claire had been expecting to see, it wasn't a *crowd*, but that was what was waiting upstairs in the hidden room on the third floor. She stared in confusion at the room full of people, then moved out of the way for Shane and Eve to join her and Michael.

Myrnin came last. 'Claire, I believe you know Theo Goldman and his family.'

The faces came into focus. She *had* met them – in that museum thing, when they'd been on the way to rescue Myrnin. Theo Goldman had spoken to Amelie. He'd said they wouldn't fight.

But it looked to Claire like they'd been in a fight anyway. Vampires didn't bruise, exactly, but she could see torn clothes and smears of blood, and they all looked exhausted and somehow – hollow. Theo was worst of all. His kind face seemed to be made of nothing but lines and wrinkles now, as if he'd aged a hundred years in a couple of days.

'I'm sorry,' he said, 'but we had no other place to go. Amelie – I hoped that she was here, that she would give us refuge. We've been everywhere else.'

Claire remembered there being more of them, somehow – yes, there were at least two people missing. One human, one vampire. 'What happened? I thought you were safe where you were!'

'We were,' Theo said. 'Then we weren't. That's what wars are like. The safe places don't stay safe. Someone knew where we were, or suspected. Around dawn yesterday, a mob broke in the doors looking for us. Jochen—' He looked at his wife, and she bowed her head. 'Our son Jochen, he gave his life to delay them. So did our human friend William. We've been hiding, moving from place to place, trying not to be driven out in the sun.'

'How did you get here?' Michael asked. He seemed wary. Claire didn't blame him.

'I brought them,' Myrnin said. 'I've been trying to find those who are left.' He crouched down next to one of the young vampire girls and stroked her hair. She smiled at him, but it was a fragile, frightened smile. 'They can stay here for now. This room isn't common knowledge. I've left open the portal in the attic in case they have to flee, but it's one way only, leading out. It's a last resort.'

'Are there others? Out there?' Claire asked.

'Very few on their own. Most are either with Bishop, with Amelie, or' – Myrnin spread his hands – 'gone.'

'What are they doing? Amelie and Bishop?'

'Moving their forces. They're trying to find an advantage, pick the most favourable ground. It won't last.' Myrnin shrugged. 'Sooner or later, sometime tonight, they'll clash, and then they'll fight. Someone will win, and someone will lose. And in the morning, Morganville will know its fate.'

That was creepy. *Really* creepy. Claire shivered and looked at the others, but nobody seemed to have anything to say.

'Claire. Attend me,' Myrnin said, and walked with her to one corner of the room. 'Have you spoken with your doctor friend?'

'I tried. I couldn't get through to him. Myrnin, are you...OK?'

'Not for much longer,' he said, in that clinical way he had right before the drugs wore off. 'I won't be safe to be around without another dose of some sort. Can you get it for me?'

'There's none in your lab—'

'I've been there. Bishop got there first. I shall need a good bit of glassware, and a completely new library.' He said it lightly, but Claire could see the tension in his face and the shadow in his dark, gleaming eyes. 'He tried to destroy the portals, cut off Amelie's movements. I managed to patch things together, but I shall need to instruct you in how it's done. Soon. In case—'

He didn't need to finish. Claire nodded slowly. 'You should go,' she said. 'Is the prison safe? The one where you keep the sickest ones?'

'Bishop finds nothing to interest him there, so yes. He will ignore it awhile longer. I'll lock myself in for a while, until you come with the drug.' Myrnin bent over her, suddenly very focused and very intent. 'We *must* refine the serum, Claire. We *must* distribute it. The stress, the fighting – it's accelerating the disease. I've seen signs of it in Theo, even in Sam. If we don't act soon, I'm afraid we may begin to lose more to confusion and fear. They won't even be able to defend themselves.'

Claire swallowed. 'I'll get on it.'

He took her hand and kissed it lightly. His lips felt dry as dust, but it still left a tingle in her fingers. 'I know you will, my girl. Now, let's rejoin your friends.'

'How long do they need to be here?' Eve asked, as they moved closer. She asked not unkindly, but she seemed nervous, too. There were, Claire thought, an awful lot of near-stranger vampire guests. 'I mean, we don't have a lot of blood in the house...'

Theo smiled. Claire remembered, with a sharp feeling of alarm, what he'd said to Amelie back at the museum, and she didn't like that smile at all, not even when he said, 'We won't require much. We can provide for ourselves.'

'He means, they can munch on their human friends, like takeout,' Claire said. 'No. Not in our house.'

Myrnin frowned. 'This is hardly the time to be—'

'This is *exactly* the time, and you know it. Did anybody ask *them* if they wanted to be snack packs?' The two remaining humans, both women, looked horrified. 'I didn't think so.'

Theo's expression didn't change. 'What we do is our own affair. We won't hurt them, you know.'

'Unless you're getting your plasma by osmosis, I don't really know how you can promise that.'

Theo's eyes flared with banked fire. 'What do you

want us to do? Starve? Even the youngest of us?'

Eve cleared her throat. 'Actually, I know where there's a big supply of blood. If somebody will go with me to get it.'

'Oh, hell no,' Shane said. 'Not out in the dark. Besides, the place is locked up.'

Eve reached in her pocket and took out her key ring. She flipped until she found one key in particular, and held it up. 'I never turned in my key,' she said. 'I used to open and close, you know.'

Myrnin gazed at her thoughtfully. 'There's no portal to Common Grounds. It's off the network. That means any vampire in it will be trapped in daylight.'

'No. There's underground access to the tunnels; I've seen it. Oliver sent some people out using it while I was there.' Eve gave him a bright, brittle smile. 'I say we move your friends there. Also, there's coffee. You guys like coffee, right? Everybody likes coffee.'

Theo ignored her, and looked to Myrnin for an answer. 'Is it better?'

'It's more defensible,' Myrnin said. 'Steel shutters. If there's underground access – yes. It would make a good base of operations.' He turned to Eve. 'We'll require your services to drive.'

He said it as if Eve were the help, and Claire felt

her face flame hot. 'Excuse me? How about a *please* in there somewhere, since you're asking for a favour?'

Myrnin's eyes turned dark and very cold. 'You seem to have forgotten that I employ you, Claire. That I *own* you, in some sense. I am not required to say please and thank you to you, your friends, or *any* human walking the streets.' He blinked, and was back to the Myrnin she normally saw. 'However, I do take your point. Yes. *Please* drive us to Common Grounds, dear lady. I would be extravagantly, embarrassingly grateful.'

He did all but kiss her hand. Eve, not surprisingly, could say nothing but yes.

Claire settled for an eye roll big enough to make her head hurt. 'You can't all fit,' she pointed out. 'In Eve's car, I mean.'

'And she's not taking you alone, anyway,' Michael said. 'My car's in the garage. I can take the rest of you. Shane, Claire—'

'Staying here, since you'll need the space,' Shane said. 'Sounds like a plan. Look, if there are people looking for them, you ought to get them moving. I'll call Richard. He can assign a couple of cops to guard Common Grounds.'

'No,' Myrnin said. 'No police. We can't trust them.'

'We can't?'

'Some of them have been working with Bishop, and with the human mobs. I have proof of that. We can't take the risk.'

'But Richard...' Claire said, and subsided when she got Myrnin's glare. 'Right. OK. On your own, got it.'

Eve didn't want to be dragged into it, but she went without much of a protest – the number of fangs in the room might have had something to do with it. As the Goldmans and Myrnin, Eve and Michael walked downstairs, Shane held Claire back to say, 'We've got to figure out how to lock this place up. In case.'

'You mean, against...' She gestured vaguely at the vampires. He nodded. 'But if Michael lives here, and we live here, the house can't just bar a whole group of people from entry. It has to be done one at a time – at least that's what I understood. And no, before you ask me, I don't know how it works. Or how to fool it. I think only Amelie has the keys to that.'

He looked disappointed. 'How about closing off these weird doors Myrnin and Amelie are popping through?'

'I can work them. That doesn't mean I can turn them on and off.'

'Great.' He looked around the room, then took a seat on the old Victorian couch. 'So we're like Undead

Grand Central Station. Not really loving that so much. Can Bishop come through?'

It was a question that Claire had been thinking about, and it creeped her out to have to say, 'I don't know. Maybe. But from what Myrnin said, he set the doorway to exit-only. So maybe we just...wait.'

Robbed of doing anything heroic, or for that matter even useful, she warmed up the spaghetti again, and she and Shane ate it and watched some mindless TV show while jumping at every noise and creak, with weapons handy. When the kitchen door banged open nearly an hour later, Claire almost needed a heart transplant – until she heard Eve yell, 'We're home! Oooooh, spaghetti. I'm starved.' Eve came in holding a plate and shovelling pasta into her mouth as she walked. Michael was right behind her.

'No problems?' Shane asked. Eve shook her head, chewing a mouthful of spaghetti.

'They should be fine there. Nobody saw us get them inside, and until Oliver turns up, nobody is going to need to get in there for a while.'

'What about Myrnin?'

Eve swallowed, almost choked, and Michael patted her kindly on the back. She beamed at him. 'Myrnin? Oh yeah. He did a Batman and took off into the night. What is *with* that guy, Claire? If he was a superhero, he'd be Bipolar Man.'

The drugs were the problem. Claire needed to get more, and she needed to work on that cure Myrnin had found. That was just as important as anything else...providing there were any vampires left, anyway.

They had dinner, and at least it was the four of them again, sitting around the table, talking as if the world were normal, even if all of them knew it wasn't. Shane seemed especially jumpy, which wasn't like him at all.

For her part, Claire was just tired to the bone of being scared, and when she went upstairs, she was asleep the minute she crawled between the covers.

But sleep didn't mean it was restful, or peaceful.

She dreamt that somewhere, Amelie was playing chess, moving her pieces at lightning speed across a black-and-white board. Bishop sat across from her, grinning with too many teeth, and when he took her rook, it turned into a miniature version of Claire, and suddenly both the vampires were huge and she was so small, so small, stranded out in the open.

Bishop picked her up and squeezed her in his white hand, and blood drops fell onto the white squares of the chessboard.

Amelie frowned, watching Bishop squeeze her, and put out a delicate fingertip to touch the drops of blood. Claire struggled and screamed.

Amelie tasted her blood, and smiled.

Claire woke up with a convulsive shudder, huddled in her blankets. It was still dark outside the windows, though the sky was getting lighter, and the house was very, very quiet.

Her phone was buzzing in vibrate mode on the bedside table. She picked it up and found a text message from the university's alert system.

CLASSES RETURN TO NORMAL SCHEDULE EFFECTIVE 7 A.M. TODAY.

School seemed like a million miles away, another world that didn't mean anything to her anymore, but it would get her on campus, and there were things she needed there. Claire scrolled down her phone list and found Dr Robert Mills, but there was no immediate answer on his cell. She checked the clock, winced at the early hour, but slid out of bed and began grabbing things out of drawers. That didn't take a lot of time. She was down to the last of everything. Laundry was starting to be a genuine priority.

She dialled his phone again after she'd dressed.

'Hello?' Dr Mills sounded as if she'd dragged him out of a deep, probably happy sleep. *He* probably hadn't been dreaming about being squeezed dry by Mr Bishop.

'It's Claire,' she said. 'I'm sorry to call so early—'

'Is it early? Oh. Been up all night, just fell asleep.'

He yawned. 'Glad you're all right, Claire.'

'Are you at the hospital?'

'No. The hospital's going to need a lot of work before it's even halfway ready for the kind of work I need to do.' Another jaw-cracking yawn. 'Sorry. I'm on campus, in the Life Sciences Building. Lab Seventeen. We have some roll-away beds here.'

'We?'

'My wife and kids are with me. I didn't want to leave them on their own out there.'

Claire didn't blame him. 'I've got something for you to do, and I need some of the drug,' she said. 'It could be really important. I'll be at school in about twenty minutes, OK?'

'OK. Don't come here. My kids are asleep right now. Let's meet somewhere else.'

'The on-campus coffee bar,' she said. 'It's in the University Centre.'

'Trust me, I know where it is. Twenty minutes.'

She was already heading for the door.

With no sounds coming from any of the other rooms, Claire figured her housemates were all crashed out, exhausted. She didn't know why she wasn't, except for a suppressed, vibrating fear inside her that if she slept any more, something bad was going to happen.

Showered, dressed in her last not-very-good

clothes, she grabbed up her backpack and repacked it. Her dart gun was out of darts anyway, so she left it behind. The samples Myrnin had prepared of Bishop's blood went into a sturdy padded box, and on impulse, she added a couple of stakes and the silver knife Amelie had given her.

And books.

It was the first time Claire had been on foot in Morganville since the rioting had started, and it was eerie. The town was quiet again, but stores had broken windows, some boarded over; there were some buildings reduced to burnt-out hulks, with blind, open doorways. Broken bottles were on the sidewalks and spots of what looked like blood on the concrete — and, in places, dark splashes.

Claire hurried past it all, even past Common Grounds, where the steel shutters were down inside the windows. There was no sign of anyone within. She imagined Theo Goldman standing there watching her from cover, and waved a little, just a waggle of fingers.

She didn't really expect a response.

The gates of the university were open, and the guards were gone. Claire jogged along the sidewalk, going up the hill and around the curve, and began to see students up and moving, even so early in the morning. As she got closer to the central cluster of buildings, the foot traffic intensified, and here and there she saw alert campus police walking in pairs, watching for trouble.

The students didn't seem to notice anything at all. Not for the first time, Claire wondered if Amelie's semi-psychic network that cut Morganville off from the world also kept people on campus clueless.

She didn't like to think they were just naturally that stupid. Then again, she'd been to some of the parties.

The University Centre had opened its doors only a few minutes before, and the coffee barista was just taking the chairs down from the tables. Usually it would have been Eve on duty, but instead, it was one of the university staffers, on loan from the food service most likely. He didn't exactly look happy to be there. Claire tried to be nice, and finally got a smile from him as he handed her a mocha and took her cash.

'I wouldn't be here,' he confessed, 'except that they're paying us triple to be here the rest of the week.'

'Really? Wow. I'll tell Eve. She could use the money.'

'Yeah, get her in here. I'm not good at this coffee stuff. Give me the plain stuff. Water, beans – can't really screw that up. This espresso is hard.'

Claire decided, after tasting the mocha, that he was right. He really wasn't cut out for it. She sipped it anyway, and took a seat where she could watch the majority of the UC entrances for Dr Mills.

She almost didn't recognise him. He'd shed his white doctor's coat, of course, but somehow she'd never expected to see someone like him wearing a zip-up hoodie, sweatpants, and sneakers. He was more the suit-and-tie type. He ordered plain coffee – good choice – and came to join her at the table.

Dr Mills was medium everything, and he blended in at the university just as easily as he had at the hospital. He'd have made a good spy, Claire thought. He had one of those faces – young from one angle, older from another, with nothing you could really remember later about it.

But he had a nice, comforting smile. She supposed that would be a real asset in a doctor.

'Morning,' he said, and gulped coffee. His eyes were bloodshot and red rimmed. 'I'm going back to the hospital later today. Damage assessments, and we've already reopened the trauma units and CCU. I'm going to catch some sleep as soon as we're done, in case any crash cases come in. Nothing worse than an exhausted trauma surgeon.'

She felt even more guilty about waking him up. 'I'll make this quick,' she promised. Claire opened her backpack, took out the padded box, and slid it across the table to him. 'Blood samples, from Myrnin.'

Mills frowned. 'I've already got a hundred blood samples from Myrnin. Why—'

'These are different,' Claire said. 'Trust me. There's one labelled *B* that's important.'

'Important, how?'

'I don't want to say. I'd rather you took a look first.' In science, Claire knew, it was better to come to an analysis cold, without too many expectations. Dr Mills knew that, too, and he nodded as he took possession of the samples. 'Um – if you want to sleep, maybe you shouldn't drink that stuff.'

Dr Mills smiled and threw back the rest of his coffee. 'You get to be a doctor by developing immunity to all kinds of things, including caffeine,' he said. 'Trust me. The second my head touches the pillow, I'm asleep, even if I've got a coffee IV drip.'

'I know people who'd pay good money for that. The IV drip, I mean.'

He shook his head, grinning, but then got serious. 'You seem OK. I was worried about you. You're just so...young, to be involved in all this stuff.'

'I'm all right. And I'm really—'

'Not that young. Yes, I know. But still. Let an old man fret a little. I've got two daughters.' He tossed his coffee cup at the trash – two points – and stood.

'Here's all I could get together of the drug. Sorry, it's not a lot, but I've got a new batch in the works. It'll take a couple of days to finish.'

He handed her a bag that clinked with small glass bottles. She peeked inside. 'This should be plenty.' Unless, of course, she had to start dosing all over Morganville, in which case, they were done, anyway.

'Sorry to make this a gulp-and-run, but...'

'You should go,' Claire agreed. 'Thanks, Dr Mills.' She offered her hand. He shook it gravely.

Around his wrist, there was a silver bracelet, with Amelie's symbol on it. He looked down at it, then at her gold one, and shrugged.

'I don't think it's time to take it off,' he said. 'Not yet.'

At least yours does come off, Claire thought, but didn't say. Dr Mills had signed agreements, contracts, and those things were binding in Morganville, but the contract she'd signed had made her Amelie's property, body and soul. And her bracelet didn't have a catch on it, which made it more like a slave collar.

From time to time, that still creeped her out.

It was getting close to time for her first class, and as Claire hefted her backpack, she wondered how many people would show up. Lots, probably. Knowing most of the professors, they'd think today was a good day for a quiz.

She wasn't disappointed. She also wasn't panicked, unlike some of her classmates during her first class, and her third. Claire didn't panic on tests, not unless it was in a dream where she also had to clog dance and twirl batons to get a good grade. And the quizzes weren't so hard anyway, not even the physics tests.

One thing she noticed, more and more, as she went around campus: fewer people had on bracelets. Morganville natives got used to wearing them twenty-four/seven, so she could clearly see the tan lines where the bracelets had been...and weren't anymore. It was almost like a reverse tattoo.

Around noon, she saw Monica Morrell, Gina, and Jennifer.

The three girls were walking fast, heads down, books in their arms. There was a whole lot different about them; Claire was used to seeing those three stalking the campus like tigers, confident and cruel. They'd stare down anyone, and whether you liked them or not, they were wicked fashion queens, always showing themselves off to best advantage.

Not today.

Monica, who usually was the centrepiece, looked awful. Her shiny, flirty hair was dull and fuzzy, as if she had barely bothered to brush it, much less condition or curl. What little Claire could see of her face looked make-up free. She was wearing a shapeless sweater in an unflatteringly ugly pattern, and sloppy blue jeans, the kind Claire imagined she might keep around to clean house in, if Monica ever did that kind of thing.

Gina and Jennifer didn't look much better, and they all looked defeated.

Claire still felt a little, tiny, unworthy tingle of satisfaction...until she saw the looks they were getting. Morganville natives who'd taken off their bracelets were outright glaring at Monica and her entourage, and a few of them did worse than just give them dirty looks. As Claire watched, a big, tough jock wearing a TPU jacket bumped into Jennifer and sent her books flying. She didn't look at him. She just bent over to pick them up.

'Hey, you clumsy whore, what the hell?' He shoved her onto her butt as she tried to get up, but she wasn't his real target; she was just standing between him and Monica. 'Hey. Morrell. How's your daddy?'

'Fine,' Monica said, and looked him in the eyes. 'I'd ask about yours, but since you don't know who he was...'

The jock stepped very close to her. She didn't flinch, but Claire could tell that she wanted to. There were tight lines around her eyes and mouth, and her knuckles were white where she gripped her books.

'You've been Princess Queen Bitch your whole life,'

he said. 'You remember Annie? Annie McFarlane? You used to call her a fat cow. You laughed at her in school. You took pictures of her in the bathroom and posted them on the Internet. Remember?'

Monica didn't answer.

The jock smiled. 'Yeah, you remember Annie. She was a good kid, and I liked her.'

'You didn't like her enough to stand up for her,' Monica said. 'Right, Clark? You wanted to get in my pants more than you wanted me to be kind to your little fat friend. Not my fault she ended up wrecking that stupid car at the town border. Maybe it's your fault, though. Maybe she couldn't stand being in town with you anymore after you dumped her.'

Clark knocked the books out of her hand and shoved her up against a nearby tree trunk. Hard.

'I've got something for you, bitch.' He dug in his pocket and came up with something square, about four inches across. It was a sticky label like a name tag, only with a picture on it of an awkward but sweet-looking teenage girl trying bravely to smile for the camera.

Clark slapped it on Monica's chest and rubbed it so it stuck to the sweater.

'You wear that,' he said. 'You wear Annie's picture. If I see you take it off today, I swear, what you did to Annie back in high school's going to seem like a Cancún vacation.'

Under Annie's picture were the words KILLED BY MONICA MORRELL.

Monica looked down at it, swallowed, and turned bright red, then pale. She jerked her chin up again, sharply, and stared at Clark. 'Are you done?'

'So far. Remember, you take it off—'

'Yeah, Clark, you weren't exactly subtle. I get it. You think I care?'

Clark's grin widened. 'No, you don't. Not yet. Have a nice day, Queenie.'

He walked away and did a high five with two other guys.

As Monica stared down at the label on her chest in utter disgust, another girl approached – another Morganville native who'd taken off the bracelet. Monica didn't notice her until the girl was right in her face.

This one didn't talk. She just ripped the backing off another label and stuck it on Monica's chest next to Annie McFarlane's photo.

This one just said KILLER in big red letters.

She kept on walking.

Monica started to rip it off, but Clark was watching her.

'Suits you,' he said, and pointed to his eyes, then to her. 'We'll be watching you all day. There are a lot more labels coming.'

Clark was right. It was going to be a really long, bad day to be Monica Morrell. Even Gina and Jennifer were fading back now, heading out in a different direction and leaving her to face the music.

Monica's gaze fell on Claire. There was a flash of fear in her eyes, and shame, and genuine pain.

And then she armoured up and snapped, 'What are you looking at, freak?'

Claire shrugged. 'Justice, I guess.' She frowned. 'How come you didn't stay with your parents?'

'None of your business.' Monica's fierce stare wavered. 'Dad wanted us all to go back to normal. So people could see we're not afraid.'

'How's that going?'

Monica took a step towards her, then hugged her books to her chest to cover up most of the labels, and hurried on.

She hadn't got ten feet before a stranger ran up and slapped a label across her back that had a picture of a slender young girl and an older boy of maybe fifteen on it. The words beneath said KILLER OF ALYSSA.

With a shock, Claire realised that the boy in that picture was *Shane*. And that was his sister, Alyssa, the one who'd died in the fire that Monica had set.

'Justice,' Claire repeated softly. She felt a little

sick, actually. Justice wasn't the same thing as mercy.

Her phone rang as she was trying to decide what to do. 'Better come home,' Michael Glass said. 'We've got an emergency signal from Richard at City Hall.'

CHAPTER TWELVE

The signal had come over the coded strategy network, which Claire had just assumed was dead, considering that Oliver had been the one running it. But Richard had found a use for it, and as she burst in the front door, breathless, she heard Michael and Eve talking in the living room. Claire closed and locked the door, dumped her backpack, and hurried to join them.

'What did I miss?'

'Shhh,' they both said. Michael, Eve, and Shane were all seated at the table, staring intently at the small walkie-talkie sitting upright in the middle. Michael pulled out a chair for Claire, and she sat, trying to be as quiet as possible.

Richard was talking.

'...No telling whether or not this storm will hit us full on, but right now, the Weather Service shows the radar track going right over the top of us. It'll be here in the next few hours, probably right around dark. It's late in the year for tornado activity, but they're telling us there's a strong possibility of some real trouble. On top of all the other things we have going on, this isn't good news. I'm putting all emergency services and citizen patrols on full alert. If we get a tornado, get to your designated shelters...'

Designated shelters? Claire mouthed to Michael, who shrugged.

'If you're closer to City Hall, come here; we've got a shelter in the basement. Those of you who are Civil Defence wardens, go door-to-door in your area, tell people we've got a storm coming and what to do. We're putting it on TV and radio, and the university's going to get ready as well.'

'Richard, this is Hector,' said a new voice. 'Miller House. You got any news about this takeover people are talking about?'

'We've got rumours, but nothing concrete,' Richard said. 'We hear there's a lot of talk going around town about taking back City Hall, but we've got no specific word about when these people are meeting, or where, or even who they are. All I can tell you is that we've fortified the building, and the barricades remain up around Founder's Square, for all the good that does. I need everybody in a security-designated location to be on the alert today and tonight. Report in if you see any sign of an attack, any sign at all. We'll try to get to you in support.'

Michael exchanged a look with the rest of them, and then picked up the radio. He pressed the button. 'Michael Glass. You think Bishop's behind this?'

'I think Bishop's willing to let humans do his dirty work for him, and then sweep in to make himself lord and master on the ashes,' Richard said. 'Seems like his style. Put Shane on.'

Michael held out the radio. Shane looked at it like it might bite, then took it and pressed TALK. 'Yeah, this is Shane.'

'I have two unconfirmed sightings of your father in town. I know this isn't easy for you, but I need to know: is Frank Collins back in Morganville?'

Shane looked into Claire's eyes and said, 'If he is, he hasn't talked to me about it.'

He *lied*. Claire's lips parted, and she almost blurted something out, but she just couldn't think what to say. 'Shane,' she whispered. He shook his head.

'Tell you what, Richard, you catch my dad, you've got my personal endorsement for tossing him in the deepest pit you've got around here,' Shane said. 'If he's in Morganville, he's got a plan, but he won't be working for or with the vamps. Not that he knows, anyway.'

'Fair enough. You hear from him—'

'You're on speed dial. Got it.' Shane set the radio back in the centre of the table. Claire kept staring at him, willing him to speak, to say *something*, but he didn't.

'Don't do this,' she said. 'Don't put me in the middle.'

'I'm not,' Shane said. 'Nothing I said was a lie. My dad told me he was coming, not that he's here. I haven't seen him, and I don't want to. I meant what I said. If he's here, Dick and his brownshirts are welcome to him. I've got nothing to do with him, not anymore.'

Claire wasn't sure she believed that, but she didn't think he was intentionally lying now. He probably did mean it. She just thought that no matter how much he thought he was done with his dad, all it would take would be a snap of Frank Collins's fingers to bring him running.

Not good.

Richard was answering questions from others on the radio, but Michael was no longer listening. He was fixed on Shane. 'You knew? You knew he was coming back here, and you didn't warn me?'

Shane stirred uneasily. 'Look—'

'No, *you* look. I'm the one who got knifed and decapitated and buried in the *backyard*, among other things! Good thing I was a ghost!'

Shane looked down. 'Who was I supposed to tell? The vamps? Come on.'

'You could have told me!'

'You're a vamp,' Shane said. 'In case you haven't checked the mirror lately.'

Michael stood up. His chair slid about two feet across the floor and skidded to an uneven stop; he leant his hands on the table and loomed over Shane. 'Oh, I do,' he said. 'I check it every day. How about you? You taken a good look recently, Shane? Because I'm not so sure I know you anymore.'

Shane looked up at that, and there was a flash of pain in his face. 'I didn't mean—'

'I could be just about the last vampire around here,' Michael interrupted. 'Maybe the others are dead. Maybe they will be soon. Between the mobs out there willing to rip our heads off and Bishop waiting to take over, having your dad stalking me is all I need.'

'He wouldn't—'

'He killed me once, or tried to. He'd do it again in a second, and he wouldn't blink, and you know that, Shane. You know it! He thinks I'm some kind of a traitor to the human race. He'll come after me in particular.'

Shane didn't say anything this time. Michael retrieved the radio from the table and clipped it to the pocket of his jeans. He shone, all blazing gold and hard, white angles, and Shane couldn't meet his stare.

'You decide you want to help your dad kill some vampires, Shane, you know where to find me.'

Michael went upstairs. It was as if the room had lost all its air, and Claire found herself breathing very hard, trying not to tremble.

Eve's dark eyes were very wide, and fixed on Shane as well. She slowly got up from the table.

'Eve—' he said, and reached out towards her. She stepped out of reach.

'I can't believe you,' she said. 'You see me running over to suck up to my mom? No. And she's not even a murderer.'

'Morganville needs to change.'

'Wake up, Shane, it *has*! It started months ago. It's been changing right in front of you! Vampires and humans working together. Trusting one another. They're *trying*. Sure, it's hard, but they've got reason to be afraid of us, good reason. And now you want to throw all that away and help your dad set up a guillotine in Founder's Square or something?' Eve's eyes turned bitter black. 'Screw you.'

'I didn't—'

She clomped away towards the stairs, leaving Shane and Claire together.

Shane swallowed, then tried to make it a joke. 'That could have gone better.' Claire slipped out of her chair. 'Claire? Oh, come on, not you, too. Don't go. Please.'

'You should have told him. I can't believe you didn't. He's your friend, or at least I thought he was.'

'Where are you going?'

She pulled in a deep breath. 'I'm packing. I've decided to move in with my parents.'

She didn't pack, though. She went upstairs, closed the door to her room, and pulled out her pitifully few possessions. Most of it was dirty laundry. She sat there on the bed, staring at it, feeling lost and alone and a little sick, and wondered if she was making a point or just running like a little girl. She felt pretty stupid now that she had everything piled on the floor.

It looked utterly pathetic.

When the knock came on her door, she didn't immediately answer it. She knew it was Shane, even though he didn't speak. *Go away,* she thought at him, but he still wasn't much of a mind reader. He knocked again.

'It's not locked,' she said.

'It's also not open,' Shane said quietly, through the wood. 'I'm not a complete ass.'

'Yes, you are.'

'OK, sometimes I am.' He hesitated, and she heard the floor creak as he shifted his weight. 'Claire.'

'Come in.'

He froze when he saw the stuff piled in front of her, waiting to be put in bags and her one suitcase. 'You're serious.'

'Yes.'

'You're just going to pack up and leave.'

'You know my parents want me to come home.'

He didn't say anything for a long moment, then reached into his back pocket and took out a black case, about the size of his hand. 'Here, then. I was going to give it to you later, but I guess I'd better do it now, before you take off on us.'

His voice sounded offhand and normal, but his fingers felt cold when she touched them in taking the case, and there was an expression on his face she didn't know – fear, maybe; bracing himself for something painful.

It was a hard, leather-wrapped case, on spring hinges. She hesitated for a breath, then pried up one end. It snapped open.

Oh.

The cross was beautiful – delicate silver, traceries of leaves wrapped around it. It was on a silver chain so thin it looked like a breath would melt it. When

Claire picked up the necklace, it felt like air in her hand.

'I—' She had no idea what to say, what to feel. Her whole body seemed to have gone into shock. 'It's beautiful.'

'I know it doesn't work against the vamps,' Shane said. 'OK, well, I didn't know that when I got it for you. But it's still silver, and silver works, so I hope that's OK.'

This wasn't a small present. Shane didn't have a lot of money; he picked up odd jobs here and there, and spent very little. This wasn't some cheap costume jewellery; it was real silver, and really beautiful.

'I can't — it's too expensive.' Claire's heart was pounding again, and she wished she could *think*. She wished she knew what she was supposed to feel, supposed to do. On impulse, she put the necklace back in the box and snapped it shut, and held it out to him. 'Shane, I can't.'

He gave her a broken sort of smile. 'It's not a ring or anything. Keep it. Besides, it doesn't match my eyes.'

He stuck his hands in his pockets, rounded his shoulders, and walked out of the room.

Claire clutched the leather box in one sweaty hand, eyes wide, and then opened it again. The cross gleamed on black velvet, clean and beautiful and shining, and it blurred as her eyes filled with tears.

Now she felt something, something big and overwhelming and far too much to fit inside her small, fragile body.

'Oh,' she whispered. 'Oh *God.*' This hadn't been just any gift. He'd put a lot of time and effort into getting it. There was love in it, real love.

She took the cross, put it around her neck, and fastened the clasp with shaking fingers. It took her two tries. Then she went down the hall and, without knocking, opened Shane's door. He was standing at the window, staring outside. He looked different to her. Older. Sadder.

He turned towards her, and his gaze fixed on the silver cross in the hollow of her throat.

'You're an idiot,' Claire said.

Shane considered that, and nodded. 'I really am, mostly.'

'And then you have to go and do these awesome things—'

'I know. I did say I was *mostly* an idiot.'

'You kind of have your good moments.'

He didn't quite smile. 'So you like it?'

She put her hand up to stroke the cross's warm silver lines. 'I'm wearing it, aren't I?'

'Not that it means we're—'

'You said you loved me,' Claire said. 'You did say that.'

He shut his mouth and studied her, then nodded. There was a flush building high in his cheeks.

'Well, I love you, too, and you're still an idiot. Mostly.'

'No argument.' He folded his arms across his chest, and she tried not to notice the way his muscles tensed, or the vulnerable light in his eyes. 'So, you moving out?'

'I should,' she said softly. 'The other night—'

'Claire. Please be straight with me. Are you moving out?'

She was holding the cross now, cradling it, and it felt as warm as the sun against her fingers. 'I can't,' she said. 'I have to do laundry first, and that might take a month. You saw the pile.'

He laughed, and it was as if all the strength went out of him. He sat down on his unmade bed, hard, and after a moment, she walked around the end and sat next to him. He put his arm around her.

'Life is a work in progress,' Shane said. 'My mom used to say that. I'm kind of a fixer-upper. I know that.'

Claire sighed and allowed herself to relax against his warmth. 'Good thing I like high-maintenance guys.'

He was about to kiss her – finally – when they both heard a sound from overhead.

Only there was nothing overhead. Nothing but the attic.

'Did you hear that?' Shane asked.

'Yeah. It sounded like footsteps.'

'Oh, well, that's fantastic. I thought it was supposed to be exit-only or something.' Shane reached under his bed and came up with a stake. 'Go get Michael and Eve. Here.' He handed her another stake. This one had a silver tip. 'It's the Cadillac of vampire killers. Don't dent it.'

'You are so weird.' But she took it, and then dashed to her room to grab the thin silver knife Amelie had given her. No place to put it, but she poked a hole in the pocket of her jeans just big enough for the blade. The jeans were tight enough to keep the blade in place against her leg, but not so much it looked obvious, and besides, it was pretty flexible.

She hurried down the hall, listening for any other movement. Eve's room was empty, but when she knocked on Michael's door, she heard a startled yelp that sounded very Eve-like. 'What?' Michael asked.

'Trouble,' Claire said. 'Um, maybe. Attic. Now.'

Michael didn't sound any happier about it than Shane had been. 'Great. Be there in a second.'

Muffled conversation, and the sound of fabric

moving. Claire wondered if he was getting dressed, and quickly tried to reject that image, not because it wasn't awesomely hot, but because, well, it was *Michael*, and besides, there were other things to think about.

Such as what was upstairs in the attic.

Or who.

The door banged open, and Eve rushed out, flushed and mussed and still buttoning her shirt. 'It's not what you think,' she said. 'It was just – oh, OK, whatever, it was exactly what you think. Now, *what*?'

Something dropped and rolled across the attic floor directly above their heads. Claire silently pointed up, and Eve followed the motion, staring as if she could see through the wood and plaster. She jumped when Michael, who'd thrown on an unbuttoned shirt, put a hand on her shoulder. He put a finger to his lips.

Shane stepped out of his room, holding a stake in either hand. He pitched one underhand to Michael.

Where's mine? Eve mouthed.

Get your own, Shane mouthed back. Eve rolled her eyes and dashed into her own room, coming back with a black bag slung across her chest, bandolier-style. It was, Claire assumed, full of weapons. Eve fished around in it and came up with a stake of her very own. It even had her initials carved in it.

'Shop class,' she whispered. 'See? I *did* learn something in school.'

Michael pressed the button to release the hidden door, and it opened without a sound. There were no lights upstairs that Claire could see. The stairs were pitch-black.

Michael, by common consent, went first, vampire eyes, and all. Shane followed, then Eve; Claire brought up the rear, and tried to move as silently as possible, although not really all that silently, because the stairs creaked beneath the weight of four people. At the top, Claire ran into Eve's back, and whispered, 'What?'

Eve, in answer, reached back to grip her hand. 'Michael smells blood,' she whispered. 'Hush.'

Michael flicked on a light at the other end of the small, silent room. There was nothing unusual, just the furniture that was always here. There were no signs anybody had been here since the Goldmans and Myrnin had departed.

'How do we get into the attic?' Shane asked. Michael pressed hidden studs, and another door, barely visible at that end of the room, clicked open. Claire remembered it well; Myrnin had shown it to her, when they'd been getting stuff together to go to Bishop's welcome feast.

'Stay here,' Michael said, and stepped through into the dim, open space.

'Yeah, sure,' Shane said, and followed. He popped his head back in to say, 'No, not you two. Stay here.'

'Does he just not get how unfair and sexist that is?' Eve asked. 'Men.'

'You really want to go first?'

'Of course not. But I'd like the chance to *refuse* to go first.'

They waited tensely, listening for any sign of trouble. Claire heard Shane's footsteps moving through the attic, but nothing else for a long time.

Then she heard him say, 'Michael. Oh man...over here.' There was tension in his voice, but it didn't sound like he was about to jump into hand-to-hand combat.

Eve and Claire exchanged looks, and Eve said, 'Oh, screw it,' and dived into the attic after them.

Claire followed, gripping the Cadillac of stakes and hoping she wasn't going to be forced to try to use it.

Shane was crouched down behind some stacked, dusty suitcases, and Michael was there, too. Eve pulled in a sharp breath when she saw what it was they were bending over, and put out a hand to stop Claire in her tracks.

Not that Claire stopped, until she saw who was lying on the wooden floor. She hardly recognised him, really. If it hadn't been for the grey ponytail and the leather coat...

'It's Oliver,' she whispered. Eve was biting her lip until it was almost white, staring at her former boss. 'What *happened*?'

'Silver,' Michael said. 'Lots of it. It eats vampire skin like acid, but he shouldn't be this bad. Not unless—' He stopped as the pale, burnt eyelids fluttered. 'He's still alive.'

'Vampires are hard to kill,' Oliver whispered. His voice was barely a creak of sound, and it broke at the end on what sounded almost like a sob. '*Jesu*. Hurts.'

Michael exchanged a look with Shane, then said, 'Let's get him downstairs. Claire. Go get some blood from the fridge. There should be some.'

'No,' Oliver grated, and sat up. There was blood leaking through his white shirt, as if all his skin were gone underneath. 'No time. Attack on City Hall, coming tonight – Bishop. Using it as a – diversion – to—' His eyes opened wider, and went blank, then rolled up into his head.

He collapsed. Michael caught him under the shoulders.

He and Shane carried Oliver out to the couch, while Eve anxiously followed along, making little shooing motions.

Claire started to follow, then heard something scrape across the wood behind her, in the shadows.

Oliver hadn't come here alone.

A black shadow lunged out, grabbed her, and something hard hit her head.

She must have made some sound, knocked something over, because she heard Shane call her name sharply, and saw his shadow in the doorway before darkness took all of it away.

Then she was falling away.

Then she was gone.

CHAPTER THIRTEEN

Claire came awake feeling sick, wretched, and cold. Someone was pounding on the back of her head with a croquet mallet, or at least that was how it felt, and when she tried to move, the whole world spun around.

'Shut up and stop moaning,' somebody said from a few feet away. 'Don't you dare throw up or I'll make you eat it.'

It sounded like Jason Rosser, Eve's crazy brother. Claire swallowed hard and squinted, trying to make out the shadow next to her. Yeah, it looked like Jason – skanky, greasy, and insane. She tried to squirm away from him, but ran into a wall at her back. It felt like wood, but she didn't think it was the Glass House attic.

He'd taken her somewhere, probably using the portal. And now none of her friends could follow, because none of them knew how.

Her hands and feet were tied. Claire blinked, trying to clear her head. That was a little unfortunate, because with clarity came the awareness of just how bad this was. Jason Rosser really *was* crazy. He'd stalked Eve. He'd – at least allegedly – killed girls in town. He'd definitely stabbed Shane, and he'd staked Amelie at the feast when she'd tried to help him.

And none of her friends back at the Glass House would know how to find her. To their eyes, she would have just...vanished.

'What do you want?' she asked. Her voice sounded rusty and scared. Jason reached out and moved hair back from her face, which creeped her out. She didn't like him touching her.

'Relax, shortcake, you're not my type,' he said. 'I do what I'm told, that's all. You were wanted. So I brought you.'

'Wanted?'

A low, silky laugh floated on the silence, dark as smoke, and Jason looked over his shoulder as the hidden observer rose and stepped into what little light there was.

Ysandre, Bishop's pale little girlfriend. Beautiful, sure. Delicate as jasmine flowers, with big, liquid eyes and a sweetly rounded face.

She was poison in a pretty bottle.

'Well,' she said, and crouched down next to Claire. 'Look at what the cat dragged in. Meow.' Her sharp nail dragged over Claire's cheek, and judging from the sting, it drew blood. 'Where's your pretty boyfriend, Miss Claire? I really wasn't done with him, you know. I hadn't even properly *started*.'

Claire felt an ugly lurch of anger mix with the fear already churning her stomach. 'He's probably not done with you, either,' she said, and managed to smile. She hoped it was a cold kind of smile, the sort that Amelie used – or Oliver. 'Maybe you should go looking. I'll bet he'd be *so* happy to see you.'

'I'll show that boy a real good time, when we do meet up again,' Ysandre purred, and put her face very close to Claire's. 'Now, then, let's talk, just us girls. Won't that be fun?'

Not. Claire was struggling against the ropes, but Jason had done his job pretty well; she was hurting herself more than accomplishing anything else. Ysandre grabbed Claire's shoulder and wrenched her upright against the wooden wall, hard enough to bang Claire's injured head. For a dazed second, it looked like Ysandre's ripe, red smile floated in midair, like some undead Cheshire cat.

'Now,' Ysandre said, 'ain't this nice, sweetie? It's too bad we couldn't get Mr Shane to join us, but my little helper here, he's a bit worried about tackling

Shane. Bad blood and all.' She laughed softly. 'Well, we'll make do. Amelie likes you, I hear, and you've got on that pretty little gold bracelet. So you'll do just fine.'

'For what?'

'I ain't telling you, sweetie.' Ysandre's smile was truly scary. 'This town's going to have a wild night, though. Real wild. And you're going to get to see the whole thing, up close. You must be all atingle.'

Eve would have had a quip at the ready. Claire just glared, and wished her head would stop aching and spinning. What had he hit her with? It felt like the front end of a bus. She hadn't thought Jason could hit that hard, truthfully.

Don't try to find me, Shane. Don't. The last thing she wanted was Shane racing to the rescue and taking on a guy who'd stabbed him, and a vampire who'd led him around by a leash.

No, she had to find her own way out of this.

Step one: figure out where she was. Claire let Ysandre ramble on, describing all kinds of lurid things that Claire thought it was better not to imagine, considering they were things Ysandre was thinking of doing to *her*. Instead, she tried to identify her surroundings. It didn't look familiar, but that was no help; she was still relatively new to Morganville. Plenty of places she'd never been.

Wait.

Claire focused on the crate that Jason was sitting on. There was stencilling on it. It was hard to make it out in the dim light, but she thought it said BRICKS BULK COFFEE. And now that she thought about it, it smelt like coffee in here, too. A warm, morning kind of smell, floating over dust and damp wood.

And she remembered Eve laughing about how Oliver bought his coffee from a place called Bricks. *As in, tastes like ground-up bricks,* Eve had said. *If you order flavoured, they add in the mortar.*

There were only two coffee shops in town: Oliver's place, and the University Centre coffee bar. This didn't look like the UC, which wasn't that old and was mostly built of concrete, not wood.

That meant...she was at Common Grounds? But Common Grounds didn't make any sense; there wasn't any kind of portal leading to it.

Maybe Oliver has a warehouse. That sounded right, because the vampires seemed to own a lot of the warehouse district that bordered Founder's Square. Brandon, Oliver's second-in-vampire-command, had been found dead in a warehouse.

Maybe she was close to Founder's Square.

Ysandre's cold fingers closed around Claire's chin and jerked it up. 'Are you listening, honey?'

'Truthfully, no,' Claire said. 'You're kind of boring.'

Jason actually laughed, and turned it into a fake cough. 'I'm going outside,' he said. 'Since this is going to get all personal now.' Claire wanted to yell to him not to go, but she bit her tongue and turned it into a subsonic whine in the back of her throat as she watched him walk away. His footsteps receded into the dark, and then finally a small square of light opened a long way off.

It was a door, too far for her to reach – way too far.

'I thought he'd never leave,' Ysandre said, and put her cold, cold lips on Claire's neck, then yelled in shock and pulled away, covering her mouth with one pale hand. 'You *bitch!*'

Ysandre hadn't seen the silver chain Claire was wearing in the dim light, as whisper-thin as it was. Now there were welts forming on the vampire's full lips – forming, breaking, and bleeding.

Fury sparked in Ysandre's eyes. Playtime was over.

As Claire squirmed away, the vampire followed at a lazy stroll. She wiped her burnt lips and looked at the thin, leaking blood in distaste. 'Tastes like silver. Disgusting. You've just ruined my good mood, little girl.'

As she rolled, Claire felt something sharp dig into her leg. *The knife*. They'd found the stake, but she guessed their search hadn't exactly been thorough; Jason was too crazy, and Ysandre too careless and arrogant.

But the knife wasn't going to do her any good at all where it was, unless...

Ysandre lunged for her, a blur of white in the darkness, and Claire twisted and jammed her hip down at an awkward angle.

The knife slipped and tore through the fabric of her jeans – not much of it, just a couple of inches, but enough to slice open Ysandre's hand and arm as it reached for her, all the way to the bone.

Ysandre shrieked in real pain, and spun away. She didn't look so pretty now, and when she turned towards Claire again, from a respectful distance this time, she hissed at her with full cobra fangs extended. Her eyes were wild and blood-red, glowing like rubies.

Claire twisted, nearly yanking her elbow out of its joint, and managed to get the ropes around her wrist against the knife. She didn't have long; the shock wouldn't keep Ysandre at bay for more than a few seconds.

But getting a silver knife to cut through synthetic rope? That was going to take a while – a while she didn't have.

Claire sawed desperately, and got a little bit of

give on the bonds – enough to *almost* get her hand into her pocket.

But not.

Ysandre grabbed her by the hair. 'I'm going to destroy you for that.'

The pain in her head was blinding. It felt like her scalp was being ripped off, and on top of that, the massive headache roared back to a new, sickening pulse.

Claire loosened the rope enough to plunge her aching hand into her pocket and grab the handle of the knife. She yanked it out of the tangle of fabric and held it at a trembling, handicapped *en garde* – still tied up, but whatever, she wasn't going to stop fighting, not *ever*.

Ysandre shrieked and let her go, which made no sense to Claire's confused, pain-shocked mind. *I didn't stab her yet. Did I?* Not that she wanted to stab anybody, even Ysandre. She just wanted—

What was going on?

Ysandre's body slammed down hard on the wooden floor, and Claire gasped and flinched away...but the vampire had fallen facedown, limp, and weirdly broken.

A small woman dressed in grey, her pale hair falling wild around her shoulders, dropped silently from overhead and put one impeccably lovely grey pump in the centre of Ysandre's back, holding her down as she tried to move.

'Claire?' The woman's face turned towards her, and Claire blinked twice before she realised whom she was looking at.

Amelie. But not Amelie. Not the cool, remote Founder – this woman had a wild, furious energy to her that Claire had never seen before. And she looked *young.*

'I'm OK,' she said faintly, and tried to decide whether this version of Amelie was really here, or a function of her smacked-around brain. She decided it would be a good idea to get her hands and feet untied before figuring anything else out.

That took long minutes, during which Amelie (really?) dragged Ysandre, whimpering, into the corner and fastened her wrists to a massive crossbeam with chains. The chains, Claire registered, had been there all along. Lovely. This was some kind of vamp playpen/storage locker – probably Oliver's. And she felt sick again, thinking about it. Claire sawed grimly at the ropes binding her and finally parted one complete twist around her hands. As she struggled out of the loops of rope, she saw deep white imprints in her skin, and realised that her hands were red and swollen. She could still feel them, at least, and the burn of circulation returning felt as if she were holding them over an open flame.

She focused on slicing the increasingly dulled knife through the rope on her feet, but it was no use.

'Here,' Amelie said, and bent down to snap the rope with one twist of her fingers. It was *so* frustrating, after all that hard work, to see just how easy it was for her. Claire stripped the ties away and sat for a moment breathing hard, starting to feel every cut, bump, and bruise on her body.

Amelie's cool fingers cupped Claire's chin and forced her head up, and the vampire's grey eyes searched hers. 'You have a head injury,' Amelie said. 'I don't think it's too serious. A headache and some dizziness, perhaps.' She let go. 'I expected to find you. I did not expect to find you *here*, I confess.'

Amelie looked *fine*. Not a prisoner. Not a scratch on her, in fact. Claire had lots more damage, and she hadn't been dragged off as Bishop's prisoner...

Wait. 'You — we thought Bishop might have got you. But he didn't, did he?'

Amelie cocked an eyebrow at her. 'Apparently not.'

'Then where did you go?' Claire felt a completely useless urge to lash out at her, crack that extreme cool. 'Why did you *do this*? You left us alone! And you called the vampires out of hiding—' Her voice failed her for a second as she thought about Officer

O'Malley, and the others she'd heard about. 'You got some of them killed.'

Amelie didn't respond to that. She simply stared back, as calm as an ice sculpture – calmer, because she wasn't melting.

'Tell me why,' Claire said. 'Tell me why you did that.'

'Because plans change,' Amelie replied. 'As Bishop changes his moves, I must change mine. The stakes are too high now, Claire. I've lost half the vampires of Morganville to him. He's taking away my advantage, and I needed to draw them to me, for their own safety.'

'You got *vampires* killed, not just humans. I know humans don't mean anything to you. But I thought the whole point of this was to save *your* people!'

'And so it is,' Amelie said. 'As many as can be saved. As for the call, there is a thing in chess known as a blitz attack, you see – a distraction, to cover the movement of more important pieces. You retrieved Myrnin and set him in play again; this was most important. I need my most powerful pieces on the board.'

'Like Oliver?' Claire rubbed her hands together, trying to get the annoying tingle out of them. 'He's hurt, you know. Maybe dying.'

'He's served his purpose.' Amelie turned her

attention towards Ysandre, who was starting to stir. 'It's time to take Bishop's rook, I believe.'

Claire clutched the silver knife hard in her fist. 'Is that all I am, too? Some kind of sacrifice pawn?'

That got Amelie's attention again. 'No,' she said in surprise. 'Not entirely. I do care, Claire. But in war, you can't care too much. It paralyzes your ability to act.' Those luminous eyes turned towards Ysandre again. 'It's time for you to go, because I doubt you would enjoy seeing this. You won't be able to return here. I'm closing down nodes on the network. When I'm finished, there will be only two destinations: to me, or to Bishop.'

'Where is he?'

'You don't know?' Amelie raised her eyebrows again. 'He is where it is most secure, of course. At City Hall. And at nightfall, I will come against him. That's why I came looking for you, Claire. I need you to tell Richard. Tell him to get all those who can't fight for me out of the building.'

'But – he *can't*. It's a storm shelter. There are supposed to be tornadoes coming.'

'Claire,' Amelie said. 'Listen to me. If innocents take refuge in that building, they will be killed, because I can't protect them anymore. We're at endgame now. There's no room for mercy.' She looked again at Ysandre, who had gone very still, listening.

'Y'all wouldn't be saying this in front of me if I was going to walk out of here, would you?' Ysandre asked. She sounded calm now. Very still.

'No,' Amelie said. 'Very perceptive. I wouldn't.' She took Claire by the arm and helped her to her feet. 'I am relying on you, Claire. Go now. Tell Richard these are my orders.'

Before Claire could utter another word, she felt the air shimmer in front of her, in the middle of the big warehouse room, and she fell...out over the dusty trunk in the Glass House attic, where Oliver had been. She sprawled ungracefully on top of it, then rolled off and got to her feet with a thump.

When she waved her hand through the air, looking for that strange heat shimmer of an open portal, she felt nothing at all.

I'm closing the portals, Amelie had said.

She'd closed this one, for sure.

'Claire?' Shane's voice came from the far end of the attic. He shoved aside boxes and jumped over jumbled furniture to reach her. 'What happened to you? Where did you go?'

'I'll tell you later,' she said, and realised she was still holding the bloody silver knife. She carefully put it back in her pocket, in the makeshift holster against her leg. It was so dull she didn't think it would cut anything again, but it made her feel better. 'Oliver?'

'Bad.' Shane put his hands around her head and tilted it up, looking her over. 'Is everything OK?'

'Define *everything*. No, define *OK*.' She shook her head in frustration. 'I need to get the radio. I have to talk to Richard.'

Richard wasn't on the radio. 'He's meeting with the mayor,' said the man who answered. Sullivan, Claire thought his name was, but she hadn't really paid attention. 'You got a problem there?'

'No, Officer, you've got a problem *there*,' she said. 'I need to talk to Richard. It's really important!'

'Everybody needs to talk to Richard,' Sullivan said. 'He'll get back to you. He's busy right now. If it's not an emergency response—'

'Yes, OK! It's an emergency!'

'Then I'll send units out to you. Glass House, right?'

'No, it's not—' Claire wanted to slam the radio down in frustration. 'It's not an emergency *here*. Look, just tell Richard that he needs to clear everybody out of City Hall, as soon as possible.'

'Can't do that,' Sullivan said. 'It's our centre of operations. It's the main storm shelter, and we've got one heck of a storm coming tonight. You're going to have to give me a reason, miss.'

'All right, it's because—'

Michael took the radio away from her and shut it off. Claire gaped, stuttered, and finally demanded, 'Why?'

'Because if Amelie says Bishop's got himself installed in City Hall, somebody there has to know. We don't know who's on his team,' Michael said. 'I don't know Sullivan that well, but I know he never was happy with the way things ran in town. I wouldn't put it past him to be buying Bishop's crap about giving the city back to the people, home rule, all that stuff. Same goes for anybody else there, except maybe Joe Hess and Travis Lowe. We have to know who we're talking to before we say anything else.'

Shane nodded. 'I'm thinking that Sullivan's keeping Richard out of the loop for a reason.'

They were downstairs, the four of them. Eve, Shane, and Claire were at the kitchen table, and Michael was pacing the floor and casting looks at the couch, where Oliver was. The older vampire was asleep, Claire guessed, or unconscious; they'd done what they could, washed him off and wrapped him in clean blankets. He was healing, according to Michael, but he wasn't doing it very fast.

When he'd woken up, he'd seemed distant. Confused.

Afraid.

Claire had given him one of the doses she'd got from Dr Mills, and so far, it seemed to be helping, but if Oliver was sick, Myrnin's fears were becoming real.

Soon, it'd be Amelie, too. And then where would they be?

'So what do we do?' Claire asked. 'Amelie said we have to tell Richard. We have to get non-combatants out of City Hall, as soon as possible.'

'Problem is, you heard him giving instructions to the Civil Defence guys earlier – they're out telling everybody in town to *go* to City Hall if they can't make it to another shelter. Radio and TV, too. Hell, half the town is probably there already.'

'Maybe she won't do it,' Eve said. 'I mean, she wouldn't kill *everybody* in there, would she? Not even if she thinks they're working for Bishop.'

'I think it's gone past that,' Claire said. 'I don't know if she has any choice.'

'There's always a choice.'

'Not in chess,' Claire replied. 'Unless your choice is to lie down and die.'

In the end, the only way to be sure they got to the right person was to get in the car and drive there. Claire was a little shocked at the colour of the sky outside – a solid grey, with clouds moving so fast it was like time-lapse on the Weather Channel. The edges looked faintly green, and in this part of the country, that was never a good sign.

The only good thing about it was that Michael didn't have to worry about getting scorched by sunlight. He brought a hoodie and a blanket to throw over his head, just in case, but it was dark outside, and getting darker fast. Premature sunset.

Drops of rain were smacking the sidewalk, the size of half-dollars. Where they hit Claire's skin, they felt like paintball pellets. As she looked up at the clouds, a horizontal flash of lightning peeled the sky in half, and thunder rumbled so loudly she felt it through the soles of her shoes.

'Come on!' Eve yelled, and started the car. Claire ran to open the backseat door and piled in beside Shane. Eve was already accelerating before she could fasten her seat belt. 'Michael, get the radio.'

He turned it on. Static. As he scanned stations, they got ghosts of signals from other towns, but nothing came through clearly in Morganville – probably because the vampires jammed it.

Then one came in, loud and clear, broadcasting on a loop.

'Attention Morganville residents: this is an urgent public service announcement. The National Weather Service has identified an extremely dangerous storm tracking towards Morganville, which will reach our borders at six twenty-seven this evening at its present speed. This storm has already been responsible for devastation in several areas in its path, and there has been significant loss of life due to tornadic activity. Morganville and the surrounding areas are on tornado watch through ten p.m. this evening. If you hear an alert siren, go immediately to a designated Safe Shelter location, or to the safest area of your home if you cannot reach a Safe Shelter. Attention Morganville residents...'

Michael clicked it off. There was no point in listening to the repeat; it wasn't going to get any better.

'How many Safe Shelters are there?' Shane asked. 'University dorms have them, the UC—'

'Founder's Square has two,' Michael said, 'but nobody can get to them right now. They're locked up.'

'Library.'

'And the church. Father Joe would open up the basements, so that'll fit a couple of hundred people.'

Everybody else would head to City Hall, if they didn't stay in their houses.

The rain started to fall in earnest, slapping the windshield at first, and then pounding it in fierce waves. The ancient windshield wipers really weren't up to it, even at high speed. Claire was glad she wasn't trying to drive. Even in clear visibility she wasn't very good, and she had no idea how Eve was seeing a thing.

If she was, of course. Maybe this was faith-based driving.

Other cars were on the road, and most of them were heading the same way they were. Claire looked at the clock on her cell phone.

Five thirty p.m.

The storm was less than an hour away.

'Uh-oh,' Eve said, and braked as they turned the last corner. It was a sea of red taillights. Over the roll of thunder and pounding rain, Claire heard horns honking. Traffic moved, but slowly, one car at a time inching forward. 'They're checking cars at the barricade. I can't believe—'

Something happened up there, and the brake lights began flicking off in steady rows. Cars moved. Eve fell into line, and the big, black sedan rolled past two police cars still flashing their lights. In the red/blue/red glow, Claire saw that they'd moved the barricades aside and were just waving everyone through.

'This is crazy,' she said. 'We can't get people out. Not fast enough! We'd have to stop everybody from coming in first, and then give them somewhere to go...'

'I'm getting out of the car here,' Michael said. 'I can run faster than you can drive in this. I'll get to Richard. They won't dare stop me.'

That was probably true, but Eve still said, 'Michael, don't—'

Not that it stopped him from bailing out into the rain. A flash of lightning streaked by overhead and showed him splashing through thick puddles, weaving around cars.

He was right; he was faster.

Eve muttered something about 'Stupid, stubborn, bloodsucking boyfriends,' and followed the traffic towards City Hall.

Out of nowhere, a truck pulled out in front of them from a side street and stopped directly in their path. Eve yelled and hit the brakes, but they were mushy and wet, and not great at the best of times, and Claire felt the car slip and then slide, gathering speed as it went.

Glad I put on my seat belt, she thought, which was a weird thing to think, as Eve's car hydroplaned right into the truck. Shane stretched out his arm to hold her in place, anyway – instinct, Claire guessed – and then they all got thrown forward hard as physics took over.

Physics hurt.

Claire rested her aching head against the cool

window – it was cracked, but still intact – and tried to shake it off. Shane was unhooking himself from the seat belt and asking her if she was OK. She made some kind of gesture and mumbled something, which she hoped would be good enough. She wasn't up to real reassurances at the moment.

Eve's door opened, and she got dragged out of the car.

'Hey!' Shane yelled, and threw himself out his own door. Claire fumbled at the latch, but hers seemed stuck; she navigated the push button on her seat belt and opted for Shane's side of the car instead.

As she stumbled out into the shockingly warm rain, she knew they were really in trouble now, because the man holding a knife to Eve's throat was Frank Collins, Shane's father and all-round badass, crazy vampire hater. He looked exactly like she remembered – tough, biker-hard, dressed in leather and tattoos.

He was yelling something at Eve, something Claire couldn't hear over the crash of thunder. Shane threw himself into a slide over the trunk of the car and grabbed at his dad's knife hand.

Dad elbowed him in the face and sent him staggering. Claire grabbed for the silver knife in her jeans, but it was gone – she'd dropped it somewhere. Before she could look for it, Shane was back in the fight, struggling with his dad. He moved the knife enough that Eve slid free and ran to grab on to Claire.

Frank shoved his son down on the hood of the car and raised the knife. He froze there, with rain pouring from his chin like a thin silver beard, and off the point of the knife.

'No!' Claire screamed, 'No, don't hurt him!'

'Where's the vampire?' Frank yelled back. 'Where is Michael Glass?'

'Gone,' Shane said. He coughed away pounding rain. 'Dad, he's gone. He's not here. *Dad.*'

Frank seemed to focus on his son for the first time. 'Shane?'

'Yeah, Dad, it's me. Let me up, OK?' Shane was careful to keep his hands up, palms out in surrender. 'Peace.'

It worked. Frank stepped back and lowered the knife. 'Good,' he said. 'I've been looking for you, boy.' And then he hugged him. Shane still had his hands up, and froze in place without touching his father. Claire shivered at the look on his face.

'Yeah, good to see you, too,' he said. 'Back off, man. We're not close, in case you forgot.'

'You're still my son. Blood is blood.' Frank pushed him towards the truck, only lightly crushed where Eve's car had smacked it. 'Get in.'

'Why?'

'Because I said so!' Frank shouted. Shane just looked at him. 'Dammit, boy, for once in your life, do what I tell you!'

'I spent most of my life doing what you told me,' Shane said. 'Including selling out my friends. Not happening anymore.'

Frank's lips parted, temporarily amazed. He laughed.

'Done drunk the suicide cola, didn't you?' When he shook his head, drops flew in all directions, and were immediately lost in the silver downpour. 'Just get in. I'm trying to save your life. You don't want to be where you're trying to go.'

Strangely enough, Frank Collins was making sense. Probably for all the wrong reasons, though.

'We have to get through,' Claire shouted over the pounding rain. She was shivering, soaked through every layer of clothing. 'It's important. People could die if we don't!'

'People are going to die,' Collins agreed. 'Omelettes and eggs. You know the old saying.'

Or chess, Claire thought. Though she didn't know whose side Frank Collins was playing on, or even if he knew he was being manipulated at all.

'There's a plan,' Frank was saying to his son. 'In all this crap, nobody's checking faces. Metal detectors are off. We seize control of the building and make things right. We shuffle these bastards off, once and for all. We can *do it!*'

'Dad,' Shane said, 'everybody in that building tonight is going to be killed. We have to get people *out*, not get them *in*. If you care anything about those idiots who buy your revolutionary crap, you'll call this off.'

'Call it off?' Frank repeated, as uncomprehending as if Shane were speaking another language. 'When we're this close? When we can *win*? Dammit, Shane, you used to believe in this. You used to—'

'Yeah. Used to. Look it up!' Shane shoved his father away from him, and walked over to Eve and Claire. 'I've warned you, Dad. Don't do this. Not today. I won't turn you in, but I'm telling you, if you don't back off, you're dead.'

'I don't take threats,' Frank said. 'Not from you.'

'You're an idiot,' Shane said. 'And I tried.'

He got back in the car, on the passenger-side front seat where Michael had been. Eve scrambled behind the wheel, and Claire got in the back.

Eve reversed.

Frank stepped out into the road ahead of them, a scary-looking man in black leather with his straggling hair plastered around his face. Add in the big hunting knife, and cue the scary music.

Eve let up on the gas. 'No,' Shane said, and moved his left foot over to jam it on top of hers. 'Go. He wants you to stop.'

'Don't! I can't miss him, no—'

But it was too late. Frank was staring into the headlights, squarely in the centre of the hood, and he was getting closer and closer.

Frank Collins threw himself out of the way at the last possible second, Eve swerved wildly in the opposite direction to miss him, and somehow, they didn't kill Shane's dad.

'What the hell are you *doing*?' Eve yelled at Shane. She was shaking all over. So was Shane. 'You want to run him over, do it on your own time! *God!*'

'Look behind you,' Shane whispered.

There were people coming after them. A *lot* of people. They'd been hiding in the alley, Claire guessed. They had guns, and now they opened fire. The car shuddered, and the back window exploded into cracks, then fell with a crash all over Claire's neck.

'Get up here!' Shane said, and grabbed her hands to haul her into the front seat. 'Keep your head down!'

Eve had sunk down on the driver's side, barely keeping her eyes above the dashboard. She was panting hoarsely, panicked, and more gunshots were rattling the back of the car. Something hit the front window, too, adding more cracks and a round, backward splash of a hole.

'Faster!' Shane yelled. Eve hit the gas hard, and whipped around a slower-moving van. The firing ceased, at least for now. 'You see why I didn't want you to stop?'

'OK, your father is officially *off my Christmas list!*' Eve yelled. 'Oh my God, look at my car!'

Shane barked out a laugh. 'Yeah,' he agreed. 'That's what's important.'

'It's better than thinking about what would have happened,' Eve said. 'If Michael had been with us—'

Claire thought about the mobs Richard had talked about, and the dead vampires, and felt sick. 'They'd have dragged him off,' she said. 'They'd have killed him.'

Michael had been right about Shane's dad, but then, Claire had never really doubted it. Neither had Shane, from the sick certainty on his face. He wiped his eyes with his forearm, which really didn't help much; they were all dripping wet, from head to toe.

'Let's just get to the building,' Shane said. 'We can't do much until we find Richard.'

Only it wasn't that simple, even getting in. The underground parking was crammed full of cars, parked haphazardly at every angle. As Eve inched through the shadows, looking for any place to go, she shook her head. 'If we do manage to get people to leave, they won't be able to take their cars. Everybody's blocked in,' she said. 'This is massively screwed up.' Claire, for her part, thought some of it seemed deliberate, not just panic. 'OK, I'm going to put it against the wall and hope we can get out if we need to.'

The elevator was already locked down, the doors open but the lights off and buttons unresponsive. They took the stairs at a run.

The first-floor door seemed to be locked, until Shane pushed on it harder, and then it creaked open against a flood of protests.

The vestibule was full of people.

Morganville's City Hall wasn't all that large, at least not here in the lobby area. There was a big, sweeping staircase leading up, all grand marble and polished wood, and glass display cases taking up part of one wall. The Licence Bureau was off to the right: six old-time bank windows, with bars, all closed. Next to each window was a brass plaque that read what the windows were supposed to deliver: RESIDENTIAL LICENSING, CAR REGISTRATION, ZONING CHANGE REQUESTS, SPECIAL PERMITS, TRAFFIC VIOLATIONS, FINE PAYMENTS, TAXES, CITY SERVICES.

But not today.

The lobby was jammed with people. Families, mostly – mothers and fathers with kids, some as young as infants. Claire didn't see a single vampire in the crowd, not even Michael. At the far end, a yellow Civil Defence sign indicated that the door led to a Safe Shelter, with a tornado graphic next to it. A policeman with a bullhorn was yelling for order, not that he was getting any; people were pushing, shoving, and shouting at one another. 'The shelter is now at maximum capacity! Please be calm!'

'Not good,' Shane said. There was no sign of Richard, although there were at least ten uniformed police officers trying to manage the crowd. 'Upstairs?'

'Upstairs,' Eve agreed, and they squeezed back into the fire stairs and ran up to the next level. The sign in the stairwell said that this floor contained the mayor's office, sheriff's office, city council chambers, and something called, vaguely, Records.

The door was locked. Shane rattled it and banged for entrance, but nobody came to the rescue.

'Guess we go up,' he said.

The third floor had no signs in the stairwell at all, but there was a symbol – the Founder's glyph, like the one on Claire's bracelet. Shane turned the knob, but again, the door didn't open. 'I didn't think they could do that to fire stairs,' Eve said.

'Yeah, call a cop.' Shane looked up the steps. 'One more floor, and then it's just the roof, and I'm thinking that's not a good idea, the roof.'

'Wait.' Claire studied the Founder's glyph for a few seconds, then shrugged and reached out to turn the knob.

Something clicked, and it turned. The door opened.

'How did you...?'

Claire held up her wrist, and the gold bracelet. 'It was worth a shot. I thought, maybe with a gold bracelet—'

'Genius. Go on, get inside,' Shane said, and hustled them in. The door clicked shut behind them, and locked with a snap of metal. The hallway seemed dark, after the fluorescent lights in the stairs, and that was because the lights were dimmed way down, the carpet was dark, and so was the wood panelling.

It reminded Claire eerily of the hallway where they'd rescued Myrnin, only there weren't as many doors opening off it. Shane took the lead – of course – but the doors they could open were just simple offices, nothing fancy about them at all.

And then there was a door at the end of the hall with the Founder's Symbol etched on the polished brass doorknob. Shane tried it, shook his head, and motioned for Claire.

It opened easily at her touch.

Inside were – apartments. Chambers? Claire didn't know what else to call them; there was an entire complex of rooms leading from one central area.

It was like stepping into a whole different world, and Claire could tell that it had once been beautiful: a fairytale room, of rich satin on the walls, Persian rugs, delicate white and gold furniture.

'Michael? Mayor Morrell? Richard?'

It was a queen's room, and somebody had completely wrecked it. Most of the furniture was overturned, some kicked to pieces. Mirrors smashed. Fabrics ripped.

Claire froze.

Lying on the remaining long, delicate sofa was François, Bishop's other loyal vampire buddy, who'd come to Morganville along with Ysandre as his entourage. The vampire looked completely at ease – legs crossed at the ankles, head propped on a plump satin pillow. A big crystal glass of something in dark red rested on his chest.

He giggled and saluted them with the blood. 'Hello, little friends,' he said. 'We weren't expecting you, but you'll do. We're almost out of refreshments.'

'Out,' Shane said, and shoved Eve towards the door.

It slammed shut before she could reach it, and

there stood Mr Bishop, still dressed in his long purple cassock from the feast. It was still torn on the side, where Myrnin had slashed at him with the knife.

There was something so ancient about him, so completely uncaring, that Claire felt her mouth go dry. 'Where is she?' Bishop asked. 'I know you've seen my daughter. I can smell her on you.'

'Ewww,' Eve said, very faintly. 'So much more than I needed to know.'

Bishop didn't look away from Claire's face, just pointed at Eve. 'Silence, or be silenced. When I want to know your opinion, I'll consult your entrails.'

Eve shut up. François swung his legs over the edge of the sofa and sat up in one smooth motion. He downed the rest of his glass of blood and let the glass fall, shedding crimson drops all over the pale carpet. He'd got some on his fingers. He licked them, then smeared the rest all over the satin wall.

'Please,' he said, and batted his long-lashed eyes at Eve. 'Please, say something. I love entrails.'

She shrank back against the wall. Even Shane stayed quiet, though Claire could tell he was itching to pull her to safety. *You can't protect me*, she thought fiercely. *Don't try.*

'You don't know where Amelie is?' Claire asked Bishop directly. 'How's that master plan going, then?'

'Oh, it's going just fine,' Bishop said. 'Oliver is dead by now. Myrnin – well, we both know that Myrnin is insane, at best, and homicidal at his even better. I'm rather hoping he'll come charging to your rescue and forget who you are once he arrives. That would be amusing, and very typical of him, I'm afraid.' Bishop's eyes bored into hers, and Claire felt the net closing around her. 'Where is Amelie?'

'Where you'll never find her.'

'Fine. Let her lurk in the shadows with her creations, until hunger or the humans destroy them. This doesn't have to be a battle, you know. It can be a war of attrition just as easily. I have the high ground.' He gestured around the ruined apartment with one lazy hand. 'And of course, I have everyone here, whether they know it or not.'

She didn't hear him move, but flinched as François trailed cold fingers across the back of her neck, then gripped her tightly.

'Just like that,' Bishop said. 'Just precisely like that.' He nodded to François. 'If you want her, take her. I'm no longer interested in Amelie's pets. Take these others, too, unless you wish to save them for later.'

Claire heard Shane whisper, 'No,' and heard the complete despair in his voice just as Bishop's follower wrenched her head over to the side, baring her neck.

She felt his lips touch her skin. They burnt like ice.

'Ah!' François jerked his head back. 'You little peasant.' He used a fold of her shirt to take hold of the silver chain around her neck, and broke it with a sharp twist.

Claire caught the cross in her hand as it fell.

'May it comfort you,' Bishop said, and smiled. 'My child.'

And then François bit her.

'Claire?' Somewhere, a long way off, Eve was crying. 'Oh my God, Claire? Can you hear me? Come on, please, *please* come back. Are you sure she's got a pulse?'

'Yes, she's got a pulse.' Claire knew that voice. Richard Morrell. But why was he here? Who called the police? She remembered the accident with the truck – no, that was before.

Bishop.

Claire slowly opened her eyes. The world felt very far away, and safely muffled for the moment. She heard Eve let out a gasp and a flood of words, but Claire didn't try to identify the meaning.

I have a pulse.

That seemed important.

My neck hurts.

Because a vampire had bitten her.

Claire raised her left hand slowly to touch

her neck, and found a huge wad of what felt like somebody's shirt pressed against her neck.

'No,' Richard said, and forced her hand back down. 'Don't touch it. It's still closing up. You shouldn't move for another hour or so. Let the wounds close.'

'Bit,' Claire murmured. 'He bit me.' That came in a blinding flash, like a red knife cutting through the fog. 'Don't let me turn into one.'

'You won't,' Eve said. She was upside down – no, Claire's head was in her lap, and Eve was leaning over her. Claire felt the warm drip of Eve's tears on her face. 'Oh, sweetie. You're going to be OK. Right?' Even upside down, Eve's look was panicked as she appealed to Richard, who sat on her right.

'You'll be all right,' he said. He didn't look much better than Claire felt. 'I have to see to my father. Here.' He moved out of the way, and someone else sat in his place.

Shane. His warm fingers closed over hers, and she shivered when she realised how cold she felt. Eve tucked an expensive velvet blanket over and around her, fussing nervously.

Shane didn't say anything. He was so *quiet*.

'My cross,' Claire said. It had been in her hand. She didn't know where it was now. 'He broke the chain. I'm sorry—'

Shane opened his fingers and tipped the cross and

chain into her hand. 'I picked it up,' he said. 'Figured you might want it.' There was something he wasn't saying. Claire looked at Eve to find out what it was, but she wasn't talking, for a change. 'Anyway, you're going to be OK. We're lucky this time. François wasn't that hungry.' He closed her fingers around the cross and held on.

His hands were shaking. 'Shane?'

'I'm sorry,' he whispered. 'I couldn't move. I just *stood there.*'

'No, he didn't,' Eve said. 'He knocked Franny clear across the room and he would have staked him with a chair leg, except Bishop stepped in.'

That sounded like Shane. 'You're not hurt?' Claire asked.

'Not much.'

Eve frowned. 'Well—'

'Not much,' Shane repeated. 'I'm OK, Claire.'

She kind of had to take that at face value, at least right now. 'What time—'

'Six fifteen,' Richard said, from the far corner of the small room. This, Claire guessed, had been some kind of dressing area for Amelie. She saw a long closet to the side. Most of the clothes were shredded and scattered in piles on the floor. The dressing table was a ruin, and every mirror was broken.

François had had his fun in here, too.

'The storm's heading for us,' Eve said. 'Michael never got to Richard, but he got to Joe Hess, apparently. They evacuated the shelters. Bishop was pretty mad about that. He wanted a lot of hostages between him and Amelie.'

'So all that's left is us?'

'Us. And Bishop's people, who didn't leave. And Fabulous Frank Collins and his Wild Bunch, who rolled into the lobby and now think they've won some kind of battle or something.' Eve rolled her eyes, and for an instant was back to her old self. 'Just us and the bad guys.'

Did that make Richard — no. Claire couldn't believe that. If anyone in Morganville had honestly tried to do the right thing, it was Richard Morrell.

Eve followed Claire's look. 'Oh. Yeah, his dad got hurt trying to stop Bishop from taking over downstairs. Richard's been trying to take care of him, and his mom. We were right about Sullivan, by the way. Total backstabber. Yay for premonitions. Wish I had one right now that could help get us out of this.'

'No way out,' Claire said.

'Not even a window,' Eve said. 'We're locked in here. No idea where Bishop and his little sock monkey got off to. Looking for Amelie, I guess. I wish they'd just kill each other already.'

Eve didn't mean it, not really, but Claire

understood how she felt. Distantly. In a detached, shocked kind of way.

'What's happening outside?'

'Not a clue. No radios in here. They took our cell phones. We're' – the lights blinked and failed, putting the room into pitch darkness – 'screwed,' Eve finished. 'Oh man, I should not have said that, should I?'

'Power's gone out in the whole building, I think,' Richard said. 'It's probably the storm.'

Or the vampires screwing with them, just because they could. Claire didn't say it out loud, but she thought it pretty hard.

Shane's hand kept holding hers. 'Shane?'

'Right here,' he said. 'Stay still.'

'I'm sorry. I'm really, really sorry.'

'What for?'

'I shouldn't have got angry with you, before, about your dad...'

'Not important,' he said very softly. 'It's OK, Claire. Just rest.'

Rest? She couldn't rest. Reality was pushing back in, reminding her of pain, of fear, and most important, of time.

There was an eerie, ghostly sound now, wailing, and getting louder.

'What is that?' Eve asked, and then, before

anybody could answer, did so herself. 'Tornado sirens. There's one on the roof.'

The rising, falling wail got louder, but with it came something else – a sound like water rushing, or—

'We need to get to cover,' Richard said. A flashlight snapped on, and played over Eve's pallid face, then Shane's and Claire's. 'You guys, get her over here. This is the strongest interior corner. That side faces out towards the street.'

Claire tried to get up, but Shane scooped her in his arms and carried her. He set her down with her back against a wall, then got under the blanket next to her with Eve on his other side. The flashlight turned away from them, and in its sweep, Claire caught sight of Mayor Morrell. He was a fat man, with a politician's smooth face and smile, but he didn't look anything like she remembered now. He seemed older, shrunken inside his suit, and very ill.

'What's wrong with him?' Claire whispered.

Shane's answer stirred the damp hair around her face. 'Heart attack,' he said. 'At least, that's Richard's best guess. Looks bad.'

It really did. The mayor was propped against the wall a few feet from them, and he was gasping for breath as his wife (Claire had never seen her before, except in pictures) patted his arm and murmured in his ear. His face was ash grey, his lips turning blue, and there was real panic in his eyes.

Richard returned, dragging another thick blanket and some pillows. 'Everybody cover up,' he said. 'Keep your heads down.' He covered his mother and father and crouched next to them as he wrapped himself in another blanket.

The wind outside was building to a howl. Claire could hear things hitting the walls – dull thudding sounds, like baseballs. It got louder. 'Debris,' Richard said. He focused the light on the carpet between their small group. 'Maybe hail. Could be anything.'

The siren cut off abruptly, but that didn't mean the noise subsided; if anything, it got louder, ratcheting up from a howl to a scream – and then it took on a deeper tone.

'Sounds like a train,' Eve said shakily. 'Damn, I was really hoping that wasn't true, the train thing—'

'Heads down!' Richard yelled, as the whole building started to shake. Claire could feel the boards vibrating underneath her. She could see the walls bending, and cracks forming in the bricks.

And then the noise rose to a constant, deafening scream, and the whole outside wall sagged, dissolved into bricks and broken wood, and disappeared. The ripped, torn fabric around the room took flight like startled birds, whipping wildly through the air and getting shredded into ever-smaller sections by the wind and debris.

The storm was screaming as if it had gone insane. Broken furniture and shards of mirrors flew around, smashing into the walls, hitting the blankets.

Claire heard a heavy groan even over the shrieking wind, and looked up to see the roof sagging overhead. Dust and plaster cascaded down, and she grabbed Shane hard.

The roof came down on top of them.

Claire didn't know how long it lasted. It seemed like for ever, really – the screaming, the shaking, the pressure of things on top of her.

And then, very gradually, it stopped, and the rain began to hammer down again, drenching the pile of dust and wood. Some of it trickled down to drip on her cheek, which was how she knew.

Shane's hand moved on her shoulder, more of a twitch than a conscious motion, and then he let go of Claire to heave up with both hands. Debris slid and rattled. They'd been lucky, Claire realised – a heavy wooden beam had collapsed over their heads at a slant, and it had held the worst of the stuff off them.

'Eve?' Claire reached across Shane and grabbed her friend's hands. Eve's eyes were closed, and there was blood trickling down one side of her face. Her face was even whiter than usual – plaster dust, Claire realised.

Eve coughed, and her eyelids fluttered up. 'Mom?' The uncertainty in her voice made Claire want to cry. 'Oh God, what happened? Claire?'

'We're alive,' Shane said. He sounded kind of surprised. He brushed fallen chunks of wood and plaster off Claire's head, and she coughed, too. The rain pounded in at an angle, soaking the blanket that covered them. 'Richard?'

'Over here,' Richard said. 'Dad? Dad—'

The flashlight was gone, rolled off or buried or just plain taken away by the wind. Lightning flashed, bright as day, and Claire saw the tornado that had hit them still moving through Morganville, crashing through buildings, spraying debris a hundred feet into the air.

It didn't even look *real*.

Shane helped move a beam off Eve's legs – thankfully, they were just bruised, not broken – and crawled across the slipping wreckage towards Richard, who was lifting things off his mother. She looked OK, but she was crying and dazed.

His father, though...

'No,' Richard said, and dragged his father flat. He started administering CPR. There were bloody cuts on his face, but he didn't seem to care about his own problems at all. 'Shane! Breathe for him!'

After a hesitation, Shane tilted the mayor's head back. 'Like this?'

'Let me,' Eve said. 'I've had CPR training.' She crawled over and took in a deep breath, bent, and blew it into the mayor's mouth, watching for his chest to rise. It seemed to take a lot of effort. So did what Richard was doing, pumping on his dad's chest, over and over. Eve counted slowly, then breathed again – and again.

'I'll get help,' Claire said. She wasn't sure there *was* any help, really, but she had to do something. When she stood up, though, she felt dizzy and weak, and remembered what Richard had said – she had holes in her neck, and she'd lost a lot of blood. 'I'll go slow.'

'I'll go with you,' Shane said, but Richard grabbed him and pulled him down.

'No! I need you to take over here.' He showed Shane how to place his hands, and got him started. He pulled the walkie-talkie from his belt and tossed it to Claire. 'Go. We need paramedics.'

And then Richard collapsed, and Claire realised that he had a huge piece of metal in his side. She stood there, frozen in horror, and then punched in the code for the walkie-talkie. 'Hello? Hello, is anybody there?'

Static. If there was anybody, she couldn't hear them over the interference and the roaring rain.

'I have to go!' she shouted at Shane. He looked up.

'No!' But he couldn't stop her, not without letting the mayor die, and after one helpless, furious look at her, he went back to work.

Claire slid over the pile of debris and scrambled out the broken door, into the main apartment.

There was no sign of François or Bishop. If the place had been wrecked before, it was unrecognisable now. Most of this part of the building was gone, just – gone. She felt the floor groan underneath her, and moved fast, heading for the apartment's front door. It was still on its hinges, but as she pulled on it, part of the frame came out of the wall.

Outside, the hallway seemed eerily unmarked, except that the roof overhead – and, Claire presumed, all of the next floor above – was missing. It was a hallway open to the storm. She hurried along it, glad now for the flashes of lightning that lit her way.

The fire stairs at the end seemed intact. She passed some people huddled there, clearly terrified. 'We need help!' she said. 'There are people hurt upstairs – somebody?'

And then the screaming started, somewhere about a floor down, lots of people screaming at the same time. Those who were sitting on the stairs jumped to their feet and ran up, towards Claire. 'No!' she yelled. 'No, you can't!'

But she was shoved out of the way, and about fifty people trampled past her, heading up. She had no idea where they'd go.

Worse, she was afraid their combined weight would collapse that part of the building, including the place where Eve, Shane, and the Morrells were.

'Claire?' Michael. He came out of the first-floor door, and leapt two flights of stairs in about two jumps to reach her. Before she could protest, he'd grabbed her in his arms like an invalid. 'Come on. I have to get you out of here.'

'No! No, go up. Shane, they need help. Go up; leave me here!'

'I can't.' He looked down, and so did she.

Vampires poured into the stairwell below. Some of them were fighting, ripping at one another. Any human who got between them went down screaming.

'Right. Up it is,' he said, and she felt them leave the ground in one powerful leap, hitting the third-floor landing with catlike grace.

'What's happening?' Claire twisted to try to look down, but it didn't make any sense to her. It was just a mob, fighting one another. No telling who was on which side, or even why they were fighting so furiously.

'Amelie's down there,' Michael said. 'Bishop's trying to get to her, but he's losing followers fast. She took him by surprise, during the storm.'

'What about the people – I mean, the humans? Shane's dad, and the ones who wanted to take over?'

Michael kicked open the door to the third-floor roofless hallway. The people who'd run past Claire were milling around in it, frightened and babbling. Michael brought down his fangs and snarled at them, and they scattered into whatever shelter they could reach – interior offices, mostly, that had sustained little damage except for rain.

He shoved past those who had nowhere to go, and down to the end of the hall. 'In here?' He let Claire slide down to her feet, and his gaze focused on her neck. 'Someone bit you.'

'It's not so bad.' Claire put her hand over the wound, trying to cover it up. The wound's edges felt ragged, and they were still leaking blood, she thought, although that could have just been the rain. 'I'm OK.'

'No, you're not.'

A gust of wind blew his collar back, and she saw the white outlines of marks on his own neck. 'Michael! Did you get bitten, too?'

'Like you said, it's nothing. Look, we can talk about that later. Let's get to our friends. First aid later.'

Claire opened the door and stepped through...and the floor collapsed underneath her.

She must have screamed, but all she heard was the tremendous cracking sound of more of the building falling apart underneath and around her. She turned towards Michael, who was frozen in the doorway, illuminated in stark white by a nearby lightning strike.

He reached out and grabbed her arm as she flung it towards him, and then she was suspended in midair, wind and dust rushing up around her, as the floor underneath fell away. Michael pulled, and she almost flew, weightless, into his arms.

'Oh,' she whispered faintly. 'Thanks.'

He held on to her for a minute without speaking, then said, 'Is there another way in?'

'I don't know.'

They backed up and found the next office to the left, which had suspicious-looking cracks in its walls. Claire thought the floor felt a little unsteady. Michael pushed her back behind him and said, 'Cover your eyes.'

Then he began ripping away the wall between the office and Amelie's apartments. When he hit solid red brick, he punched it, breaking it into dust.

'This isn't helping keep things together!' Claire yelled.

'I know, but we need to get them out!'

He ripped a hole in the wall big enough to step through, and braced himself in it as the whole building seemed to shudder, as if shifting its weight. 'The floor's all right here,' he said. 'You stay. I'll go.'

'Through that door, to the left!' Claire called. Michael disappeared, moving fast and gracefully.

She wondered, all of a sudden, why he wasn't downstairs. Why he wasn't fighting, like all the others of Amelie's blood.

A couple of tense minutes passed, as she stared through the hole; nothing seemed to be happening. She couldn't hear Michael, or Shane, or anything else.

And then she heard screaming behind her, in the hall. *Vampires*, she thought, and quickly opened the door to look.

Someone fell against the wood, knocking her backward. It was François. Claire tried to shut the door, but a bloodstained white hand wormed through the opening and grabbed the edge, shoving it wider.

François didn't look even remotely human anymore, but he did look absolutely desperate, willing to do anything to survive, and very, very angry.

Claire backed up, slowly, until she was standing with her back against the far wall. There wasn't much in here to help her – a desk, some pens and pencils in a cup.

François laughed, and then he growled. 'You think you're winning,' he said. 'You're not.'

'I think you're the one who has to worry,' Michael said from the hole in the wall. He stepped through, carrying Mayor Morrell in his arms. Shane and Eve were with him, supporting Richard's sagging body between them. Mrs Morrell brought up the rear. 'Back off. I won't come after you if you run.'

François' eyes turned ruby, and he threw himself at Michael, who was burdened with the mayor.

Claire grabbed a pencil from the cup and plunged it into François' back.

He whirled, looking stunned…and then he slowly collapsed to the carpet.

'That won't kill him,' Michael said.

'I don't care,' Eve said. 'Because that was *fierce*.'

Claire grabbed the vampire's arms and dragged him out of the way, careful not to dislodge the pencil; she wasn't really sure how deep it had gone, and if it slipped out of his heart, they were all in big trouble. Michael edged around him and opened the door to check the corridor. 'Clear,' he said. 'For the moment. Come on.'

Their little refugee group hurried into the rainy hall, squishing through soggy carpet. There were people hiding in the offices, or just pressed against the walls and hoping not to be noticed. 'Come on,'

Eve said to them. 'Get up. We're getting out of here before this whole thing comes down!'

The fighting in the stairwell was still going on — snarling, screams, bangs, and thuds. Claire didn't dare look over the railing. Michael led them down to the locked second-floor entrance. He pulled hard on it, and the knob popped off — but the door stayed locked.

'Hey, Mike?' Shane had edged to the end of the landing to look over the railing. 'Can't go that way.'

'I know!'

'Also, time is—'

'I know, Shane!' Michael started kicking the door, but it was reinforced, stronger than the other doors Claire had seen. It bent, but didn't open.

And then it did open…from the inside.

There, in his fancy but battered black velvet, stood Myrnin.

'In,' he said. 'This way. Hurry.'

The falling sensation warned Claire that the door was a portal, but she didn't have time to tell anybody else, so when they stepped through into Myrnin's lab, it was probably kind of a shock. Michael didn't pause; he pushed a bunch of broken glassware from a lab table and put Mr Morrell down on it, then touched pale fingers to the man's throat. When he found nothing, he started CPR again. Eve hurried over to breathe for him.

Myrnin didn't move as the refugees streamed in past him. He was standing with his arms folded, a frown grooved between his brows. 'Who are all these people?' he asked. 'I am not an innkeeper, you know.'

'Shut up,' Claire said. She didn't have any patience with Myrnin right now. 'Is he OK?' She was talking to Shane, who was easing Richard onto a threadbare rug near the far wall.

'You mean, except for the big piece of metal in him? Look, I don't know. He's breathing, at least.'

The rest of the refugees clustered together, filtering slowly through the portal. Most of them had no idea what had just happened, which was good. If they'd been part of Frank's group, intending to take over Morganville, that ambition was long gone. Now they were just people, and they were just scared.

'Up the stairs,' Claire told them. 'You can get out that way.'

Most of them rushed for the exit. She hoped they'd make it home, or at least to some kind of safe place.

She hoped they had homes to go back to.

Myrnin glared at her. 'You do realise that this was a *secret* laboratory, don't you? And now half of Morganville knows where it is?'

'Hey, I didn't open the door; you did.' She reached

over and put her hand on his arm, looking up into his face. 'Thank you. You saved our lives.'

He blinked slowly. 'Did I?'

'I know why you weren't fighting,' Claire said. 'The drugs kept you from having to. But...Michael?'

Myrnin followed her gaze to where Eve and Michael remained bent over the mayor's still form. 'Amelie let him go,' he said. 'For now. She could claim him again at any time, but I think she knew you needed help.' He uncrossed his arms and walked over to Michael to touch his shoulder. 'It's no use,' he said. 'I can smell death on him. So can you, if you try. You won't bring him back.'

'No!' Mrs Morrell screamed, and threw herself over her husband's body. 'No, you have to try!'

'They did,' Myrnin said, and retreated to lean against a convenient wall. 'Which is more than I would have.' He nodded towards Richard. 'He might live, but to remove that metal will require a chirurgeon.'

'You mean, a doctor?' Claire asked.

'Yes, of course, a doctor,' Myrnin snapped, and his eyes flared red. 'I know you want me to feel some sympathy for them, but that is not who I am. I care only about those I know, and even then, not all that deeply. Strangers get nothing from me.' He was slipping, and the anger was coming back. Next it would be confusion. Claire silently dug in her pockets. She'd put a single glass vial in, and miraculously, it was still unbroken.

He slapped it out of her hand impatiently. 'I don't need it!'

Claire watched it clatter to the floor, heart in her mouth, and said, 'You do. You know you do. Please, Myrnin. I don't need your crap right now. Just *take your medicine.*'

She didn't think he would, not at first, but then he snorted, bent down, and picked up the vial. He broke the cap off and dumped the liquid into his mouth. 'There,' he said. 'Satisfied?' He shattered the glass in his fingers, and the red glow in his eyes intensified. 'Are you, little Claire? Do you enjoy giving me orders?'

'Myrnin.'

His hand went around her throat, choking off whatever she was going to say.

She didn't move.

His hand didn't tighten.

The red glow slowly faded away, replaced by a look of shame. He let go of her and backed away a full step, head down.

'I don't know where to get a doctor,' Claire said, as if nothing had happened. 'The hospital, maybe, or—'

'No,' Myrnin murmured. 'I will bring help. Don't

let anyone go through my things. And watch Michael, in case.'

She nodded. Myrnin opened the portal doorway in the wall and stepped through it, heading – where? She had no idea. Amelie had, Claire thought, shut down all the nodes. But if that was true, how had they got here?

Myrnin could open and close them at will. But he was probably the only one who could.

Michael and Eve moved away from Mayor Morrell's body, as his wife stood over him and cried.

'What can we do?' Shane asked. He sounded miserable. In all the confusion, he'd missed her confrontation with Myrnin. She was dimly glad about that.

'Nothing,' Michael said. 'Nothing but wait.'

When the portal opened again, Myrnin stepped through, then helped someone else over the step.

It was Theo Goldman, carrying an antique doctor's bag. He looked around the lab, nodding to Claire in particular; and then moved to where Richard was lying on the carpet, with his head in his mother's lap. 'Move back, please,' he told her, and knelt down to open his bag. 'Myrnin. Take her in the other room. A mother shouldn't see this.'

He was setting out instruments, unrolling them in

a clean white towel. As Claire watched, Myrnin led Mrs Morrell away and seated her in a chair in the corner, where he normally sat to read. She seemed dazed now, probably in shock. The chair was intact. It was just about the only thing in the lab that was – the scientific instruments were smashed, lab tables overturned, candles and lamps broken.

Books were piled in the corners and burnt, reduced to scraps of leather and curling black ash. The whole place smelt sharply of chemicals and fire.

'What can we do?' Michael asked, crouching down on Richard's other side. Theo took out several pairs of latex gloves and passed one set to Michael. He donned one himself.

'You can act as my nurse, my friend,' he said. 'I would have brought my wife – she has many years of training in this – but I don't want to leave my children on their own. They're already very frightened.'

'But they're safe?' Eve asked. 'Nobody's bothered you?'

'No one has so much as knocked on the door,' he said. 'It's a very good hiding place. Thank you.'

'I think you're paying us back,' Eve said. 'Please. Can you save him?'

'It's in God's hands, not mine.' Still, Theo's eyes were bright as he looked at the twisted metal plate embedded in Richard's side. 'It's good that he's unconscious, but he might wake during the procedure. There is chloroform in the bag. It's Michael, yes? Michael, please put some on a cloth and be ready when I tell you to cover his mouth and nose.'

Claire's nerve failed around the time that Theo took hold of the piece of steel, and she turned away. Eve already had, to take a blanket to Mrs Morrell and put it around her shoulders.

'Where's my daughter?' the mayor's wife asked. 'Monica should be here. I don't want her out there alone.'

Eve raised her eyebrows at Claire, clearly wondering where Monica was.

'The last time I saw her, she was at school,' Claire said. 'But that was before I got the call to come home, so I don't know. Maybe she's in shelter in the dorm?' She checked her cell phone. No bars. Reception was usually spotty down here in the lab, but she could usually see something, even if it was only a flicker. 'I think the cell towers are down.'

'Yeah, likely,' Eve agreed. She reached over to tuck the blanket around Mrs Morrell, who leant her head back and closed her eyes, as if the strength was just leaking right out of her. 'You think this is the right thing to do? I mean, do we even know this guy or anything?'

Claire didn't, really, but she still wanted to like

Theo, in much the same way as she liked Myrnin – against her better sense. 'I think he's OK. And it's not like anybody's making house calls right now.'

The operation – and it was an operation, with suturing and everything – took a couple of hours before Theo sat back, stripped off the gloves, and sighed in quiet satisfaction. 'There,' he said. Claire and Eve got up to walk over as Michael rose to his feet. Shane had been hanging on the edges, watching in what Claire thought looked like queasy fascination. 'His pulse is steady. He's lost some blood, but I believe he will be all right, provided no infection sets in. Still, this century has those wonderful antibiotics, yes? So that is not so bad.' Theo was almost beaming. 'I must say, I haven't used my surgical skills in years. It's very exciting. Although it makes me hungry.'

Claire was pretty sure Richard wouldn't want to know that. She knew she wouldn't have, in his place.

'Thank you,' Mrs Morrell said. She got up from the chair, folded the blanket and put it aside, then walked over to shake Theo's hand with simple, dignified gratitude. 'I'll see that my husband compensates you for your kindness.'

They all exchanged looks. Michael started to speak, but Theo shook his head. 'That's quite all right, dear lady. I am delighted to help. I recently lost a son myself. I know the weight of grief.'

'Oh,' Mrs Morrell said, 'I'm so sorry for your loss, sir.' She said it as if she didn't know her husband was lying across the room, dead.

Tears sparkled in his eyes, Claire saw, but then he blinked them away and smiled. He patted her hand gently. 'You are very generous to an old man,' he said. 'We have always liked living in Morganville, you know. The people are so kind.'

Shane said, 'Some of those same people killed your son.'

Theo looked at him with calm, unflinching eyes. 'And without forgiveness, there is never any peace. I tell you this from the distance of many centuries. My son gave his life. I won't reply to his gift with anger, not even for those who took him from me. Those same poor, sad people will wake up tomorrow grieving their own losses, I think, if they survive at all. How can hating them heal me?'

Myrnin, who hadn't spoken at all, murmured, 'You shame me, Theo.'

'I don't mean to do so,' he said, and shrugged. 'Well. I should get back to my family now. I wish you all well.'

Myrnin got up from his chair and walked with Theo to the portal. They all watched him go. Mrs Morrell was staring after him with a bright, odd look in her eyes.

'How very strange,' she said. 'I wish Mr Morrell had been available to meet him.'

She spoke as if he were in a meeting downtown instead of under a sheet on the other side of the room. Claire shuddered.

'Come on, let's go see Richard,' Eve said, and led her away.

Shane let out his breath in a slow hiss. 'I wish it were as simple as Theo thinks it is, to stop hating.' He swallowed, watching Mrs Morrell. 'I wish I could, I really do.'

'At least you want to,' Michael said. 'It's a start.'

They stayed the night in the lab, mainly because the storm continued outside until the wee hours of the morning – rain, mostly, with some hail. There didn't seem to be much point running out in it. Claire kept checking her phone, Eve found a portable radio buried in piles of junk at the back of the room, and they checked for news at regular intervals.

Around three a.m. they got some. It was on the radio's emergency alert frequency.

All Morganville residents and surrounding areas: we remain under severe thunderstorm warnings, with high winds and possible flooding, until seven a.m. today. Rescue efforts are under way at City Hall, which was partially destroyed by a tornado that also levelled several warehouses and abandoned buildings, as well as one building in Founder's Square. There are numerous reports of injuries coming in. Please remain calm. Emergency teams are working their way through town now, looking for anyone who may be in need of assistance. Stay where you are. Please do not attempt to go out into the streets at this time.

It started to repeat. Eve frowned and looked up at Myrnin, who had listened as well. 'What aren't they saying?' she asked.

'If I had to guess, their urgent desire that people stay within shelter would tell me there are other things to worry about.' His dark eyes grew distant for a moment, then snapped back into focus. 'Ibid nothing.'

'What?' Eve seemed to think she'd misheard.

'Ibid nothing carlo. I don't justice.'

Myrnin was making word salad again – a precursor to the drugs wearing off – more quickly than Claire had expected, actually, and that was worrying.

Eve sent Claire a look of alarm. 'OK, I didn't really understand that at all—'

Claire put a hand on her arm to silence her. 'Why don't you go see Mrs Morrell? You too, Shane.'

He didn't like it, but he went. As he did, he jerked his head at Michael, who rose from where he was sitting with Richard and strolled over.

Casually.

'Myrnin,' Claire said. 'You need to listen to me, OK? I think your drugs are wearing off again.'

'I'm fine.' His excitement level was rising; she could see it – a very light flush in his face, his eyes starting to glitter. 'You worry over notebook.'

There was no point in trying to explain the signs; he never could identify them. 'We should check on the prison,' she said. 'See if everything's still OK there.'

Myrnin smiled. 'You're trying to trick me.' His eyes were getting darker, endlessly dark, and that smile had edges to it. 'Oh, little girl, you don't know. You don't know what it's like, having all these guests here, and all this' – he breathed in deeply – 'all this blood.' His eyes focused on her throat, with its ragged bite mark hidden under a bandage Theo had given her. 'I know it's there. Your mark. Tell me, did François—'

'Stop. Stop it.' Claire dug her fingers into her palms. Myrnin took a step towards her, and she forced herself not to flinch. She knew him, knew what he was trying to do. 'You won't hurt me. You need me.'

'Do I?' He breathed deeply again. 'Yes, I do. Bright, so bright. I can feel your energy. I know how it will feel when I...' He blinked, and horror sheeted across his face, fast as lightning. 'What was I saying? Claire? What did I just say?'

She couldn't repeat it. 'Nothing. Don't worry. But I think we'd better get you to the cell, OK? Please?'

He looked devastated. This was the worst part of it, she thought, the mood swings. He'd tried so hard, and he'd helped, he really had – but he wasn't going to be able to hold it together much longer. She was seeing him fall apart in slow motion.

Again.

Michael steered him towards the portal. 'Let's go,' he said. 'Claire, can you do this?'

'If he doesn't fight me,' she said nervously. She remembered one afternoon when his paranoia had taken over, and every time she'd tried to establish the portal, he'd snapped the connection, sure something was waiting on the other side to destroy him. 'I wish we had a tranquilliser.'

'Well, you don't,' Myrnin said. 'And I don't like being stuck with your needles, you know that. I'll behave myself.' He laughed softly. 'Mostly.'

Claire opened the door, but instead of the connection snapping clear to the prison, she felt it shift, pulled out of focus. 'Myrnin, stop it!'

He spread his hands theatrically. 'I didn't do anything.'

She tried again. The connection bent, and before she could bring it back where she wanted it, an alternate destination came into focus.

Theo Goldman fell out of the door.

'Theo!' Myrnin caught him, surprised out of his petulance, at least for the moment. He eased the other vampire down to a sitting position against the wall. 'Are you injured?'

'No, no, no—' Theo was gasping, though Claire knew he didn't need air, not the way humans did. This was emotion, not exertion. 'Please, you have to help, I beg you. Help us, help my family, please—'

Myrnin crouched down to put their eyes on a level. 'What's happened?'

Theo's eyes filled with tears that flowed over his lined, kind face. 'Bishop,' he said. 'Bishop has my family. He says he wants Amelie and the book, or he will kill them all.'

CHAPTER FOURTEEN

Theo hadn't come straight from Common Grounds, of
course; he'd been taken to one of the open portals – he
didn't know where – and forced through by Bishop. 'No,'
he said, and stopped Michael as he tried to come closer.
'No, not you. He only wants Amelie, and the book, and
I want no more innocent blood shed, not yours or mine.
Please. Myrnin, I know you can find her. You have the
blood tie and I don't. Please find her and bring her. This
is not our fight. It's family; it's father and daughter.
They should end this, face-to-face.'

Myrnin stared at him for a long, long moment,
and then cocked his head to one side. 'You want me
to betray her,' he said. 'Deliver her to her father.'

'No, no, I wouldn't ask for that. Only to – to let
her know what price there will be. Amelie will come.
I know she will.'

'She won't,' Myrnin said. 'I won't let her.'

Theo cried out in misery, and Claire bit her lip. 'Can't you help him?' she said. 'There's got to be a way!'

'Oh, there is,' Myrnin said. 'There is. But you won't like it, my little Claire. It isn't neat, and it isn't easy. And it will require considerable courage from you, yet again.'

'I'll do it!'

'No, you won't,' Shane and Michael said, at virtually the same time. Shane continued. 'You're barely on your feet, Claire. You don't go anywhere, not without me.'

'And me,' Michael said.

'Hell,' Eve sighed. 'I guess that means I have to go, too. Which I may not ever forgive you for, even if I don't die horribly.'

Myrnin stared at each of them in turn. 'You'd go. All of you.' His lips stretched into a crazy, rubber-doll smile. 'You are the best toys, you know. I can't imagine how much *fun* it will be to play with you.'

Silence, and then Eve said, 'OK, that was extra creepy, with whipped creepy topping. And this is me, changing my mind.'

The glee faded from Myrnin's eyes, replaced with a kind of lost desperation that Claire recognised all too well. 'It's coming. Claire, it's coming, I'm afraid. I don't know what to do. I can feel it.'

She reached out and took his hand. 'I know. Please, try. We need you right now. Can you hold on?'

He nodded, but it was more a convulsive response

than confirmation. 'In the drawer by the skulls,' he said. 'One last dose. I hid it. I forgot.'

He did that; he hid things and remembered them at odd moments – or never. Claire dashed off to the far end of the room, near where Richard slept, and opened drawer after drawer under the row of skulls he'd nailed to the wall. He'd promised that they were all clinical specimens, not one of them victims of violence. She still didn't altogether believe him.

In the last drawer, shoved behind ancient rolls of parchment and the mounted skeleton of a bat, were two vials, both in brown glass. One, when she pried up the stopper, proved to be red crystals.

The other was silver powder.

She put the vial with silver powder in her pants pocket – careful to use the pocket without a hole in it – and brought the red crystals back to Myrnin. He nodded and slipped the vial into his vest pocket, inside the coat.

'Aren't you going to take them?'

'Not quite yet,' he said, which scared the hell out of her, frankly. 'I can stay focused a bit longer. I promise.'

'So,' Michael said, 'what's the plan?'

'This.'

Claire felt the portal snap into place behind her, clear as a lightning strike, and Myrnin grabbed the front of her shirt, swung her around, and threw her violently through the doorway.

She seemed to fall a really, really long time, but she hit the ground and rolled.

She opened her eyes on pitch darkness, smelling rot and old wine.

No.

She knew this place.

She was trying to get up when something else hit her from behind – Shane, from the sound of his angry cursing. She writhed around and slapped a hand over his mouth, which made him stop in mid-curse. 'Shhhh,' she hissed, as softly as she could. Not that their rolling around on the floor hadn't rung the dinner bell loud and clear, of course.

Damn you, Myrnin.

A cold hand encircled her wrist and pulled her away from Shane, and when she hit out at it, she felt a velvet sleeve.

Myrnin. Shane was scrambling to his feet, too.

'Michael, can you see?' Myrnin's voice sounded completely calm.

'Yes.' Michael's didn't. At *all*.

'Then *run*, damn you! I've got them!'

Myrnin followed his own advice, and Claire's arm was almost yanked from its socket as he dragged her with him. She heard Shane panting on his other side. Her foot came down on something springy, like a body, and she yelped. The sound echoed, and from the darkness on all sides, she heard what sounded like fingers tapping, sliding, coming closer.

Something grabbed her ankle, and this time Claire screamed. It felt like a wire loop, but when she tried to bat at it, she felt fingers, a thin, bony forearm, and nails like talons.

Myrnin skidded to a halt, turned, and stomped. Her ankle came free, and something in the darkness screamed in rage.

'Go!' He roared – not to them, but to Michael, Claire guessed. She saw a flash of something up ahead that wasn't quite light – the portal? That looked like the kind of shimmer it made when it was being activated.

Myrnin let go of her wrist, and shoved her forward.

Once again, she fell. This time, she landed on top of Michael.

Shane fell on top of her, and she gasped for air as all the breath was driven out of her. They squirmed around and separated. Michael pulled Eve to her feet.

'I know this place,' Claire said. 'This is where Myrnin—'

Myrnin stepped through the portal and slammed it shut, just as Amelie had done not so long ago. 'We won't come back here,' he said. 'Out. Hurry. We don't have much time.'

He led the way, long black coat flapping, and Claire had to dig deep to keep up, even with Shane helping her. When he slowed down and started to pick her up, she swatted at him breathlessly. 'No, I'll make it!'

He didn't look so sure.

At the end of the stone hallway, they took a left, heading down the dark, panelled hall that Claire remembered, but they passed up the door she remembered as Myrnin's cell, where he'd been chained.

He didn't even slow down.

'Where are we going?' Eve gasped. 'Man, I wish I'd worn different shoes—'

She cut herself off as Myrnin stopped at the end of the hallway. There was a massive wooden door there, medieval style with thick, hand-hammered iron bands, and the Founder's Symbol etched into the old wood.

He hadn't even broken a sweat. Of course. Claire windmilled her arms as she stumbled to a halt, and braced herself against the wall, chest heaving.

'Shouldn't we be armed?' Eve asked. 'I mean, for a rescue mission, generally people go armed. I'm just pointing that out.'

'I don't like this,' Shane said.

Myrnin didn't move his gaze away from Claire. He reached out and took her hand in his. 'Do you trust me?' he asked.

'I will if you take your meds,' she said.

He shook his head. 'I can't. I have my reasons, little one. Please. I must have your word.'

Shane was shaking his head. Michael wasn't seeming any too confident about this, either, and Eve – Eve looked like she would gladly have run back the other way, if she'd known there was any other choice than going back into that darkness.

'Yes,' Claire said.

Myrnin smiled. It was a tired, thin sort of smile, and it had a hint of sadness in it. 'Then I should apologise now,' he said. 'Because I'm about to break that trust most grievously.'

He dropped Claire's hand, grabbed Shane by the shirt, and kicked open the door.

He dragged Shane through with him, and the door slammed behind him before any of them could react – even Michael, who hit the wood just an instant later, battering at it. It was built to hold out vampires, Claire realised. And it would hold out Michael for a long, long time.

'Shane!' She screamed his name and threw herself against the wood, slamming her hand over and over into the Founder's Symbol. 'Shane, *no*! Myrnin, bring him back. Please, don't do this. Bring him *back*...'

Michael whirled around, facing the other direction. 'Stay behind me,' he said to Eve and Claire. Claire looked over her shoulder to see doors opening, up and down the hall, as if somebody had pressed a button.

Vampires and humans alike came out, filling the

hallway between the three of them, and any possible way out.

Every single one of them had fang marks in their necks, just like the ones in Claire's neck.

Just like the ones in *Michael's* neck.

There was something about the way he was standing there, so still, so quiet...

And then he walked away, heading for the other vampires.

'Michael!' Eve started to lunge after him, but Claire stopped her.

When Michael reached the first vampire, Claire expected to see some kind of a fight – *something* – but instead, they just looked at each other, and then the man nodded.

'Welcome,' he said, 'Brother Michael.'

'Welcome,' another vampire murmured, and then a human.

When Michael turned around, his eyes had shifted colours, going from sky blue to dark crimson.

'Oh *hell*,' Eve whispered. 'This isn't happening. It can't be.'

The door opened behind them. On the other side was a big stone hall, something straight out of a castle, and the wooden throne that Claire remembered from the welcome feast was here, sitting up on a stage. It was draped in red velvet.

Sitting on the throne was Mr Bishop.

'Join us,' Bishop said. Claire and Eve looked at each other. Shane was lying on the stone floor, with Myrnin's hand holding him facedown. 'Come in, children. There's no point anymore. I've won the night.'

Claire felt like she'd stepped off the edge of the world, and everything was just…gone. Myrnin wouldn't look at her. He had his head bowed to Bishop.

Eve, after that first look, returned her attention to Michael, who was walking towards them.

It was not the Michael they knew – not at all.

'Let Shane go,' Claire said. Her voice trembled, but it came out clearly enough. Bishop raised one finger, and Michael lunged forward, grabbed Eve by the throat, and pulled her close to him with his fangs bared. 'No!'

'Don't give me orders, child,' Bishop said. 'You should be dead by now. I'm almost impressed. Now, rephrase your request. Something with a *please.*'

Claire licked her lips and tasted sweat. 'Please,' she said. 'Please let Shane go. Please don't hurt Eve.'

Bishop considered, then nodded. 'I don't need the girl,' he said. He nodded to Michael, who let Eve go. She backed away, staring at him in disbelief, hands over her throat. 'I have what I want. Don't I, Myrnin?'

Myrnin pulled up Shane's shirt. There, stuffed in his waistband at the back, was the book.

No.

Myrnin pulled it free, let Shane up, and walked to Bishop. *I'm about to break that trust most grievously*, he'd said to Claire. She hadn't believed him until this moment.

'Wait,' Myrnin said, as Bishop reached for it. 'The bargain was for Theo Goldman's family.'

'Who? Oh, yes.' He smiled. 'They'll be quite safe.'

'And unharmed,' Myrnin said.

'Are you putting conditions on our little agreement?' Bishop asked. 'Very well. They go free, and unharmed. Let all witness that Theo Goldman and his family will take no harm from me or mine, but they are not welcome in Morganville. I will not have them here.'

Myrnin inclined his head. He lowered himself to one knee in front of the throne, and lifted the book in both hands over his head, offering it up.

Bishop's fingers closed on it, and he let out a long, rattling sigh. 'At last,' he said. 'At last.'

Myrnin rested his forearms across his knee, but didn't try to rise. 'You said you also required Amelie. May I suggest an alternative?'

'You may, as I'm in good humour with you at the moment.'

'The girl wears Amelie's sigil,' he said. 'She's the only one in town who wears it in the old way, by the old laws. That makes her no less than a part of Amelie herself, blood for blood.'

Claire stopped breathing. It seemed as if every head turned towards her, every pair of eyes stared. Shane started to come towards her.

He never made it.

Michael darted forward and slammed his friend down on the stones, snarling. He held him there. Myrnin rose and came to Claire, offering her his hand in an antique, courtly gesture.

His eyes were still dark, still mostly sane.

And that was why she knew she could never really forgive him, ever again. This wasn't the disease talking.

It was just Myrnin.

'Come,' he said. 'Trust me, Claire. Please.'

She avoided him and walked on her own to the foot of Bishop's throne, staring up at him.

'Well?' she asked. 'What are you waiting for? Kill me.'

'Kill you?' he repeated, mystified. 'Why on earth would I do such a foolish thing? Myrnin is quite right. There's no point in killing you, none at all. I need you to run the machines of Morganville for me. I have already declared that Richard Morrell will oversee the humans. I will allow Myrnin the honour of ruling those vampires who choose to stay in my kingdom and swear fealty to me.'

Myrnin bowed slightly, from the waist. 'I am, of course, deeply grateful for your favour, my lord.'

'One thing,' Bishop said. 'I'll need Oliver's head.'

This time, Myrnin smiled. 'I know just where to find it, my lord.'

'Then be about your work.'

Myrnin gave a bow, flourished with elaborate arm movements, and to Claire's eyes, it was almost mocking.

Almost.

While he was bowing, she heard him whisper, 'Do as he says.'

And then he was gone, walking away, as if none of it meant anything to him at all.

Eve tried to kick him, but he laughed and avoided her, wagging a finger at her as he did.

They watched him skip away down the hall.

Shane said, 'Let me up, Michael, or fang me. One or the other.'

'No,' Bishop said, and snapped his fingers to call Michael off when he snarled. 'I may need the boy to control his father. Put them in a cage together.'

Shane was hauled up and marched off, but not before he said, 'Claire, I'll find you.'

'I'll find you first,' she said.

Bishop broke the lock on the book that Myrnin had given him, and opened it to flip the pages, as if looking for something in particular. He ripped out a page and pressed the two ends together to make a circle of paper, thickly filled with minute, dark writing. 'Put this on your arm,' he said, and tossed it to Claire. She hesitated, and he sighed. 'Put it on, or one of the many hostages to your good behaviour will suffer. Do you understand? Mother, father, friends, acquaintances, complete strangers. You are not Myrnin. Don't try to play his games.'

Claire slipped the paper sleeve over her arm, feeling stupid, but she didn't see any alternatives.

The paper felt odd against her skin, and then it sucked in and clung to her like something alive. She panicked and tried to pull it off, but she couldn't get a grip on it, so closely was it sticking to her arm.

After a moment of searing pain, it loosened and slipped off on its own.

As it fluttered to the floor, she saw that the page was blank. Nothing on it at all. The dense writing that had been on it stayed on her arm – no, *under the skin,* as if she'd been tattooed with it.

And the symbols were *moving.* It made her ill to watch. She had no idea what it meant, but she could feel something happening inside, something…

Her fear faded away. So did her anger.

'Swear loyalty to me,' Bishop said. 'In the old tongue.'

Claire got on her knees and swore, in a language she didn't even know, and not for one moment did she doubt it was the right thing to do. In fact, it made her happy. Glowingly happy. Some part of her was screaming, *He's making you do this!* but the other parts really didn't care.

'What shall I do with your friends?' he asked her.

'I don't care.' She didn't even care that Eve was crying.

'You will, someday. I'll grant you this much: your friend Eve may go. I have absolutely no use for her. I will show I am merciful.'

Claire shrugged. 'I don't care.'

She did, she knew she did, but she couldn't make herself feel it.

'Go,' Bishop said, and smiled chillingly at Eve. 'Run away. Find Amelie and tell her this: I have taken her town away, and all that she values. Tell her I have the book. If she wants it back, she'll have to come for it herself.'

Eve angrily wiped tears from her face, glaring at him. 'She'll come. And I'll come with her. You don't own jack. This is *our* town, and we're going to kick you out if it's the last thing we do.'

The assembled vampires all laughed. Bishop said, 'Then come. We'll be waiting. Won't we, Claire?'

'Yes,' she said, and went to sit down on the steps by his feet. 'We'll be waiting.'

He snapped his fingers. 'Then let's begin our celebration, and in the morning, we'll talk about how Morganville will be run from now on. According to *my* wishes.'

Author's Note

I had an especially great track list to help me through this book, and I thought you might enjoy listening along. Don't forget: musicians need love and money, too, so buy the CDs or pay for tracks.

'On and On' .... Nikka Costa
'Everybody Got Their Something' .... Nikka Costa
'Above the Clouds' .... Delirium & Shelly Harland
'2 Wicky' .... Hooverphonic
'Is You Is or Is You Ain't My Baby' ....
         Rae & Christian Remix, Dinah Washington
'Enjoy the Ride' .... Morcheeba
'Hate to Say I Told You So' .... The Hives
'See You Again' .... Miley Cyrus
'Fever' .... Sarah Vaughn, Verve Remix
'Peter Gunn' ..... Max Sedgley Remix, Sarah Vaughn
'Blade' .... Spacekid & Maxim Yul Remix,
                            Warp Brothers
'Aly, Walk with Me' .... The Raveonettes

'Hunting for Witches' .... Bloc Party
'Cuts You Up' .... Peter Murphy
'Hurt' .... Christina Aguilera
'Run' .... Gnarls Barkley
'Electrofog' .... Le Charme
'Where I Stood' .... Missy Higgins
'Children (Dream Version)' .... Robert Miles
'Grace' .... Miss Kittin
'Walkie Talkie Man' .... Steriogram
'Living Dead Girl' .... Rob Zombie
'Saw Something' .... Dave Gahan
'Boy with a Coin' .... Iron & Wine
'Fever' .... Stereo MC's
'Kaybettik' .... Candan Ercetin
'Playing with Uranium' .... Duran Duran
'Staring at the Sun' .... TV on the Radio
'The Moment I Said It' .... Imogen Heap
'This Is the Sound' .... The Last Goodnight
'Juicy' .... Better Than Ezra
'One Week of Danger' .... The Virgins
'Wolf Like Me' .... TV on the Radio
'Poison Kiss' .... The Last Goodnight
'Beat It' .... Fall Out Boy
'Old Enough' .... The Raconteurs
'I Will Possess Your Heart' .... Death Cab for Cutie

The Morganville Vampires series so far...